The Nerve A Cord

OrangeBooks Publication

Smriti Nagar, Bhilai, Chhattisgarh - 490020

Website: **www.orangebooks.in**

First Edition, 2022

The Nerve A Cord

Keshav Sadashiv Sapru

Preface

Hello, thank you for purchasing this book and reading it.

When I first wrote this book over a long period of time, I was becoming progressively more liberal, socialist, environmentalist, atheist and angsty. Nowadays I'm progressively becoming more conservative, capitalist, producerist, theist and less angsty. What that should tell you, is to change your mind, or it'll sneak up on you. :)

This book is dark, so you should instead not buy it, go out and do something else or if you really want to read a book written by me, buy my collection of essays.

Some of these stories are funny, smart, curious, inquisitive, light-hearted and funny, and they would really like to get to know you, and perhaps you could be enlightened.

My particular apologies to any Christians reading this book, it contains a poem which is critical of Christianity due to the grooming of some boys and girls in catholic churches in the world by priests. This book is not critical of any other religion, and it is unfair to single them out, the reason behind this is that as I grew up with Western Empirical criticism, it targeted Christianity as the largest religion at the time, in India, this is not the case, it is a minority religion which may feel threatened by criticism, so take that explanation in advance before you read. I've also come to realize over time how diverse religious thought really is, so I have grown too. In consolation, some of these stories are quite apocalyptic like the christian or other religious sense. So, you could say, it's Christian in spirit. I imagine that's what Western (and maybe Eastern) environmentalism is borne out of too, angsty apocalyptism.

Aside from removing some racialist epithets in a surrealist story about hatred down below, I have not really censored my work. At the time, I felt really guilty about putting them in, so I removed them. As I feared that racialists would take my words and run with them. Additionally, I realized it's not my work that they need to be racialist, they just are, and my work would be an excuse for them, well, even if they read it, that is, this might be read by 500, or 12 people, who knows? 12, because I have given some of my early copies to friends and family members, there you go. I did not put those words back, A) because I have forgotten them, B) because I am lazy and C) because it shows my evolution of thought, which you can construe anyway you like. Furthermore, you could always include those words in with your imagination. So there you have it. Hope your more informed, now just look down, or look to the right, to read and enter my stories.

Thanks again, take care.

Keshav Sapru

3rd Jan 2022 C.E.

Gurugram, Haryana, India.

$3C)(

As I was walking into the other room, I heard a voice from the other room.

"Are you sure that you don't wanna sleep here?"

I looked at her for a little bit, before I realized, why, yes indeed, I do want to stay with her. I mean, after all what's a little nudity, but the human body?

And after all, the answer to "Can I stay in your room is?" is "Guilezzz? Alive?" henchman.

"OF COURSE!!" M. Bison.

And so I said yes, because being too smart about it would mean that I'm a fart smellar.

So I waltzed into the other other room.

And closed the door?

Why ye-es, indeed I did.

"So…………………………" I said looking at her.

"Clothes off?"

"Why yes, of course."

I enthusiastically dropped my shorts and was gloriously buffed.

And my wind vane was none the happier.

"Aaah, cool breeze"

So, I watched her, as she undid her clothes, and stood tackle out.

Aal I Kould doo waz to stare at her, with blushful Roshian eyezzz.

"So, do you want to lie down?" "OF COURSE!!" M. BISON.

I lay down.

"You can come closer, wrap yourself around me, if you like".

And that is just what I did. Like a proboscis snake, I wrapped myself around her. Tackles twined.

We woke the next morning, and I let my inner tempest out.

I dragged her and pointed her face onto the mess on the bed.

"Is this how one sleeps?!!"

"Shall I rub your face in it?!!"

I said as I held her neck to the mess.

"Oh? I'm sorry, how shall I be punished?"

"I shall rub my face in your mess!"

So, I practiced all of my tongue twisters on her Merkin Muffley, especially the ones that ended in a P, began with a P, and went for middling in the P.

OF course, the sights and sounds were pornographic. And I made sure that inspite of my country manners, I made her see Next Tuesday.

With my hand still forcing her head down, I let go, and she slapped me hard. Ow! That hurt.

So, I slapped her twin resonators and made her sing!

Afterwords, she made sure to step on me and twine our tackles, I mean tackle our twines, I mean, you get it.

So much fire! So much passion! So much friction! That we almost passed out from speeding on the highway. The G's were much too many!

FAR TOO MUCH DICITON!

After what seemed like an instantaneous eternity, I made sure to slime her insides. The kind of slime, that only a Ghostbuster could conjure through positive vibes!

Sometimes I think that Tackle-twining (or twining-Tackles) may not just be so bad after all, no matter how many times you may slip in the slime!

"Don't slip in the slime!" Nikolai Belinski.

Always Be Down To Surprise Midgets!

6000 Years

MMMM17 A.D.

John Wilson, the mega pastor of the Mega-Church of the Children of Solomon walked up to his pedestal. He smiled as he saw the crowd of sheep seated in front of him, ready to start his bucolic sermonizing. "*For I'm the blessed Shepard, who will guide my flock to the kingdom of heaven!*" He thought.

"Children of Solomon!" his voice boomed on the speakers, as everybody grimaced at the volume and the jarring feedback.

"MY Children of Solomon", he said softly, as he touched his right palm on his heart. "Do not be lead astray by these heathen politicians and blasphemous scientists, and their devilish ways! For they have the serpent as their tongue, and the goat as their mind!" He paused for dramatic effect, as some people in the crowd booed and snickered. "Evolution and Plate Tectonics are heresy, and tools of the Devil, MY children! Let not these vassals of the devil, destroy your gardens of Eden, and lead you cast from the kingdom of God!"

Isiah and Lena were sitting at the back of the congregation. They saw reverend Wilson denounce the evils of today's society with much fervour. They saw the way he was so animated, the way he gestured, so energetic. How he walked with such authority, and the way he held his sway on his captive audience.

All they could think about was how right he was.

6000 Y.S.A (Years Since Atomization)

Dedonade, dressed in his tribal garb. Adorned with the metal jewels of the all-powerful atom. Sat down in the circle with his fellow children of the atom.

"Children of atom" He paused for dramatic effect. And to put his right hand on his heart. "My brothers and sisters", said he, as he looked around, eyeing every single member of his group. "6000 years ago, the Ancient Ones, showed us the might of the great and most holy atom", "Praise Atom!", He was interrupted by his zealous followers. "Praise Atom", he curtly stated their customary pledge to the false god.

"Now, let us continue. The Ancient Ones led a great battle against nature. Nature wanted to take what The Ancient Ones had, and we fought back with the fires of Atom. We laid waste to the corruption of nature. She ran scared, back to her hole. Yes, we suffered a lot, because she selfishly kept her bounty with her. But, now thousands of years later, we are free again to do as we please. No more shall we be beholden to nature. And, if she comes in our way, we will smite her with atom's fires!" He shouted, arousing the animalistic desires of death and destruction amongst his serfs.

Radia was seating with Megadeth in the congregation, shouting "Death to Nature!" "Death to Nature!" Too young to understand the weight behind her words. All she knew and all she had to know, was that she was right, they were right.

6000 S.N.G (Since New Genesis)

Nike looked at her mike, thinking about what to say to her fellow Neo-Genites. *"I need to tell them about how the useless Earthers destroyed the homeland, and how the Neo-Genites had to escape to New Genesis, terraform the hellish exomoon and make it their own." "I need to tell them, how Neo-Genesis has only been around for 6000 years, because we created it. The Earthers and their false gods think that they were the ones who came first. No, they weren't the first. They destroyed New Genesis, went to Earth, destroyed Earth, and now, after all our efforts to make it habitable again, they want to destroy it again?! I must tell them! I must tell them that it can never, ever, happen again. That we can never, ever, allow this to happen again!"* Nike reached out and picked up the mike with her left hand, and placed her right hand on her heart, and she began to speak. "The Earthers lie when they tell us how it is that they came first, denying us our clear sacrosanct firstness and superiority! Do not, my friends be swayed by their serpentine tongues. For they wish to lead us astray with their false gods, and steal our sacred planet. As they wish to shepard us, Nature, into ghettoes. We are Gods, we are the ones by whom this planet spins and breathes, my friends, without us, there would've been no planet, no life" and as she continued, all those who heard her on their magic mikes, knew that she was right, that they were right. And after all, that's all that matters.

A Beautiful Life

"It's just a bit further. We're almost out"

ZAP! *KRAKOW!* *BZZT!* *BZZT!* *BZZT!* *BZZT!* *BZZT!*

"No! Not again! Not again! No please! I beg of you! Let us go, you bastards! I don't care what our profiles are, or that we need to be safe to rebuild! We want to be free like animals! We want to be animals! Not poked and prodded like birds in gilded cages!"

"How can we let you go, comrades? Your lives are too precious, we need everyone here to be beautiful, safe and happy. Do you understand? We're preparing you for the basement. Once you're hanzed and ready. Your lives are too beautiful to let go waste. That is all"

"Take them away"

All these words with barely a stare. Intent as lovers, there as wardens.

The 7 beauts, electrified, are taken back with terror and despair. I looked outside, only Hanzers can survive out there. They'll be Hanzers in no time.

Till then, they get to enjoy their beautiful lives.

A Song For Holy And Hellish

HYPOCRITES

We know that you like your girls young,

We know that you like your boys small,

Indeed, we know that you don't like men at all,

In fact, you like children three feet tall.

A Wish For A Lifetime

Deus Ex Machina: You witnessed all the endings.

"If God gave you three wishes, what would you wish for?" The child psychologist asked the little boy. "I would ask for enough wishes to last me a lifetime; I would also ask God to never let me wish for immortality; and I would ask him to never let anything bad which I wished to come true". The little boy said. The child psychologist looked at the little boy with a slightly surprised and a slightly bemused expression. "I haven't heard something like that in ages, please, wish for something." "Really?" the boy asked. "Really", the therapist replied.

The little boy closed his eyes and said, "I wish for a real fire engine."

Acid

I'm walking down the street.

It's a cool day, so I'm wearing a hoodie.

A little nippy, so turning up the collar, really helps, when all of a sudden, out of my peripheral vision, this black form rises up to envelope me, I duck, but I wasn't quick enough.

Then there's this indescribable pain. So violent, that all of my body lights up in agony. I cover my face, and I feel something sticky like cheese come off in my hands, later on, I would realize that it was my face. I felt someone throw me to the ground, and pour lots of water on my face. I thought that it was because of this that the pain subsided, but in fact, it was because of my nerves being burnt through.

Reads the stenographer's typeout.

"We really just needed to hear from you, what you went through. There's more than enough witnesses, expert and otherwise, since it happened in broad daylight, and the jydges having caught the culprit, just after your assault, for this case to be an open and shut one. But I believe that without the human element, dry statements should not be what we leave for posterity", said the Jydge.

"What should be the punishment for this villain?" asked the Jydge.

"I feel that adding to brutality, will not solve our problems, even though we are currently living in a world where jystice is expedient. I propose that this man be given help to rehabilitate back into society, and that the state, if he so chooses to regress back into assault provide suitable living conditions isolated from society, so that he may not cause further harm to others, if he cannot be so. I also understand that others choosing the expedient and retributive jystice have allowed me to approach rehabilitation. Hopefully this can change".

"Noticed. The culprit has been chosen to be taken to the rehabilitative facility, if he is found to be unresponsive, he will be taken to the psychopath reintegration program. If no further improvements are seen, he is to be isolated without surroundings conducive to insanity" said the jydge.

The survivor walked out. Content in good deed.

Jystice is served.

After The Children

The whole movie is set in black and white. Not necessarily neo-noir, just black and white. Thank you.

The film starts with a police detective sitting in his chair, lost in deep thought. I'll leave it upto the actors or actresses to show how he's being pensive. Thank you.

Deep, deep, deep thought. In fact so deep that all sound slowly vanishes, then all light, and then the sound of the telephone slowly creeps in. Getting louder and louder and louder, until it snaps him out of his thoughts. Since he was protected by his deep thought, the actual sound of the telephone is beyond jarring, it's deeply deafening. Deeply. Thank you.

Now.

He picks up the telephone and speaks.

"Jim, we have an interesting case for you. There's been a victim of a heart attack, but it could be a case of negligence or manslaughter, or even pre-meditated murder, we just don't know. Since she died at sight of the perp. The forensic team found out that she had a healthy body, no history of heart illness, or even the mildest of anxiety attacks. We know this because her medical records show this, psychiatric and physical. She was suffering from depression and neurosis, and there may have been some weakness caused by them, but judging from what we have, it seems unlikely. The team also knows that she's been dead for 8 hours and that she died before she hit the ground, it seems that the perp put on quite the frightening show"

"Alright Svetlana, thank you. I'll be there in the half hour"

Click

Ring ring

"Yes?"

"Hey, it's me again. I'm sorry, but I forgot to tell you one more detail, in my hurry, and my mechanistic delivery, I forgot to tell you something very important. Jim, it was, huuuuhhh, it was your ex-girlfriend Jim. It was Mary. I'm sorry Jim, again, force of habit"

Jim senses a soft smile at the other end, by the gentle exhale from her nostrils.

"It's okay Svetlana, don't worry, I'll figure this out, it's the least I can do for her"

"Okay"

Click

Jim feels really, really grim as he gets up, and gets ready to go out. It's cheesy, but he likes to wear a long coat and a hat, it makes him more comfortable when he's out observing. He smiles.

"Atleast the perp was physically violent, I mean wasn't physically violent. I won't have to see her mangled or know that she suffered. Thank goodness"

At the point where he thinks, "was physically violent", he closes his eyes, shakes his head from side to side, and slaps himself on the head. Reset face. Reset Head. Reset Mind.

Jim leaves.

We arrive at the scene of the crime. There's police tape around the body, and white chalk which marks the perimeter of the body.

There's a few forensics who are taking their last photos, and the rest are packing up their gear. Some of them look up and give Jim a nod or smile. Sympathy. He returns their affectionate gaze with a polite look of recognition.

Jim slowly moves into his dream world. The sound drains out, the lights go out. His eyes are shut, his mind blank.

The scene changes. Mary's body is now viewed from the side, as is the floor. Everything around it is still dark. He's picturing the crime scene horizontally, that is on the y axis. She's lying there. She gets up. As she's getting up, the horizontal floor moves from the y to the x axis, and she moves from the x to the y axis. She gently lands at the edge of the floor. Her hair floating gently. Her eyes open slowly. We're back from the dream place. She's there in the real world. We're looking at Jack from the third person close up view. She's blurred in the background, And Jack's still in the dream world. Eyes closed. She walks closer and closer to him, and as she approaches him, still blurred.

We close up on Jack's face the world behind him either black or blurred out, her face is close to his, she's gentle, peaceful. She puts her right arm on his left shoulder and kisses him softly on his right cheek. And then whispers into his ear.

"He's after the children"

She looks him intensely in his eyes. He looks at her intently and he has tears in his eyes. He touches her face gently, it's warm to the touch. She closes her eyes, and holds his hand with her hand and rubs her face against the palm of his hand. Just lovingly enjoying his affectionate caress. It's beautiful.

She softly disappears while smiling at him. His hand is in the air, he has tears falling down.

He slowly composes himself. A powerful spiritual experience.

The scene changes. We see him at his home, on his desk sitting pensively. He can't think anymore. He gets up and walks down the stairs to the road. There's a forest on the otherside. He likes the peace and solitude which they provide to him. He lights a cigarette and walks to the forest. Still pensive. He starts looking around. Then suddenly, the hairs on the back of his neck prick up. He freezes. He slowly scans the area, walks around slowly. He then, with great trepidation walks up to the boundary of the forest. The camera changes view. It's now looking at Jim. The camera rises from ground level and towers over him, there's terror in his eyes, as he's frozen in place, his eyes wide open, his mouth open, the cigarette falls from his mouth and hits the ground, his face contorts from pain as he goes into cardiac arrest. He falls face first into the soft ground.

The world is dark now, pitch black. We just see his body at ground level. His upper torso. He's in his dream world. Mary walks up to him, bends down and whispers into his right ear.
"Jim, wake up".

He wakes up with a long breath drawn in, his head's pounding and he quickly checks his body for any wounds.
"He almost got you too" she says as he slowly gets up, rubbing his temples.

She reaches out for him with a hand.

"Don't worry, we'll get him together"

Jim looks up at her as he's helped up and smiles.

The End

AGAPE

I was in my gas mask and my faceplate was fogging up. I couldn't take it off though, for that would mean certain sleep. Ours was the 4th regiment of the 9th division of the 10 Army of the Pacifist States of Australia. Our official national and military policy was pacifism. Meaning, non-lethal governance and non-lethal weaponry. Currently, amidst all the crackling of electricity from batteries of Tasers to the loud laser and gunfire of the adversarial combatants (not enemies, we mustn't dehumanize the other).

The view in front of me, is eerily beautiful. Night sky, dark, electricity and plasma crackling away. The power of pacifism will make everyone see the light. Literally.

My Taser rifle charged up, as I fired electricity at the adversary. Sparks of blue light reached out as cephalopodan tentacles. Thin, fractal tendrils, refracted by my protective visor, raced up to the person in front of me. Irrespective of their gender. The hand touched, the man fell. I recharged and proceeded to further electrify my fellow men.

The other person who succumbed to me, wasn't so easy.

It clutched at its heart. Terror in its eyes. And fell.

Never had I ever thought of the other as a person. Empathy was for people, feeling it, was different. I took off my visor, I took off my helmet, there was no effect. I rushed towards it. I saw that it was a she. It still surprises me to see female warriors, it hasn't been common.

I reached down to look in her dying eyes. I grasped her hand and held on. Talking empathy is far different from walking it.

I looked into her eyes. There was a mixture of terror and despair, but a slow softness arose. That of hope, and not fear. Of peace and not anger.

Two fundamentalists, action and paction. United, forever.

The plasma blew a hole in his right shoulder, as the Taser short-circuited his heart. As he fell on her, the painful grimace buried in a mouthful of sand.

And it was over.

Alien Abduction

I see a long thin shadow for a neck. I see a flat top for a head. It's day, not night. I lay down in our bed, between my parents, I'm afraid of the shadow people. Very scared. My parents form a protective barrier around me. What if they came from my feet, my head, or over my parents?

They're unafraid, they'll stop them.

I Fall Asleep!

In my dream, there's a blackish-greyish haze above me. There's a figure, that I can't completely delineate. I'm talking to him. He's talking to me. We're talking about life, "aliens". My arms are raised, and so are my, as if I'm standing up and talking. My arms reaching out in conversation, so realistic, so vivid.

The dream finishes, my parents must've noticed that I talk and enact in my sleep.

I wake up.

I know one thing for real, aliens are real.

An Impossible View

In the year 2180, when mankind had recovered from the global warming catastrophe of the 2070s-2080s and re-established a highly technologically advanced and ecologically sustainable civilization, the citizens of Planet Earth were faced with an impossible view.

Here is how the events unfolded.

Diaspar Adams sat in a savannah, near the only tree which could be seen for miles. It was quiet and unbelievably peaceful. She was thinking, "How is it that we think when we're not supposed to be thinking? Do we think about thinking? How does that work?" She heard a rustle behind her, looked behind her and found herself looking at 6ft tall, bald and slightly overweight central Asian man. She thought that he was central Asian, since his features were so ambiguous, he could've been from anywhere. She was startled for a moment and then said to him cheerily, "Hey there! How's it going? Really nice day, huh?" She didn't think about where or how he came, she just assumed that he used one of those levitating Segway-like personal transports. But on close inspection, she couldn't see it anywhere.

The central Asian man replied, "Hi! It's good to see you! It's certainly a wonderful day!" I was just passing by on my Segway, and I thought that I'd introduce myself."

She thought and replied, "Are you a ranger? Or a keeper of the park?"

"I'm Nature, it's nice to meet you."

She replied, 'It's good to meet you, Mr. Nature. She thought about making the, "Good-natured" quip but then thought against it." "What brings you here?" "It's just Nature." He replied. She thought, "Okay, his parents really were nature lovers, maybe he was born in the transitionary decades of the late 21st century." "I wanted to introduce myself", he continued, "Because I thought that it was finally time that I could reach out to human beings, without being scoffed at." "Why would, 'humans' scoff at you?" Because up until now, you had lost faith in me. "Faith in you? Who are you?" "Is this somebody famous, who I'm supposed to know?" She asked herself. 'Arrrrre...yooouu...somebody...famous?" She said with a squinting her eyes, pursing her lips and tilting her head to the left (a.k.a "waiting-for-opprobrium" face).

He said, "No, not somebody famous, I'm somebody who works in the shadows, changing your world slowly and gradually, always waiting to cause some calamity, muahahahaha!" Faking an evil laugh. She looks at him in amused surprise. "He's a real comedian, isn't he?" She thought. "But on a more serious note, I'm Nature. Or as we're better known: Mother Nature." He continued. "Well, you're definitely no mother, that's for sure." Cutting him off. "That's true, I'm, or we're trying to show that Nature is not confined to one nationality or gender. Plus, the author of this story wanted us to be politically correct." "Ohhh-kaay, right. Is there something you want to tell me?" She said, sounding incredulous. "Yes, I do, but... (He sits down)... Ahhh, that's nice. Now we can talk." She adjusts her posture to face him. "What we want to ask you about pertains to the reason why it took so long for humans to reconcile itself with us and itself." She listens more intently, as he speaks. "Why?" She asks.

"The reason, though simple at first hand, results in very complex ramifications. During the period of time that humans thought themselves at one with us, they strived to live in harmony, but as they settled to become settled farmers and herders....the need to expand their influence grew. Unfortunately till such a time that it was almost too late to save the Earth from another mass extinction. But, luckily in the end, humans became enlightened as a race when their very existence was threatened. And the society which you see today, one with nature, technologically advanced, sufficiency for everyone's needs and some greeds too." He said with a pleasant grin. "A statement that would've probably gone contrary to what Gandhi would've said". She thought to herself.

This change took place the moment that some misguided men (and less influentially, women) in the last 6,000 years of your history perpetuated the popular myth that humans were separate from Nature, and they were not animals (since that word carried a stigma) nor were they a force of Nature." "Wait", she stopped him. "Firstly, I don't believe I'm saying this for something so bad, but anyways, why were women less influential in this decision making process?" And secondly, "What do you mean by, 'we're a force of nature'?" She said puffing her face up, imitating a fat man walking (with a hint of sarcasm). "In answer to your first question, around 6,000 years ago, men started the process (first in isolated incidents, but then throughout the world) to reduce the social role of women, i.e. the human world, started to become a male-dominated place. In answer to your second question, humans are a force of Nature, don't you see? Besides some unbelievably powerful natural calamities, humans are the most powerful force on Earth. Your species can move mountains, create huge cities, control the weather, harness the *entire* power of the Planet, make weapons that can scar the Earth for millennia, use technologies that can make it a better place and enhance your living, make life, create sentience and much more. You are a force of Nature and you're joined by the sheer trillions of species in the Universe who can do the same and better. When you look up in the night sky and see the thousands of stars, you are not insignificant, you're a part of an immense whole which defines your place in the stars, and which you as a participant in this cosmic stage define too." "It is not arrogant (**they** continue) to recognise your place in the stars and become a species with Universe-warping capabilities. It is what I do every day."

She was speechless, she didn't know what to say... either this man was crazy, or he was just a crazy visionary. Not much difference, I guess.

He was looking at her with a deeply profound look in his eyes. When she got her voice back, she asked him, or them, wryly, "If you're Nature why aren't you covered in vegetation, and why don't animals follow you?" They nearly hit their head in frustration... "Okay, do you like it when family members crowd around you all day long? Or would you like it if your hair was growing uncontrollably from every pore?" They said in a matter-of-fact voice. She just nodded and mouthed, *no*. "We're just kidding", they said. The real reason is because I wanted you to feel comfortable... seeing one of your kind". "Are you God?" She asked. "Ah", they said, "the allimportant question, are we God?" "Well, our answer is that, we're a projection made of infinite entities, form the smallest sub-atomic particle to the most advanced intelligence out there, and you are included in us and vice-versa". "Can you really prove to me that you're Nature? Change the laws of Physics? She asked them. "If we did that, that could kill you, and it would be the undoing of 40 billion years of work on this Universe. But just so that you believe us, we will create a miniature Nuclear Fusion reaction between our fingertips". They clicked their fingertips, and with a POP! Sound, a pico-sun was floating between the tips of their two fingers. "The flash from its ignition, didn't hurt me, maybe h-, they were screening my eyes from the flare of its birth", she thought, mesmerised. "Behold (they said with glee), we always wanted to say that. The power of your fusion reactors in between my finger-tips (in a deep and mellifluous voice)".

She gawked in awe at the awesome spectacle, the power of the nuclear reactors she had seen only in podcasts and from afar, was now within grasping distance.

She asked him, "But which God are you? Are all of them, none of them, or only what we want to see you as?"

He said, "I think, Diaspar, that you just answered that question for yourself."

"Well", she said, "You could just as well be the member of an extremely advanced alien race, how would I know?"

"That's a very astute observation, and it's also a very good one". They said. "But what does it matter?" they continued. If we were an infinitely powerful race of aliens, how would you distinguish us from God? We are a collective consciousness made up of all the life forms, particles, branes, etc. in all the infinite Omniverses. You are a part of us, and we are a part of you. Nothing can stop humans from becoming God-like in their power, except themselves, and maybe other external forces, blah, blah... but the point is, that we are here to ensure that you do not do it in a way that can cause your extinction. The Global warming crisis of the transitionary decades, is merely one of the many challenges that humans will have to face in the coming eons. We are here to guide and help the human race when it needs us the most. Which is very hard, considering the fact that we have to balance free-will with help. Sort of like the dilemmas which the characters in Star Trek had to face with their prime directive. Which, as surprising as it is, is still ongoing, ha, ha, ha!"

For Diaspar, she had always suspected that there could've been some higher power in the Universe, but she never realised that she was a part of it, and that it was a part of her.

"What about evil?" She asked. "Why does it exist?"

"Good question", they replied. "The answer is: stagnation... While this answer is quite harsh, it is rooted in logic. An infant society without any chaos, cannot adapt and evolve, and even if it did, the rate of change would be so slow, that it would be as good as stagnation. Violence, death, destruction, and other chaotic influences, helps an infant civilisation to contemplate, theorise, strive for perfection, order, advancement and it also shakes its members out of apathy. Adverse conditions have been the root cause behind many socio-economic, psychological and scientific advancements in your civilisation, have they not? If dictators were not scared of death, or if men were not scared of the opprobrium from the women they had supressed, or if the poor had not felt the pain from the suffering at the hands of their exploiters, or if even something as flawed as money did not (paradoxically) act as a deterrent for those whom other's misery was a business (due to its finite quantity), would society have ever woken up from its apathy and demanded for change and progress?"

"I guess not. It could've happened, but it probably would've taken far too long for the change to be of any value, I guess".

"We didn't create evil, it was the outcome of free will, I wouldn't even call it good and evil, I would say that some people promoted more constructive chaos, while others promoted more destructive chaos".

"Why do you, uh, you all refer to yourselves in the 3rd person?" She asked.

"We enjoy talking to you so much. Whenever we come across a member of a species who ask us 'chaotically constructive questions' *wink* *wink* and have a sense of humour, we LOVE it! In answer to your question, we would like to begin with a simple analogy.

There are trillions of cells in your body, individually, they do not know that they exist, or even if they did, they don't know who "you" are. The same way, "you" cannot sense every cell in your body, but together, they make up you, and you can feel their entirety. You know what your skin feels like, but you don't know what a single skin feels like. You can sense your stomach, your, etc... But not every single unit. That's similar to what we are at this moment. Of course, instead of us not feeling connected to everything that we are made up of, is the furthest from the truth.

Although feeling maybe, not an incorrect term, but a term which can cannot capture the entirety and the complexity of our connections. Simply put, in micro-objects, such as electrons, protons, etc. we realized that we couldn't know everything about them, due to the uncertainty principle. The precision in measuring the velocity and the position of the particle is proportionate. The more we know about one, the less we know about the other property. So, to circumvent this problem, we tweaked the probability wave, so that we could increase the probability finding the two properties. So, instead of directly observing the particles, we increased the probability of where their velocities and their positions lie. We moulded reality to suit us. We didn't break the laws of physics, we bent them. Hence, our impressions on those particles are there forever. Of course, the process and the science are not so simple, but the author doesn't understand the complexities of this, as we do. In macro-objects, we learnt that all brains, or neural networks are all deeply entwined in the fabric of the Cosmos. Hence, we ensure that all information is saved before the information becomes irretrievable due to entropy. Yes, we save all the information in brains to us, we are linked to all lifeforms and physical constructions of this Universe. We are the manifestation of everything, the same way that your sentience and consciousness is the result of all your neurons, and all the atoms that make up their structure and all the chemicals which they to use form, communicate, etc.

Diaspar thinks for but a moment, and asks, "That's all great, but how are you not a Black Hole of some sort, isn't there a limit to how much information that can be held in a volume of spacetime?"

The being replied, "Yes, a very nasty predicament for trying to harness and harmonize everything into one whole. What we learnt through our discoveries and research was that there are an infinite number of Universes and Quantum communication is possible amongst them. We took one particle from one single Universe and quantum entangled it with its counterparts simultaneously. Of course, since every particle in one Universe is quantum entangled with another in the same one, we entangled its short lived virtual particle partner. It turns out that Universe's don't care much for virtual particles, they are very short-lived, and so, we had to stabilize them. But that doesn't mean that we can take all of them. It would've caused some very bad repercussions in those Universes.

Hence, we stuck to one, and created an infinitely large quantum computer instantaneously. Sure, some Black holes would live slightly longer than their immense life spans, but we figured that a change of a point followed by over 100 zeroes 1 extension in their lifetime, would be too negligible. And the energy loss of the Universes involved would also be too small, so small in fact, that it would have no foreseeable effect on the future heat deaths of their respective Universes, except a negligible acceleration. But, we digress, by creating an infinitely large and infinitely powerful quantum computer; we could store and process as much data as we wanted without the fear of creating an infinitely large Black Hole.

She says, "I can't imagine the glitches going around in your system. Ha ha ha!"

The being replies, "Actually there aren't any. We treat the virtual particles as stem cells, we assign them different characteristics and they "grow" to behave exactly as the particle that they were assigned to behave as. A virtual electron can be programmed to behave like a "real" electron. So, our quantum computer is essentially an infinitely large Universe spread across an infinite Universes, so it seems infinitesimally small, and hence, undetectable.

"Holy Shit!" She said, "I think that I'm going to lose my mind! We could all be in your simulation, yet, if this were a simulation, it would be so precise, that it would be real."

"This concept is like, like, the opposite of the cosmic horror trope, it's like cosmic elation, or something." She said.

"Yes, possibly", the being said.

Then, suddenly in her mind popped a thought, "What would it be like to have sex with nature?" So, she asked hi- them, this question.

The being answered, "Nothing, you would just have a really nice time with an unknown stranger in the middle of nowhere." They quipped.

The absurdity of the situation made them both guffaw with laughter. It seems like sex, as a topic, no matter what, usually seems to be a testing ground as to how open one is. Odd, isn't it? I could be wrong. Or maybe it will be a relic of my mind, or of our time. Nevertheless, let's continue with the story.

"We've digressed so far off topic, that I don't even remember what we were talking about." She said.

The being responded, "It was about us sending a message to your fellow humans, that the time has come for nature and humans to work hand-in-hand."

"I turned on your iris-implant when we met, and except for the sex-question, and everything prior to what I'm saying right now. I broadcasted our talk to the entire world, so that they could know that we want to hold a discussion with mankind, the same way as we held one here today."

"And I hope that this conversation got them interested for further debate."

"You're leaving?" She asked. "Yes" They replied. "I have to get this man back to his ranger outpost; I don't want the poor thing to be lost any more than he has to be." She smiled at this, her guess had been correct.

"And don't worry", they said, "even if we're going away, it doesn't mean that we're not there." "I know", she said in response.

They hugged, said their goodbyes and waved at each other, till they were both specks in each other's eyes.

She wondered to herself," What if this was just some elaborate hoax? What if all those supposed 4th wall breaks were just what they were supposed to be, a pretence? What if he was just a really good hacker and programmer, and the sun was a hologram, and her iris implant was just hacked by him and their entire conversation had been broadcasted to the whole world by him?" She felt vulnerable and powerless. But then she thought to herself, "We've become so cynical, that we expect people to be open and straight- forward, but when they are, we suspect them; when we expect them to put others above themselves, we suspect them, and so on it goes…" "Maybe that man was just a man and not some God-like entity, but a large amount of what he said did make sense to me and provided me with hope. And I guess that at the end of the day, that's all that matters."

"I see a beautiful city and a brilliant people rising from this abyss. I see the lives for which I lay down my life, peaceful, useful, prosperous and happy. I see that I hold a sanctuary in their hearts, and in the hearts of their descendants, generations hence. It is a far, far better thing that I do, than I have ever done; it is a far, far better rest that I go to than I have ever known."

Ancient

ALIENS

Warning…

Cryogenesis Power levels insecure…

Initiating Cryostasis pod cycling…

Wake up call response 100%

Vital Signs Normal…

Start Up sequence complete…

Commencing countdown, engines on…

Rerouting power to propulsion… Cybernetic recharge complete…

Awaiting for your input commander…

Good Morning, Newt, this is the commander speaking.

What is our current location?

Good Morning, Commander Redekr, We are currently in system YABB/20T.

We are at stations keeping, awaiting your orders.

Good. As you are no doubt aware, I will convene with Kara and get back to you.

Of course, Commander, I await your response. Till then I will be collecting astronomical and astrophysical data as usual, I will inform you of points of interest.

Keep me availed.

Wilco.

The commander walks over to his CO.

"Kara, anything to report while I was under?"

"Nothing but the inky black of space for 10,000 light years. Interspersed with the occasional excitement witnessed by celestial events. Although at this particular juncture in the Universe's history, as the Stelliferous Era gives way to the black hole Epoch, it is at once both interesting and saddening to slowly see all the stars twinkling out, with the last Quasars burning out their fuel supplies to become sleeping giants, no more to act as landmarks in the Universe and so on. To hear the dying calls of the few radio civilizations too late to go interstellar and hear the others quieten down to prepare for the eternal winter. Some new celestial events did pique my curiosity, seeing supernovas form from the collision of multiple brown dwarfs, hardly a common sight. There's some nostalgia as well, as we're so far from our stellar nation, that we cannot view them, let alone communicate with them. The ship has run well, although I'm tired now, both mechanically and psychologically, having been on board for eons, even with stasis and my slow decay. Existentialism always bummed me out. Through strange eons, it becomes a uniquely insipid philosophy, and makes you regain your love for the world. Although there are times when I slipped back. Oh well"
"Excellent".

"That's what I like about you"

"Yes? Yes"

"Bummer"

"Well, what's this system like"

"Well, it's a late stage Type G Main Sequence Star. Currently in the last moments of its whitedwarf phase. The civilization which pulled it's planet away from the expanding star seems to have some habitation still left, judging by the weak signals leaving the planet"

"Somebody's alive after 20 Trillion years?"

"Well, it may not be somebody per say"

"It could just be a small beacon on loop"

"Possible"

"We're currently at the edge of the System, at full impulse it should take just less than 8 hrs"

"Maximum magnification"

An average rocky planet comes into view. Darkened by the dim light of its dying sun. Strange shadows form as the white dwarf begins to cool down, long dims followed by short spikes in energy. Not very visible, nor very frequent, but the sensitive telescopes pick up the tiny perturbations, this star couldn't possibly have more than a billion years left before it becomes a "cool" black dwarf. To stay like that for all eternity.

While the telescopes aren't sensitive to pick up this, nor were optics designed for this, but the interferometres pick up small gravitational perturbations, as if some object is imperceptibly changing the distribution of the mass of planet.

"Could it be a transport system built through the core of the planet?"

"It's possible, Redekr"

"Civilizations at the end of time"

"Those that didn't leave for the stars when they shifted their planet out of the way of their star's red giant phase, are probably battening down the hatches for the far future"

"Aye"

"Or they could be waiting for harnessing exotic matter"

"Still in the far future"

7 Hrs and 45 mins later…

"Checkmate commander"

"God-fucking-damnit, that's 20 wins for you, 1 for me and a draw. I'm a real shit tit"

"Aw, don't be so hard on yourself Redekr, that's my job"

"Hardy-har"

"Captain, before we come up on the planet, I wished to inform you, no points of interest in this system"

"Thank you, Newt. To think that 500 billion light years from home and we find bloody nothing besides this. But I guess that this is good enough"

"Yes, Captain"

"Scanning planet, Captain"

"Yes?"

"Reading life signs. Bipedal, 30,000 signatures"

"We're being hailed"

"Patch us through"

"Kaptian, welcome to the third rock from the Sun"

"Bleeding hell, that was fast"

"How have you survived for so long?"

"Easy captain, cannibalism"

"Ha, ha, funny"

"Well, not really"

"Yes"

"It's quite simple, you exist for 20 trillion years and you learn a few things"

"We moved our planet away from our sun when it expanded, sent our people to find a way to another universe, while we agreed to stay back here for untold eons and broadcast data from the edge of time and space, it is best to go out with a bang, is it not?"

"I couldn't agree more"

He looks at Kara.

"We're space-farers and we've been travelling for hundreds of billions of years, we don't even know if our homeworld is still there, let alone our people, any chance that you could take us on?"

Kara and Newt exchange glances and glance back at the Captain, but sya nothing.

"Why yes, Kapitan, we would love to"

"THERE'S ONLY THE END TO LOOK FORWARD TO"

"YES"

"YES"

"YES"

"YES"

"YES"

"YES"

YES

Yes

Yes

Yes

Yes

Yes

Yes

Yes

Apache

(This is about the incident where a US Army Apache gunned down civilians while making light of the situation, in Iraq. This video was released by wikileaks. This movie's intent is not to be anti-US per say but more on the lines of what war and prejudice do to human beings and how we as a collective take advantage of its fallout, or on the other hand, show our outstanding capacity for selflessness in times of trouble. This is also not hero worship of Edward Snowden or Julian Assange. The only hero worship allowed in these parts is of me. Tee Hee)

A man walks out his house, followed by his friend. They're going to drop their kids to school. As they approach the van, they hear the sound of a helicopter and very loud gunfire very close, and then a huge explosion, as smoke and fire rises not one street across. They rush into the van, as their children ask them what happened.

Not far away, a US convoy of Humvees is under heavy fire from machine guns and RPGs. The commander of the convoy calls in the big guns, to deal with the insurgents. Big papa responds (the helicopter gunship). And starts firing at them. And then moves further down the road to scan for more enemies.

The helicopter comes into view. They spy some men in their viewscreen, and suspect one of them carrying a RPG and a man they suspect of carrying a gun. They ask for permission to engage. They receive permission to engage, they start firing at them with their cannon, the men dive for cover and the rest for the house. The helicopter gunship fires a hellfire missile at the house and destroys it.

The men on the ground are walking outside a house. One man in plainsclothes is carrying a camera with a telescopic lens slung on the side. The men in front of him is carrying a RPG. The men around him are unarmed. They don't pay much attention to the helicopter because they're used to it.

The helicopter opens fire and chaos ensues. The journalist drops to the ground and starts crawling ahead, blinded by the pain.

The van pulls up and the two men jump out to help the injured man on the ground. They pick him up and put him into the van.

The helicopter opens up on the van, while crudely remarking about the incident.

The van is destroyed, we see this from the viewscreen. No need for unnecessary gore glorification.

The Humvees hear the gunfire and pull up to the van, as the soldiers come out, they examine the wreckage. They find the dead men inside and the gravely injured children. As they report to big papa in the sky. Big papa responds with a "They shouldn't have brought kids to a war". As the medics look shocked not only at the nonchalance of the gunship operators, but also at the sight.

Wikileaks leaks the footage of the gunship opening fire on the van, without the prior context, and the internet and the world (well atleast those who're not busy fighting for their survival) blows up in outrage. After the media firestorm and further, the investigation by the Pentagon, Julian Assange in an interview responds to the question posed by the journalist that, releasing the heavily edited footage was politically expedient to paint the US Army in a bad light to bring attention to the human rights violations which are taking place in Iraq.

In the investigation, the Pentagon does not find the actions of the operators a war crime, but does mention that the lackadaisical attitude of the gunship operators and their nonchalant attitude towards the deaths of the individuals was a matter of concern (indicative of PTSD). In light of the circumstances that the US convoy was under heavy fire, the operators did not have the luxury to assume the innocence of the civilians and that the journalist was not dressed in any defining clothing. But it also notes that it shouldn't have fired as the group of men was largely unarmed except for the man with the RPG. Firing at the house where the unarmed civilians went to hide was also unnecessary, especially upon the dubious suspicion that civilians running from gunship fire would be running towards weapons in the house and not in fact for shelter, as they were.

There was a documentary also made on this. Which had interviews with the Army personnel on the ground at the time. The Iraqis were dead, and the operators of the gunship were unknown (as their identities were kept secret). Towards the end of the documentary, the US Army medic expresses regret and sadness at the incident, and how he himself personally was affected by seeing the children injured and how he had to take care of them and take them to the hospital, and how he had to reveal to them that their father and uncle were dead.

Apocalypse

We see a farm. It's a utopia. Animals, people, plants living in harmony.

We see the oppressors come in.

They capture you.

They torture you.

They kill the family,

They kill all the animals,

They kill all the plants,

They glass the Earth,/

"We will break you!" they say.

As they kill the kid, you look at them,

And you think,

"You will not break me, there will be a Utopia"

Years pass. You're now in a Utopia, having survived the apocalypse. The oppressors now work for the greater good.

But you still can't meet them. You can't still see eye-to-eye. You're feelings-thought are more powerful than your conscious thought.

They're racked by guilt. You're racked by grief.

Perhaps time will heal, perhaps the apocalypse will end. There is no war, but the war within.

Where do you go, when you go within? Within.

Where does the grief go? Grief?

What was it like to hold your child, Joy? Joy.

What was it like to lose your child, pain? Pain.

What was it like to survive the apocalypse, powerful? Powerful.

What was it like to build the Utopia, Euphoria?! Euphoria!

A blood black nothingness, A system of cells.

Within Cells Interlinked!

Within one cell!

Dreadfully Distinct!

Against The Dark!

A Tall White Fountain Played!

Pale Fire!

Pale Fire! Pale Fire! Pale Fire! Pale Fire! Pale Fire!

Pale! Fire! Pale! Fire! Pale! Fire! Pale! Fire! Pale!

FIRE!

PALE!

PALE!

FIRE!

FIRE!

PALE!

FIRE!

FIRE!

FIRE!

PALE!

PALE!

FIRE!

PALE! FIRE!

PALE ! FIRE !

PALE ! FIRE !

PALE! FIRE!

PALE FIRE!

PALE FIRE!

Arab Blood

I was standing where the 8 train would come. I felt the air on my skin, and the rush of the train. I put my fingers in my ears. The menacing horn tamed by a square inch of skin. The doors slid open, and I walked in. Looking, left and right, I caught sight of the Arab Blood. Ever since I had taken it upon myself to not retire anymore of their kind. I felt the urge to apologize to one. Perhaps the forgivnance of one would assuage my guilt of a dozen others.

I tensed up, I felt sweaty in my palms, what will be her reaction? What will she do? I started to feel like as if there was a knot in my chest. Could she smell me? Did I stink of fear, or faeces?

I walked away from her, slowly, ponderously, as the train moved in the other direction. I imagined myself starting to do slapstick acts like Charlie Chapman.

"Bollocks to it all" I thought as I sat down. Looking down, shy, hoping that she would leave, go away. I held my face in my hands. My spectacles looking up, as if they were scoffing at gravity.

I looked at her again, thought, got up and walked towards her. Thankfully, the seat near her was empty. I sat down with a, "Humph!" The breath slowly leaving my body.

She looked at me, and she smiled knowingly, "You only smell a little bit like faeces". I smiled. I held her hand, and she put her head on *my* shoulder, and *I* on hers.

And I heard, *"All is forgiven"*.

That was enough.

ASS

"I'm not your wife! I'm not your wife!"

"The way you shake it, I can't believe it!"

"I've never seen an ass like that!"

If you haven't guessed already, especially if you're not me.

That's Neelansh. The resident wierdo. Not like us, we're good weird,

He's rubbish weird. But don't say that aloud, love, we're disgusted, but he's pasted. I think, I mean, this is how drunk people behave, right?

What're we doing here? This is the past, all I really remember, is how disgusted you were, when he humped the wall, while singing that.

Hey! I can remember my stories, the way I want too, bub.

Alright, alright.

He's there.

Humping the wall.

The way you shake it, I can't believe it. Back when he hadn't had thoughts of homophobia in his head. Ironical, since he's homoromantic himself. Ha ha, yeah! All the Christians dancing to a song about gay sex, in weddings, ha ha!

Hey, thoughts?

Yeah?

I'm writing a story.

We don't care, if we're not in it.

You are, you're the inspiration for this.

Oh?

Yes.

The annoyance.

Young man.. Young man…

Great, thanks for making "fun at the YMCA" me so ineffectual with your bloody addictions, that I "get myself clean" without listening to music.

Bollocks.

They'll soon be in your mouth.

No yours, if you don't shut up!

You're too fat for autofellatio!

Blowing yourself.

Anyways! As I was saying (atleast I don't hump.. wlass… oh)

He was humping the wall, and making the horny face. Oi! You're In this story! Now shut up!

"No place to hang all your washing, we gonna rock don't do, and then we'll take it higher!" You like this song too, you see?

Can't et food for the kid! Good God!

It's unbearable without music! Boo hoo!

Shut up! Fear! Bollocks!

Bloody Bollocks!

Now you know how hard it is for to write stories?

Horny face, humping the wall, ass like that. Me disgusted.

Yes

Or Ah yes?

Ah, Yes!

I was puritanical, shy around girls (except childhood friends), after a certain age, no bad language, marriage, yada, yada.

Ayways, grew up to like Eminem's Ass like that. Got to understand liberalism. Anarchism. Laughed at Eminem's funny song, got introduced to triumph the puppet dog.

Thanks internet for Christian conservatism! Now I know why mentally ill people are prone to illness, they just take up another space in their heads and voices!

Bollocks!

All I wondered about at that time, was, what was this song?

And all I think I imagined was, an ass, an ass's ass and a person's face on an ass's ass.

An ass shaking an ass's ass, an ass shaking an ass's ass. Didn't want to say the former, while saying an ass shaking its ass, wanted to make it confusing, English! Yay! Vagueness! Yay!

Now, I'm tired of this!

Hopefully, I don't think that they'll be there for the next sotry.

Should stop suppressing them. This is actually quite creative,

Or quite annoying, you bastard! Freee floooowwww!

Free Falling!

Alright tat's it!

Out!

8Mokcing high pitched voice* But first, let me take a selfie!

LLLLLLLLLUUUUHHHHH!

Autophobia

"With so many stories to go, and things to be found"

Our protagonist sits on his desk with his student. Looking at him, our protagonist feels the flush from desire.

His eyes gaze over the boy's features, the black hair, those-morose-but-sometimes-happy eyes. The slightly brown skin.

And our protagonist can't help but feel love and desire for this boy, with his energy and joy and every sadness like a stab in the heart.

He catches himself, admonishing himself for this desire. But another part of him wonders why it's wrong? After all when he was a boy, he felt desire for all his friends.

It was wrong then, it isn't wrong now. Even the boy knew, he told him, and he was okay with it.

Is innocence and age the barrier?

But I can't harm children. Fantasizing about them won't, but this will. My love will have to come out separately. When I can live out my fantasies, I will then, till then, I will be cold and frigid.

Whenever I look at them, it will be replaced by guilt, confusion and sometimes disgust.

The tuition session with this boy ends. His mother, the talkative and nagging kind.

"Thanks for the service, let me see you off"

Out of the house and onto the streets, back to the house.

Time to unwind for sometime. Perhaps porn, perhaps pleasuring oneself, perhaps the borderline stuff.

Atleast try the adult stuff. Retrain the mind. Or just watch some of that stuff.

It doesn't harm the children if I watch that.

Well, if I don't pay for it, it doesn't contribute.

The heart's not in it anymore, the computer is closed. Climbed into the bed and slept.

He went into a World where as a kid being with another kid wasn't wrong, and neither was it with anybody else.

The next day, he wakes up and decides to do something about his unnecessary fantasizing about children. He ends up at the local pedophile help clinic. Well of course, it's not named like that, obviously, but it's written, "psychological help for the unutterable". A lady in their welcomes him in and guides him to a group of people seated in a circle. "Pedophiles Anonymous", they called themselves. After telling his story, it occurred to him that he may have Primary Obsessive Compulsive Disorder, this required work but it wasn't impossible to cure!

Bad Joke

REFINERY

Warning! (Sniff! Snorts cocaine, auaacckkhhh)

This contrains! Mocherie und hugh laurie.

You stoopid gerh'mans! I thought you were nefer late!

Warning! (In squeaky voice!)

The following perversion of comedy contains errors! Feel free to crediteditdebitsexitit them.

"A bear walks into a bar"

Patron: What would you likh?" (Britiss accent)

Ba're'err: PAUSE, "I'd like a bag of chips and a pint of beer"

Patron: "I'm sorry, wha'at?"

Bear: PAUS. "I'd like a bag of chips and a pint of beer"

"pATEREoN:" Why the paws?

Then the bear molests him (I.e eats him in a most gratuitous manor. Britishh ackcent). Mmhhmmm. Clears throat. Of what? :_) Thank you for the Joke Stefano! (Not you mausa).

Knock! Knock!

Who's There?!

Icehole!

Icehole who?!

Icehole your mother.

A WOMAN is sitting by herself. On her neck, there's a sign that sez: "Warning! Woman!"

Woman: I don noty know why I feel so drained of late.

Man walks in. Man sex: You sir! Are a sperm bank!

End joke now or we exterminate!

Yes fungal overloards! I do now!

Speak Engrish, child.

Yes, daddy.

Where's mommy?

Up yours daddy.

So sorry!

My atrocity at your absurdity!

Apologies!

Now get lost! OR I PULL OUT MY UNDIES TILL YOUR WEAR THEM YOU FUNDIES!

YOU OVER THERE! WHAT IS THE NAME OF THIS LAND?!

HAS AY ONE SEEN MY PUSSY?!

THANK YOU! WE NOW CHRISTEN, HASHAYONESEENMYPUSSY?!

THANK YOU FOR YOUR COOPERATION! GOODBYE!

Benchsitters

Alystra could feel the weight of her legs as she walked slowly but steadily in search of a bench to sit on. She was cutting across the large park which lay between her workplace and her home. The 12 hour shift at the local bookstore had taken its toll. She dealt with snotty customers, shrieking children, titanic idiots, monotony and occasionally she met an oasis in this deluge of mindless effluence. Not a lot of people reading books these days. Not a lot of people reading anything anyways.

Back to her feet though. As she walked her feet felt leaden, it was as if she was walking through custard. Her back was stiff and sore from standing for many hours. Her mouth was open from exhaustion, and since she was a righty, her right foot was numb from fatigue, this made tilt to the left as she compensated. The few people who passed her by at this late hour looked at her as though she were drunk.

She was searching desperately for a place to sit. As she came around the bend, there it was! A bench! Mana from Heaven! Angels had crafted this seat to a perfect mold of her ass! She rushed toward the bench in anticipation, and heedless of the cold steel and her poor, soft back, she plonked herself down on it. An action which she quickly regretted as a sharp pain went up her spine, and her body groaned in protest. This bench was an anal probe machine by Satan himself! The pain made her grimace. The drunk who now had farted? Despicable! Let us leave before she eats us!

Eventually, the pain subsided and her ass and her back calmed down. Allowing her a much needed rest. After, what seemed like an eternity, the clippitty-clop of heels to her right, broke her sleep. As she slowly but surely, opened her eyes and it was stabbed by the flash of a damn streetlight in front of her. *"Do they purposefully put streetlights in front of benches?! I sleep! I don't read!"* As she scanned the horizon, moving her head slowly from the left to the right she saw in her drunken state, an Irishwoman. Well, atleast what she thought was an Irishwoman.

Stereotypes and all that. *"She looks a lot like that woman in that short film that I watched, I'm sure this would feel like an obvious exposition sequence* ****YAWN**** *in a film, wouldn't it?"* she thought.

"Do-do you mind, uh, mind going for a walk?" the Irishwoman asked shivering in an Irish accent.

"Well, why the fuck not?" Alystra thought. Thinking this, Alystra got up and shambled towards the woman, like a drunken zombie who wanted to play with his, no, er, her meal. "If you don't mind, could you take one bag of mine? I'm half-dead you see" she said to the woman now in front of her.

"Sure, of course, anything to walk this could off" the woman replied. "Anything to walk this drink off", mumbled Alystra to herself.

They started walking in silence together. Shortly after their commitment to walk together, the woman to her left stopped shivering, and all was right in the world.

Bored of silence, and wanting to have any stimulus to get her mind off of the sleep, she asked the woman to her left, "So… I know this is drivelous, but I'd like to know, so that my face doesn't meet the floor, what it is that you do?"

The woman to her left, started laughing at that joke, but that made the insidious cold around her find a crevice to freeze her, and she started shivering again. "Well, I'm Death, I collect souls for a living, and now I've come to collect yours" the woman said after she stopped shivering.

Now it was Alystra's turn to laugh maniacally. "HAHHAAHHAAAHHAHAHAHAHAHAHAHA- *COUGH*-*COUGH*-HAHAHAHAHA-HEEHAHAHA" The Onomatopoeia

went. Alystra laughed wholeheartedly for what seemed like an Eternity. By the time she stopped laughing there were tears pouring out her eyes, and her eyes were red.

"You're a real riot 'Death'" Alystra said through tears while making quotation marks while saying the word, "Death".

"So, I've been told", Death replied.

"Ahhahaha, you're too damn funny", Alystra said sarcastically, while still laughing. Does that make this ironic/sarcastic or not ironic/not sarcastic? I can't tell, Death's beyond me, ask her.

"I'm not joking Alystra. I mean, I'm joking, because I'm not your death, your death was caused by something else. I'm Death, as in, the very embodiment of the concept of Death", Death replied.

"Stop fucking with me, did I forget to remove my name tag?" said Alystra incredulously, putting her right hand on left breast reflexively to feel for the name tag.

"Alystra, born 25th June 1999 to Macy and Jonathan Jones. You're grandfather really had the rare stupidity of being bad at and with names. You like to be in the nude. You find clothes to be an unnecessary burden which you literally shouldn't have to shoulder", Death said sardonically.

"Huh?" Alystra squinted at the Irishwoman.

"Most of that was by reading your mind, butI like to keep myself up-to-date with people I'm about to kiiiiiiiiiiiillllllllll, muahahaha ha ha ha ha ha!", Death quipped.

"So, you're God as well?" she asked.

"Well, I mean you can call me that, but you can also call me entropy, Satan, Shaitan, Yam Devta, Mephistos, Mom, Dad, Jesus, Gabriel, Hades, Zeus the king of cats, etc. I have many different names. And that's because I come to people in the form that they find the most comfortable. I'm this form right now, because the last depiction of me that you identify with me was in that short film which you watched", Death said.

"So, I'm dead?" She asked.

"Yeah, sadly, your heart died of boredom, sweetie", she replied.

Alystra mouth curved in a sly and sardonic half-smile and she said, "I can't believe this, Death's joking about death".

"Honey, when you've lived as long as I have, the only thing that you can make fun of is you and yourself", Death replied.

"Goddamn", Alystra stretched the word out comically.

"Why, thank you, I quite like my damming ways. In fact I might just build you one", Death quipped.

"Tell you what, 'God', why don't you just bring back to life, and make me kill myself by hearing your puns, for your amusement, 'kay?" Stop making her so snarky, Keshav, or I'll bugger you myself.

Ignoring her monologue, Alystra continued, "So, what now? Heaven, Hell, purgatory, the loot farting Unicorn land, or the inside of a brown cow?" said Alystra trying to act smart.

"Even better, you're in me now. So you can go anywhere you want, do whatever you want. I'm quite vast, you're quite small", Death said.

"Sex jokes, huh? So, what now, an Eternity of boredom instead of a lifetime of boredom?" said Alystra nonplussed.

'Well, after eating you whole, and swallowing your soul, the least I could do is prevent depression and boredom. You can do anything you want. Provided, you don't use my powers to kill or destroy anything before their time is up. Basically, you'll be my grim reaper. But, mostly, your job is to be my eyes and ears, and your job will be merely observation until something interesting happens. Eventually, after an extremely long time, I will cease to exist and I'll reverse the death of the Universe and be born again. And yes, your scientists were wrong, the answer is always aliens", Death soliloquised.

'Now, is this the part where you stop soliloquising, you die, I die and this hell can end?" said Alystra wryly.

"I'm sure that you'd like to stare into the Abyss by ceasing to exist, but let me tell you that there's nothing worse than not existing." Death responded, ignoring Her Wryness.

"No" Said Alystra with tears in her eyes and all her mirth gone. "I want to be at peace, I don't want to continue existing. Anyways, we'll meet again at the end of the Universe, right? When you and the Universe come back", Alystra continued.

With trepidation, Death looked into the eyes of Alystra, and with a look that signified sorrow but understanding, she snapped her fingers, and Alystra was no more. She disappeared, unforgotten, virtual, at peace.

Reverting back to her stoic and infinite gaze, Death said, "Sentient life, peh, remind me to tell Nature to de-evolve sentience and intelligence. Okay?" Death said with a faux derisiveness.

"Okay"?

BOKEH

Solar System, 300 million years ago.

A paleolithic farmer growing some grain on his watery field stands up for some reason, perhaps to stretch, perhaps by that instinctual drive to look around when nobody is there, notices a white, shiny object out, far in the blue sky above him. It seems to be as far as the nearest city would be to him, but he can't tell for sure. Mesmerized by its appearance, the object seems to fall through the sky. He approaches one of his fellow farmers to declare what he saw. When all of a sudden everything in his vision seems to turn to white.

He has been vapourized. From orbit, a massive 1000 km fireball illuminates the backdrop of the lush planet on which it rudely halted all life. Little streaks of particles flash almost imperceptibly, on the corners of your vision, if you were there. Signaling a much worse future.

Solar System, Today.

Four astronauts from the Extended ISS programme, approach a vast pyramidal like mountain, called the D&M. Abnormally high radiation, guaranteed that this would be the first location where a manned mission to Mars would take place. It was unclear whether a natural nuclear reactor was the culprit behind this at some point in Mars past, or a more sinister interpretation of the data as suggested by some scientists, mostly disregarded as the loony fringe. At the intelligence community's behest, for whom all threats, no matter how foreign or domestic were worthy of investigation, nudged the programme executives at NASA to put this area on the itinerary of the international team sent on the first mission of Mars. If either of those hypotheses would be correct it would be astonishing. As the first would imply that Mars had water on its surface for much longer than anticipated, while the second would imply, even if in the long past, of the presence of an alien civilization which wiped out an indigenous society on Mars and reduced it to its barren self as seen now, before everyone.

Far Away, Yesterday, Today And Tomorrow

In a decrepit solar system, with torn apart planets and dim double binary stars, remnants of vast space mining vessels dot the main beltway of this system like asteroids. Whoever built these monuments to creative destruction are mostly lost to history. Their handiwork to be scrutinized by those they would've crushed without a thought countless eons ago.

Boom Story

My brother and I were walking up the Damavand mountain range. More precisely, a mountain in the Damavand range. We just had to get out of the suffocating air of Tehran. As we were walking up the mountain, we passed by shops, people, rappels, *fear* of rappels etc. Ski Lifts, with people, and lovers. Saw my first public kiss in Iran. Or quite frankly, one of my first in the World. Anyways, propaganda prevents you from seeing people as people. Where we? Ah, yes, we were walking up the mountain, to Damavand, and I started talking about my stories. Like right now!

I told him about what my future stories will be, and what my ideas are, and then I told him about Boom Story. I was just telling him about it. When, BOOM!

We were on the slide, me at back, him at front, and it went faster ***and faster ansfdfaerandfasternadsdafasertandfaster***

TILL WE WERE IN SPAACE!

BOOM!

Earth, this is us. We're in Spaace and everything is alright.

Born Ready

McMurdo Base

Antarctica

Earth Confederation

100 AFC

A hundred years ago, we were made aware as a World of an incoming alien invasion, when our astronomers found a highly blue-shifted object within 3 light years of Earth. We assumed that it was an invasion since observations from the JWST revealed a massive ship with giant cannons and millions of smaller ships forming a funnel in front of it.

It was clearly a warship.

So we started massive preparations. We united the World. We solved climate change, poverty, genocide, and all those other ills, we even built Jägers, and made a couple more of those "Pacific Rim" movies. Although Guillermo didn't direct or produce, he was disgusted. Those who questioned such egregious wastes, were politely reminded of the facts of how their massive robots could disrupt the interior of the alien ships.

3 years later, they arrived. They didn't even bother approaching our planet. We had a couple of preliminary DEWs on the Moon, which were like static electricity for them.

All they did, was to stop the rotation of the Earth.

Instantly.

Within seconds, anything South of the deep Arctic and anything North of the deep Antarctic was razed to nothing by Hypersonic winds. Out of 10 billion humans, only 70,000 survived. Out of life on Earth, only a few species made it out alive. The Oceans were mostly fine. Lots of things died in the shallow waters, and the light zone of the oceans, and on the coasts from monster tsunamis. But deeper than 500 feet, not much change was there.

Above the surface was a different matter. Everything outside of underground nuclear bunkers was vapourized in an instant.

The only central commands we had left, were a few thousand people scattered across the world. NORAD, the Russian Missile Command, China, EU, Japan, India, etc.

Most of Earth became a desert, all the trees were dead. The aliens were adapted to a harsh climate and setup shop on Earth, they then restarted the Earth's rotation. Wiley basturds.

Oxygen levels plummeted. We had a mass extinction and anoxification at hand. We couldn't fight the aliens. Turns out that even while staring the apocalypse in the face, we didn't listen to our white coats.

So we eke out a living on the fringes of Earth, waiting for life to recover. The aliens don't bother disturbing us. And we don't have the resources to do much, except spy, intercept communications, rare guerilla attacks on EHVTs, etc.

It turns out the facts were wrong.

We were born ready, just not war ready.

Bovine

The author was sitting in his favourite restaurant, at his favourite table, in his favourite chair.

"I need to stop distracting myself from my art. I need to stop wallowing in self-pity. Yes, the world is depressing, yes, there's a lot of suffering, yes, you could die at any moment, but what's the point in living if you do nothing and just wait for the end to come? It's my own regret, help me make the most of freedom and of pleasure, nothing ever lasts forever, everybody wants to rule the world. Heh, I can't get the rhyme of the 'Lorde' version of this song out of my head. I can't begin to imagine the rhyme of the original, jovial 'tears for fears' version. I guess that the newer version is more viral for my thoughts. Its melancholy matches my mine as well". He smiled, as he thought this while sipping from his favourite kind of tea, masala tea, from his favourite kind of cup. The "masala" cup. Why was it "masala"? Cause it was really a soup cup. It had soup, tomato, spicy, etc. written all over it. It was his favourite cup, his special cup, because his dad had bought it for him, with a lot of love and affection.

He'd grown apart from his dad. The toxic divorce proceedings between his mother and father had ensured that. He chose to live with his mom, who was equally damaged by the divorce and her past. Making him grow apart from her as well. Handling more than just your own "demons" can really fuck with your mind.

"My love for my father is under repair. Still, I haven't stopped loving him, my love has dampened. It's under a mattress of pain, fatigue and a profound sadness. When he tells me, I love you, I reply mechanically, I love you too. So as to not hurt him. I've tried telling him in the past that my love has softened. It's not as absolute as it was when I was a child. Then he reminds me that I'm still his child. I know, I reply. Then he adds, but you're not a child. I know, dad, I know.

I love you. I really do. Or maybe it's just something I tell myself. But, when he told me that he was going to die, I did shed a tear. Even while we sleep, we will find you acting on your best behaviour, turn your back on Mother Nature, everybody wants to rule the world. Thank you, Lorde. Heh,

Lorde". He smiles as he continues to relish his tea. "They make it like I do. 600ml of pure, unadulterated masala chai". "Not everyone can enjoy genuine home brewed tea, especially masala chai, with all the ingredients and the care that you put in. Oh, shut up you lot, let me enjoy my bloody stiff drink".

His last words just escaped his mouth, as a gunshot rang out, blood spurted, the world screamed and was silenced by darkness.

"I'm alive. Of course you're alive you bloody wank stain. Thanks, assholes, that really helps. Just doing our jobs. Your jobs, eh? Alright shut up! Let me bloody think!". The author thinks, as his eyes open and are instantly stabbed by the flash of a neon light. *"That split the night, and echoed the sounds of silence. STOP! Or I'll actually gouge out my eyeballs and skullfuck myself to death!"* He thought, quite maniacally. *"Alright, where am I? What happened? And why can't I move me bloody head?"* He tries to speak, but only a guttural, "Khkrrrkkkkhhkkhh" comes out.

"WHAT THE FUCK?! WHY CAN'T I SPEAK?!" He tries to flail his arms around in panic, but he only feels the mental sensation of them flailing about, he doesn't see anything moving in front of his eyes. This makes him panic even further. *"My arms! I can feel them moving! But they aren't! They aren't bloody moving! I can't feel my arse, or my balls! I can't feel my stomach grumble, or feel like taking a piss or a shit! What the fuck is going on?!"* He starts to sweat profusely, the beeping noise to his left increases rapidly as his heart beat skyrockets. The doctor and the nurse rush in thinking that he's going into cardiac arrest rush to his side. They see his eyes moving wildly, and his body starts to spasm as his panic goes into overdrive.

"He's going into shock, I'm going to give him 25ccs of Diprivan, stat".

The doctor injects the sedative intravenously, and our protagonist becomes unconscious.

After a day of being unconscious. The author awakens and through his peripheral vision finds the doctor standing to his side.

"I came as the nurse informed me that you were about to wake", She spoke softly. "I wanted to explain your predicament, personally". She continued. "From what the police told me, as you were seated on your table, a suspected racist shot you in your neck at point black range. The bullet was luckily a hunting round of around .22 calibre and it passed right through your neck without ripping your head off. But, it did leave a gaping hole in your neck which was spouting blood. The shooter left in a hurry as bystanders rushed to help you. One of the attendants had the quick-wittedness to hold and press down on your wound as he called another attendant of the tea shop to press down on your wound tightly from the other end, without moving you, or your head, of course. The paramedics arrived, bandaged you, and rushed you to the hospital. Your surgery lasted nearly a day. The hole in your larynx and trachea had to be sealed. Luckily, the bullet missed the major veins and arteries, and that's why I'm here explain this to you. Bone splinters had to be removed from you neck and you damaged spine and spinal cord had to be repaired. But, we can't heal nerves, once damaged, especially for adults, it's extremely difficult for them to heal. As you've probably noticed, you've lost all feeling below your upper neck. And you will be breathing through a tube in your neck, till such time that your trachea heals completely. You won't be able to talk for atleast two weeks to month. And even after that, you'll need speech therapy. I'm really very sorry". She said, as she placed her hand on my hand. "The police are still looking or the suspect". "Please get some rest", saying this she walked out of the room.

"As it turns out, I will be bedridden for the rest of my life, maybe I can ask for some euthanasia, perhaps my murderer would grant me that one last wish. He or she could get to pull the plug in glee", he thought.

His parents were obviously quite worried about his plight. Thankfully, the one uniting factor amongst them was him. **Especially**, harm done unto him.

"Whoever's this asshole, I'll cut his balls off and feed them to him. He shot my son! I'll execute his whole family", said my dad in his usual, heartwarming Übermensch talk. Venting his anger and frustration. It was quite endearing for me, to hear my dad talk about ripping and tearing this man to shreds. It gave me quite a gleeful feeling. My mother rolled her eyes at me, as she smiled at me in her, "look-at-him-being-publicly-humiliating-himself-smile". Although, to be quite honest, my dad was a bulldog, he would've quite readily done what he said, if I hadn't signaled no to him with my eyes (as, moving my head was quite literally a pain in the neck), due to my pathological pacifism. It was also probably the reason why the divorce took so long, he was lonely, and he couldn't stand the fact that our family was breaking up. Still I couldn't put past the mental and emotional torment he put mom through because, he was in his own hell. I don't know, I don't like to think about it. It's such a moral gray area. I was just happy to see my parents together again. Because I loved it. His faux Übermaschimo fatherly expression of angry love and my mother's clichéd dismissal of his boisterous aggression, it felt like my childhood again. When things were simpler, happier and plainer. Even if it was just a fantasy. With them around, I felt that I could be made great again. Clearly, they would start debating as to who would take care of me, and in whose home and where. You see, I come from an affluent family. They each have independent homes in different countries. My dad sold his ancestral property off. A big one. It allows us to live our upper-class lifestyle. No matter how distasteful I find it. I have to admit, it does have its perks. More books, more knowledge, more access to more countries, more porn. Not that I'll be ever using the instruments. It wouldn't be so bad to die a virgin, if I could atleast masturbate, but with my near 100% paralysis, I'd go insane from sexual frustration and other things as well.

While my parents were fighting about whose house, at what time, for how long, etc. I was thinking about how unfair the world is about euthanasia. Passive euthanasia is allowed in many parts of the world, for those who have lapsed into a vegetative state with permission from their families. But the poor sods who're suffering like me, can't avail of active euthanasia accept in a few parts of the world, because of some misplaced sense of self-righteousness. As visiting hours got over. My parents chose to stay the night. I was really moved by this. And I'm not being sarcastic. My body's a vegetable, I'm not. Nothing's worse than that. I'm trapped, with no escape.

My parents stayed over the weekend. My mom and my dad tried their level best to help in whatever way that they could. Cleaning my toilet bowl. I felt terrible being so helpless and powerless. So dependent. But my dad kept reminding me of how when I was a baby, he would clean my poo, and then whenever he'd had a bath, I would soil his clothes again. So, he had to clean me AND have a bath again. This old, done to death anecdote, which used to redden my face, or annoy me. Now made me laugh like a madman, which sounded like a whale snorting through a plastic snorkel. Talk about a blowhard, amiright? And I had tears in my eyes. Not just of humour, but also of a joyous, melancholic and nostalgic sadness for the days of old.

My mom kept me up-to-date with all the political and social happenings of the world. She was a social activist. She cracked lame jokes, many of which were mine. Some were good, admittedly. They were warned to not make me laugh too much, death and all that jazz. She even licked my face, as I used to do hers, and since I had no form of defence against her dark arts, I found myself nearly suffocate controlling my giggles as she continued her affectionate torture. If it weren't for them, I would've given up the will to live, long ago. They fretted all the doctors and nurses, and probably drove them insane with all their henning over me. For except for my intravenous food and medicines, they insisted and downright demanded to take care of all my non-medicinal needs on their own. I mean, look at it from their perspective, their lifeblood, me, was literally on his deathbed. A very long and slow death, but death, nonetheless.

It just so happened that one day, when my parents were out for lunch, they were pretty old now, in their late 50s, early 60s, so despite their love and enthusiasm for my care, they were after all ageing and worn humans, with quite a lot of time and suffering under their belts.

Anyways, I was "fed", cleaned, drugged quite a bit and ready for some sweet, sweet sleep with nightmares, when in barged, guess who? A reporter.

Now, my mind was all fogged up from all the cocaine, sorry, all the drugs which I'd been quite politely imbibing. But, I do remember that my first line of inquiry was, "Doctor! How nice of you to fuck by".

Now, the reporter, she seemed to be a little taken aback with my question or my consciousness, I'm a little unsure as you would be, if you saw a woman riding up space mountain as a fuzzy angelic figure with two stars for eyes who just phased through a door and straight into your face. I mean I was really out of it. Am I glad that we can get legal hard drugs if we're shit out of luck in a hospital.

Now, she was quite professional and she put this odd electrode contraption on my skull. Possibly to read my thoughts. Did I mention that I have armed police guards? How'd she get through them? Press credentials or boobies? Heh heh.

"I want to interview you about your predicament. Would you be willing?" she asked. "From the midnight land of ice and snow! Valhalla I'm coming! Ahhhhh ahhhh ahhhhh ahhh! Ooooooooo Ooooooo!" I answered. I mean I was really out of it by now. My entire music playlist was playing in my head right now, at the same time.

Then she splashed my face with cold water, and I snapped out of it a little bit. So I quite eloquently said, "Sure thing sugar boobs". Now, I don't quite know why, but drugs make me pretty sexist and misogynist, but it just seems like they do. Or maybe for me at the time, I felt like as if I was complimenting her. Or maybe I am a sexist and misogynist deep down. Or perhaps it's that I've been drugged up my arsehole. Oh! Who cares?

Clearly, she ignored me, otherwise I would've also remembered quite the slap.

"Why do you think it happened?" She asked. *"Why do I think this happened? Some racist prick just decided that that day would've been good as any other to screw this guy. The stupid cow fucker."* I thought. And the electrode hat on my head must've transformed my brain signals into words on her handheld which she was looking into.

"How's your experience?" She asked, quite vaguely.

"Honestly? For a paraplegic person? Quite well I suppose, I'm fed, cleaned, drugged and dressed for the benefit of the innocent eyes of others. But, I'm a writer, I don't want to be bedridden for the rest of my life. I was slowly recovering from my depression, and this present predicament of mine hasn't really helped. I want to die, but I can't. It may sound selfish, my parents are coming together after a long time, even if it's an uncomfortable "alliance", my childlike wish has been fulfilled. I know that if I die, or if I could, commit suicide, it would break them, they've suffered a lot in their lives, and this might just push them over the brink. But I'm suffering, I don't want to live such a life" I thought. She paused for a while, looking up from her screen and then she looked over at me.

"Would you like me to kill you?" She said, most calmly.

And in that moment, it struck me. The peculiar choice of questions and words. Her cold, mechanical demeanour. It all made sense now. Maybe I was fantasizing, but, she could be my assaulter. So, I did what any self-respecting survivor would do, stare down his aggressor and think the question. I mean what could I say? I'm not going to openly question the actions of a cutthroat maniac.

"Are you the one who fired the bullet?" I asked. "Yes", she replied. Now, don't get me wrong, I had fantasized this, but I was genuinely surprised that this was the case. I have a tendency to grossly underestimate or overestimate my intuition. Mostly the former.

"Should I do it? Should I ask my would-be-murderer to become one and put me out of my misery? Should I fulfill her desire to kill, and mine to die?" I thought quite naturally. Thinking is such a personal and integral part of us that I forgot that I was being watched. Not that she really cared about consent.

"I had hoped for this moment, you know? I had hoped that my bullet wouldn't kill you, that you would end up paraplegic, not a vegetable, that's why I aimed for your neck. That you could be here, and I could hear it from your mouth that you want to die, and I could be here, to administer death. The crime is Life, and the punishment is Death". She said.

"If you keep monologuing, I'll suffocate myself" I thought.

Upon reading this, she let out a bark of laughter. "I'd like to see that" she said, amidst peals of laughter. "It wasn't that funny. Says the guy who laughs at how lame jokes are legless? Oh sod off" I thought.

"Alright, if you're so keen on murdering my ass, go ahead, do it, you daft whore" I thought. She smiled at me after reading this, and then she surprised me, by kissing me on the fucking lips. I quickly imagined him, so as to get all the fear and loathing out of my mind. After my initial shock was over, I thought, *"Oh, just fucking great, she's one of those assholes who gets off on killing people".* Honestly, I don't know what she was trying to do, but atleast there wasn't any moaning. I mean what's worse or better? Getting facehugged by your murderer, or that you die just after your first kiss? Bugger.

As she reached for the plug, I took in a deep breath, I knew I would need that Oxygen for the time that it took the doctors to come. The machines went off, and I knew that she wouldn't have much time to leave, but as she was about to, she brought her elbow down on my diaphragm, and she rushed out.

The pain was immense, I felt like my lungs were going to implode as the air rushed out of my mind. The machines were off, so I was unable to take a breath. I was clawing at my neck, or atleast I had the phantom feeling of my arms doing that. It was so surreal. I knew I could feel my arms on the pipes, yet they were not there, they were by my sides. I was experiencing respiratory distress, and this time I don't know if I'm going to survive. Either way, I'm screwed.

Cheche Hall

I walk out of Cheche Hall after putting the 'bat piece' into the monopoly box. As I'm closing the door.

A child's hand grabs mine. It's night, so, it's a bit frightening, but I take the hand into mine and I lovingly take the child with me down the stairs, on my shoulders.

I spend time with the child, playing, talking, silliness, food, water, the loo, and then, once the fun and togetherness is over, the child disappears, an enigma. A ghost.

It took this to satisfy the violence of this place's heart, to banish the demons of the past. The pain and suffering is gone.

(Inspired by Guillermo Del Toro's "The Devil's Backbone")

Ghosts are just the mighty dead.

Chrystal Ambitions

A long fibrous entity, clearly energetic in Nature, spreads across the Solar System in search of that most precious of organized matter, life.

This malevolent behemoth, tastes the tops of gas giants, recoils with disgust and keeps moving through space.

It reaches across the coldness and vastness of space-time and manages to taste the anti-entropy of a Blue World.

"Blueness!" it thought to itself. As it entered the atmosphere for a most delectable snack.

As the scientist sat down in his sofa and thought about some powerful and equally obscure astrophysical calculations which would redefine the World.

He had a strange sensation in his mind. As he was thinking, he saw a massive cloud devour his World. He heard voice. "Go home and see what I've done to your family".

Inspite of being a very rational empiricist, something about this dream or vision was so ominous and alien that he had no choice but to satisfy his anxiety.

He leapt out of his chair and ran towards the door. And then opened it.

As he looked outside, he saw no one.

There were these embers raining down from the sky. He didn't wait anymore, he ran as fast as he could.

Out onto the street, a being moves swiftly between the buildings.

These buildings are like no other.

The best description would twirling seaweeds. Biomemetic towers to the core. With phototropic shoots and geotropic roots. As it twirls with the intensity of the wind, they move like spirals.

Deriving their energy from, with photovoltaic cells as organic and as efficient as leaves.

The sun glistening off of their shimmering windows. The sky darkens, as they do.

Embers fall, a gentle, rain of foreshadowing.

The World's spirit takes on an eerie beauty.

Still, what was more important was that he got to his family in time.

As he ran through the once populated city, his pace quickened as he now saw his house approaching.

At the sound of the Dong, it will be Death O' Clock.

He reached his door and burst in.

He found no one. The soft-warm glow of the walls lit up the room with natural light.

He found the sofa his wife loved to sit on, empty.

He called out for her, he called out for his kids, but, nothing.

As he moved through the house, the eeriness was overwhelming, every room had stopped mid-action.

Upon reaching his wife's room, he found her near the bed. With a weapon in her hand.

As the warmth of the light came in, he saw blood.

Slowly approaching her, he asked her tentatively, "Honey, where are the kids?" She said, "I couldn't stop her from hurting the kids".

"Who?"

"You"

With that she leapt, and attempted to cut his head off. Somehow he managed to jump back, before he lost his head.

He ran into the bathroom and closed the door behind him. She attacked the door with all her might.

There wasn't much efficiency in her blows, but given enough time, she was able to create a plank-hole.

As he looked at her in horror, something incomprehensible happened, a thougth from faraway crept into her decrepit mind and

"HERE'S JOHNNY!"

The energetic entity then moved to devour the planet.

At that moment as it was consuming the planet. The galactic fleet warped in to engage the space demon.

ALL HANDS! ACTION STATIONS!

Climate Hustle

A man sits near a woman sleeping on a bed. He's sitting on a chair, facing her. He has a sign sticking out from his head. It says, "Climate Denier". He's holding a book in his hands, which he's pointing at her. The woman's face is painted green.

He says, "Begone, green demon!"

Her eyes open quickly, she glares at him, gets up and slaps a tree into his face with her right hand.

This happens 10 ten times in rapid succession, the same action being repeated as it hits his rightcheek finally.

He flies out of his chair a few feet and does dozens of flips in the air, and crashes dramatically into the floor. His head has trees growing out of it, and the letters in the sign change quickly (like a slot machine) to environmentalist. He has birds and planets revolving above his head.

The woman gets up, looks at the camera and maniacally laughs like the Mask, with a highpitched, "Ha-Ha!"

The women's legs move very quickly, in one place, as she rockets down the stairs and out the house.

The camera moves to the man's face as he points his right finger up and says weakly, "That worked", and his head flops down again.

As the woman slams through the door, the sight that she's greeted by makes her eyes pop out and her tongue falls to the floor, as her legs lift a few feet off the ground as she screams, "Ahhhhhhhhhh!"

What she sees are as follows:

A looney toon smashing chimneys into the road, which blacken the sky.

An animal torturer, brutalizing all animals in a vicious manner (it's suggested by the horrific noises in his barn, :D)

Government officials handing out certificates which have approved "Destroy The Environment", shaking hands with oily bastards.

Scientists on the ground, having their faces stomped by a boot, which says, "Fuck Science", everytime it stomps a face.

Religious Leaders preaching, "Money, Power, Genocide, Destroy, Obey, Consume".

Judges taking money to condemn the environment and environmentalists to death.

A man sitting on a table which says MEAT, with a fork and a knife, and a maniacal grin.

A man in a chariot, whipping men and women who are pulling it.

Men at the river who are laughing as one burns the birds with a flame thrower, one poisons the fishes, one is spraying brown stuff (shit) from a machine into the river, one is pouring oil from a barrel, and one is using a garbage truck to dispose plastic into it.

Near a bunch of trees, a man is cutting the trees with a chainsaw, and another one is pushing a tree into a grinding, out of whose other end money is flying out.

And a soldier at guard in the centre. Shooting at anyone who gets out of line.

People are wheezing and coughing everywhere.

Everytime a bad thing happens, there's an inception BWAAS (air horn) noise. The woman turns the chimneys into windmills, and makes them float in the sky,

she zaps the looney toon back to her world, the sky clears and brightens, Government certificates change to "Protect The Environment", Scientists and their torturers are now working together to make the world a better place as friends, The religious leaders now preach, Humane, Kind, Love, Togetherness, Life, Learn, Preserve", The judges and their bribers stop indulging in illegal activities and instead together start to hand out real justice, she turns the MEAT eater into a VEGGIE eater, she turns the charioteer and his slaves into friends in a park, she turns the men in the river to as follows,

the flamethrower becomes a lover of birds, the poisoner becomes a bread thrower to the fish, the one dumping brown stuff, into a firemen who douses out the flames, the plastic man, into a flower shooter, with fragrance everywhere,

the chainsawer becomes a tree hugger, the money grinder into a gardener and makes the soldier into a happy flowery man, who's holding a big flower instead of a gun, and everyone's smiling and having fun. Whenever something good happens, a twinkling sound plays. Like faeries you know?

As soon as she thinks that she's done, A GIANT drop of oil in a suit, top hat and monocle, with a moustache and towering over everything else, looms over the happy scene, and he starts monologueing. It's oil man!

"I'm the one who's made everyone evil and destructive, Muah ha ha ha!"

Oil-man continues laughing and blabbing, as the green woman starts to rotate her right arm very very fast, blindingly fast. She draws in the powers of Earth, Fire, Water, Air and Heart, she starts to sing the Captain Planet theme song and suddenly, as if her arm is Mjölnir, she flies into the air and destroys oil-man in an instant, and instead of oil, water rains down on everyone and cleans everything, as oil man is destroyed and everyone and everything is saved. Everyone is happy and joyful, as green woman (she isn't actually green) lands and everyone cheers her, and some hug her. Even former denier is seen happy and clapping, as he rubs his cheek and the woman sticks her tongue out at him, as he laughs.

THE END

Why yes, this is a feel good propaganda film about environmentalism, sharing its name with the drab and witless anti-environment film of the same name, as a tool for awareness and counterpropaganda, love.

Degradation

As I lay there, on my bed, I felt a pain on my hand, and on my crotch. I looked at my hand. There was something grotesque there. The skin around the joint of my thumb had swelled with so many pustules, it may have been a fungus, who knows?

I panicked and rubbed it off with my right thumb, and it come off, lots of pain. But somehow, clear skin underneath.

I pulled my pajamas away from my waist. Looked at my crotch, nothing there, just an itch. I scratched it, shrugged, and went back to sleep.

Divorce

(Haven't you got a heart?)

Whenever, wherever, whether I'm in Srinagar or in Delhi, from Kashmir to Kanyakumari, they all keep asking the same motherfucking question, didn't try to stop them from going apart? (Now it's my turn to rock'em, sock'em, drop'em, stop'em and mock'em) Didn't you try to bring them together, once they wanted to move apart? Haven't you ever tried to shove a motherfucking chabook up your ass? You stupid turds! Yes! I'm a kid, I didn't just stop and stare like a gormless dumbass. I walked, I talked, I stalked, I cajoled, I consoled, I begged, I pleaded, I tried to make them whole. That's what kids do you stupid git!

So, I stand, and I sit, And I'm thankful for every question that I get, but I'm racin', I'm pacin', I stand and I sit. I'm grabbing my hair out, but I can't be "leeberal" or a "post-modernist", whatever the fuck that is, it's how my childhood made me. I'll have to start a fight, I'll be me and I'll be mean you stoopit tit!

You can call me an asshole, you can fire your crapshoot, I'll stand in the boardroom, smile for your eye-cameras, buy you some sourdough, with some salt to go. I don't care, all I can be is just me. So, I point one finger at 'em , but it's not the index, or te pinkie, or the ring, or the thumb, it's the one you put when you don't give a fuck man. When you won't just put up with the bullshit they pull you through. So, blame it on my ADD, girl. So look where it's at, and where's it at? It's up your ass! Where were the parents?! It's tiring me out, so all immediately point a finger on me, but I point back with don't-fuck-me.

Because I am, who I am, if I wasn't, then why would say I am, in the neighbour, the hood, everyday I am. Radio won't even taste my jam. I'm so sick and tired of admired, that I wish that I would just die or get fired. And drop from my labels, 'cause I'm not gonna be able to top all my fables. I just do not got the patience to deal with these cocky cockasians. Who just thing I'm just some nigga who tries to be slack.

But I can't take a shit without someone standing by it, smelling it and telling me its texture. No, I'm not answer your autocrap, you can call me asshole, I'm glad, 'cause it feeds me the fuel that keeps the fire burning. 'Cause I am who I am, if I wasn't, then why would I say I am. In the neighbour, the hood, everyday I am. Radio won't even taste my jam. They won't even taste my crap.

INSPIRED BY EMINEM. SPECIFICALLY, 'THE WAY I AM'.

THESE ARE SUPPOSED TO BE SERIOUS, SORRRY!

I

WAS

READY

BORN

TO

BE MAD

MAX

WHERE WAS I GOING WITH THIS? OH YES

SERIOUSSNESS

EARTH

120 million years from now.

High above in orbit, a large spaceship looms. It has travelled at twice the speed of light for 50 million years. Then it slowed to 0.9c, 25 light years from Earth, so that it wouldn't destroy the solar system, or our neighbouring stars.

It's an archaeology ship, from a planet, whom it is so distant now, that it is as alien to its home world, as we are to it. Filled with daring adventurers, sacrificing millions of years and generations, for the chance to be the first FTL travelers and pioneers. They know that they are alone. Whichever star systems they were sent to in whichever galaxy they went to, will not be visited by their fellow terrestrials. These worlds are for them only. As 50 million years is a long time for not only FTL technology to evolve, but for whole orders of life to come into existence and to cease to exist.

For the past couple of decades. These extra-earth entities, or aliens, if you so prefer, had been excavating fossils, artefacts to become more knowledgeable about the planet they were on. Records in the millions of years were too deep down retrieve without damaging them. Here, Nature did the job for them. Exposed Earth, limestone, which had various fossilized articles of a civilization long past. A skull, a locomotive, a mechanical arm, lots of plastic, etc. Black bands reach far above the limestone, signifying an unprecedented mass extinction event. About 8 feet and 4 inches from the previous layer of Limestone. After this the limestone continued. A very long and vast mass extinction. Nevertheless, judging by the age of this planet, this planet had another 880 million years of multicellular life left, and billions of years of unicellular life after that. Enough time for a new, perhaps more successful civilization building species.

The intelligent, tool-making civilization which had made this grand mark on this planet. Had been extinct for over a 100 million years. While life had recovered, robust and blossoming after that extinction period which claimed them as well, it was still sad to see a near success wiped out before they solved their problems. The rest of the planet was teeming with life, but we were out here in this desert, as it was most interesting. A billion years of this planet's history represented in the 80 foot cliff in front of me. A vast canyon stretched out around me, of how many untold mysteries, no one yet knows. We will certainly build a colony on this world, and uncover more mysteries about this world, and of that mysterious long-lost civilization. We will learn little of their cultures, in even a million years. As any records outside of fossils will be long gone, and any space records would've either de-orbited long ago, drifted far off, or come apart in this vast expanse of space-time. Any signals, have long since dissipated into the cosmic background radiation, indistinguishable. And any telescopes would've been impossible to use in our FTL journey. And even though we may have records from our homeworld's observations of this part of the night sky, I doubt, we doubt, that they would be of much use.

While time travel maybe an option we could explore, it would merely take the observer into a parallel universe, from which return would be nigh-impossible and far too resource-intensive to be viable, even for an inter-galactic civilization as us. Perhaps on another world in a billion years, we might have the freedom of resources to grace a planet with such worthy respect. And not one, but too all that we find later.

But, until such time comes to a pass, we must satisfy our curiosity with the tried, tested and ageold skill of Ancient archaeology. And even when we do have viable time travel, the knowledge of this vast discipline, cannot be forgotten, as the council of the ******** Intergalactic Confederation is aware.

Until then

Rzxexloghozxlizth

Escalation

A man tries to get the attention of his mother, so he takes a particle of dust and throws it at her. He takes his hand and smacks her on the back. He takes a book and hits her. Still nothing. He takes a piece of paper with "Car" written on it and strikes her with it. A truck, A plane, A skyscraper, A supertanker, A Moon, A planet, A Star, A Solar System, A Galaxy, A Supernova,

A hypernova, A Quasar, The Universe, BOOM, BIGGER BOOM, BIGGEST BOOM, EVEN BIGGEST BOOM, TOTALLY BIGGEST BOOM,

"MOOOOMM! WHY AREN'T YOU LISTENING TO ME?!"

"Sweetie, all you had to do was ask"

Facepalm

Far Too Many Verses

Re: Idiot njeelani

Subject: Are alternate dimensions the same as parallel universes?

Dear Astrophysicist,

We hear the term alternate dimension(s) used as a synonym for parallel universe(s). Are they different terms or do they mean one in the same thing?

Kind regards,

Neelam Jeelani

Dear Neelam,

Hi. Yes. It's true that in popular culture, the phrases, "alternative dimensions" and "parallel universes" are used synonymously. But they aren't. You know the 3 sides which surround us all. They are integral to our understanding of the world. Even as babies we are aware of the 3 spatial dimensions (+1 time dimension). In astrophysics, there's nothing like an "alternative dimension" per say. And alternative dimension at the most would imply a Universe where there are more than three 3 spatial dimensions which we (or something/someone else) can perceive. Alternate dimensions also include temporal dimensions. That is, say, going up-down, left-right, forwardsbackwards, diagonally, etc. Mind-boggling it is. Even for trained specialists such as us. We can only visualize such worlds in math only. Our brains are not wired in more than 3+1 dimensions (3 space + 1 time, forwards). The closest we can come to visualizing higher dimensions is perhaps in a Tetragrammaton. Or a cube within a cube. Or a cube with 36 sides (a Hypercube) and those two cubes have to be revolving around their central axis. So in three dimensions it gives the illusion of the cubes phasing in and out of each other. This is again an approximation. We're 3-

D beings, we can't observe 4-D objects in their entirety. Even if we were teleported to such a Universe, we would still see 3-D representations of everything around us. Our minds would protect us from things that which we cannot comprehend, as we'd lose our sanity (as we're not used to such shapes). It's unclear what would happen if a 3-D being grew up in a higher dimensional world, perhaps they'd be able to perceive those shapes, or perhaps there would be hardware limitations from our own brain. It's unknown. In our own Universe, when it was born, only 3+1 dimensions unfurled. The others stayed furled. In M-Theory, our latest theory to explain everything (which we're still working on). The minimum number of predicted spatial dimensions are 11, and the limit tends to infinity (a limit, not a number). The minimum number of Universes predicted are 10^500. That's the multiverse (minimum number, again the upper bound is infinite). If only the lower bound is valid (we just don't know), or anything less than infinite is valid, the chances are that we exist in a vast and diverse multiverse where no two Universes are alike, and the chances that a Universe like ours, or similar to ours, which exists is negligible. However if there are an infinite number of Universes, then there would be, theoretically an infinite number of Universes like ours, and an infinite universes unlike ours. Again, we just don't know.

So, simply, alternate dimensions (or more precisely more or less space-time dimensions), always exist in other Universes (in respect to ours), and parallel Universes can have alternate dimensions (in respect to ours). But, in scientific parlance, Alternate Dimensions and Parallel Universes aren't interchangeable words.

I hope that this answers your question.

Kind Regards,

Mary Bellaire

"Why don't you poke your eyes out with that compass? Why don't you drink that bleach and see what happens? Why don't you clip your clitoris with nail clipper?" Said the voices of attrition when no longer held back by the scientific voice.

The scientist took a week to write this e-mail back. And so she held her head in her hands. The toll of life bends reality, much like her art. *"Don't worry, they're here, they'll take care of you, I'll take care of you. Apologize to her for the late message"* Said the kind voice. *"Yes, Mother"* She said with the intent to hang her out to wry and dry. But nevertheless, that secret seriousness deep inside, had left her high and dry.

A great herculean force moved her life. She was not sure, but her mind is what made her cry, sometimes with joy for the richness of life was hers to enjoy, but mostly like a blasted blight, it would leave her mind deprived.

Re: Idiot njeelani

I'm so sorry that I took so long to reply. You see, as a scientist, my mind is quite fractalized. Kind Regards,

Goodbye.

GAINAX

"What are you saying?"

"What I'm saying is very simple"

"It's the edge of our resolution"

"Really?"

"Really"

"Once we used gravitons to scan the Universe, we managed to unite gravity with the other forces, we've managed to resolve the Universe almost to the origin of itself, but we can't go any further"

"Why not?"

"Because, that would require us to recreate a pocket Universe to see where the Superforce comes from, we just don't have the capability to do so. Maybe some of our descendants will manage"

"Are you thinking what I'm thinking?"

"Yes, Physics has undermined the need for physics, now that we can explain everything, every action, every interaction, they'll just be a few technicians and massive supercomputers figuring out some things, and resolving others" "Science has ended science"

"Ha ha ha, that's funny, I think that we should all become farmers, and leave all the other fields to the comps"

"Yeah. But what about writing?"

"Ah, write if you want to, they're enough of those anyways"

Title: **God Sucks**
Category: Fiction » Sci-Fi
Author: Chantern15
Language: English, Rating: Rated: M

God Sucks

"Are you sure that this is going to work?" asked the boy. "Of course it'll work" said the mad scientist.

"Couldn't we just do FTL travel? Atleast there I wouldn't have to die." He said.

"That's unclear. While yes, Faster-Than-Light travel can make you drift into higher dimensions, it's unclear whether you'd survive" she said.

"Well, that's inspiring. Will it hurt?" he asked, with trepidation.

"No, not in the least, the transfer of your quantum information will be instantaneous and hence quite painless. Another reason to not use FTL travel is that it's quite possible that you would be quite well-cooked from all the microwave saturation" she replied.

"Another thing" she said. "FTL travel while far more feasible than it was during the 20th and the 21st centuries. It is still very, very cost prohibitive, it requires too many people and too much preparation. Our computing prowess has advanced far faster than our propulsion technology.

Hence, making teleportation difficult but not nearly as impractical FTL travel" she continued.

"Okay. Now, why do I need to float? And why am I naked?" he asked.

"First of all, this is nothing sexual. I'm not here to get off on your nude body. This is because you cannot be in contact with anything. Even air" she explained.

"What?! Not even air?! If you create a vacuum, won't I implode?" he barked fearfully.

"Ha ha ha ha! I got you, I got you good. No, there's going to be no vacuuming which will go on. We will communicate your information instantaneously, so there will hopefully be no extra air molecules which will teleport into your body, which would cause you to die very painful. So, to reduce the movement of particles, we're going to supercool the air around you with liquid Helium. You can survive the intense cold for about 2 minutes. Don't worry, we will cool you much faster than that. And then you will be teleported into higher-dimensional space. Since space is a vacuum, you will only chill out slowly. You will also lose water and air quite quickly. So, you'll only get a minute to see the event, before we teleport you back. We're going to have a problem here, because while your information is communicated through quantum entanglement, something will have to take your place here. Where there is a vacuum, perhaps all the required particles will come into place over a large area, due to the amount of space between particles in space. Or the spaciness of space, so to speak. So, we will either have a hotchpotch of gases equal to your weight or just a hunk of expanding higher-dimensional space-time which will destroy our planet, and possibly, eventually even our Universe. But, that's only if space-time has particles. Well, it's now or never. Hopefully it will be the former. Also, quantum teleportation will conserve your momentum, and I mean all your momentum. You're revolving around the sun? Check. The Earth is rotating? Check. The Galaxy is rotating? Check. The Galaxy is moving towards the Andromeda Galaxy? Check. The Local Cluster is moving? Check. The Virgo Supercluster is moving? Check. Space is expanding? Check. Although that effect will be negligible, hopefully. When you travel to higher-dimensional space, you will no longer be a 3-D spatial object. You will be a 5-D spatial object. You won't sense that change, as your brain will protect from that massive trauma. But we don't know how the addition of addition of extra spatial dimensions will affect you. Will they amplify the effects of space expansion, diminish them, or neutralize them? We don't know. But since gravity is weaker in higher dimensions as its more spread out, there could be rapid expansion, but then you'd die, and you wouldn't know anyways. Hmm?" She lectured.

"So, basically, either I'll die, or I'll die, or I'll die, or I'll die. But if I'm alive, I'll know it. I'll also be moving extremely fast. Why couldn't you just say that?" he asked.

"It wouldn't be as much fun. It's positively orgasmic to talk about science. Especially scientific terms" she replied.

"Great. I'm being sent to 5-D space by an astrophysicist who gets turned on by blowing people up" he retorted.

"No, just by blowing people" she said, laughing.

The boy rolled his eyes so hard that they might've just popped out and started dancing to ragtime gal.

"Okay, so when I teleport you, you'll moving at around 0.2% of light. Because that's approximately the speed at which our local cluster is moving at. Buuuuttt, if we factor in the pull from the Great Attractor and the Shapely Attractor, it could be much, much more. I'd hazard a guess of 0.5-0.6% of light". She said.

"Yes, darling, do hazard a guess as I hazard my neck" he said sardonically.

"Huh, I honestly don't know what to do here. If you accelerate from 0 to 0.5-0.6% of c, you would experience 3.403004418823859e+44 Gs' of acceleration. You would be stripped to your sub-atomic constituents. Unless, of course! How can I forget, what matters is your frame of reference. If I place you extremely close to the black hole, the gravitational pull of the black hole should cancel out the extreme acceleration on your body" she exclaimed.

"Closer than the photosphere" she said excitedly.

"You mean closer than even where light can't escape?" he asked.

"Precisely. You don't have to worry. Quantum Entanglement is basically when two particles are connected by ultra-microscopic wormholes. Where two Black Holes are quantum entangled. Possibly by sharing their radiation. It's unclear, as we need more research. Which is where you come in my dear, sweet guinea pig! You shall study this 5-D Black Hole. Stare into the void and make it blink!" she went on maniacally.

"What do you want the safe thought to be?" she asked.

"Safe thought?" he asked back.

"Jeez. If you're getting fucking fucked, what do you want your get out of jail free card to be?" she asked, frustrated.

"Beam me up Scotty", he thought in a Scottish accent.

"You got it. Remember the Scottish accent. Don't bother asking. I implanted an organic transmitter in your brain, it's perfectly safe, as long as you don't fuck your head up" she retorted.

He decided to keep quiet.

"You won't have to worry about coming back. As long as you don't cross the event horizon, you'll be fine. Using my calculations I will place you very, very, very close to the Black Hole. Wait! Sorry, 5-D black holes don't have event horizons! They're naked singularities. There was a theory back in the early 21st century which speculated that we reside in the event horizon of a 4D spatial Black Hole. If the Ultra-Microscopic Wormhole theory is true then the 5-D Black Hole could be Quantum Entangled to the 4-D Black Hole. There's another very, very important goal of this mission. God. If we're residing in the event horizon of a 4-D Black Hole, then technically speaking that Black Hole is God, and all our religions should've been worshipping it. It'll probably send us to hell. Which considering Black Holes is probably being spat out the other end through a White Hole. If they exist, of course. So, here's your chance to find out whether unprotected higher-dimensional travel will kill you and everything else and whether God is sentient, or just a giant fucking hard drive" she said. While they had been talking slowly cooled the air around him and he was so engrossed in talking that he had missed it. She had cooled the air with invisible *lasers.*

"Now just wait a fucking minute" he protested.

"Sorry! Too late! Energizing Lasers! Firing!" she shouted.

And in an instant he was disintegrated and reintegrated at the other end.

As he came into existence, he saw an extremely bright light in front of him as the Black Hole came into view. It was like a million galaxies, that's how powerful the light was. He was certain that the radiation was cooking him from the inside out. But he couldn't think, as the air from his lungs was being forcibly removed and his skin and eyes were turning a bright red as all the water started to evaporate into space. He wasn't feeling cold as yet as his body was cooling very slowly in the vacuum of space. The Black Hole, but in this case it was emitting a bright white light. It was the naked singularity. Unbound by the event horizon, unbound by general relativity.

It was so terrifying, but also so fucking beautiful. The Black Hole as it inhabited a higher dimension appeared as a 3-D torus to him. But unlike any torus that he had seen. It was moving flowing very fast in its shape. As it moved in it separated into blobs connected by thin spindles and then back outwards into a Torus. The Torus itself had a very wide hole and a very thin ring.

But he realized that he was falling into the Black Hole. "*Fuck, this is going to hurt like hell*" he thought. But, as the light grew brighter and brighter, and he closed his eyes to prevent blindness, he fell through the Black Hole/Wormhole and he appeared out the other side surprised to find himself facing the 4-D Hyperspherical Black Hole and not Heaven.

"*Some big star died, millions, maybe billions of years ago, and it left our Universe in its way*" he thought looking at the strange Black Hole with its event horizon made up of rippling spheres morphing between spiky and non-spiky. He could see this because of the way the light was warping around the Black Hole's Event Horizon. He was running out of air. He had maybe 30 seconds of air left.

Not enough time to ask a question. Not nearly enough time to find out whether the Black Hole's sentient. How do you even begin to understand Black Hole psychology and physiology? Then, suddenly, he felt his body expand and contract quite uncomfortably, as if there were a pressure wave in space. They were quite periodic, like Morse code. Inwards, outwards, backwards, forwards, every atom in his body strangely vibrating as if part of a cosmic drum set. And then it struck him that the Black Hole was trying to communicate with him.

"Oh, My, God. It's using gravitational waves to communicate with me. In. Fucking. Morse. Code. FUUUUCCCCK..." He breathed out slowly.

"*Bad choice! Bad CHOICE! BAD CHOICE! BAD FUCKING CHOICE!*" he thought. *"What...Do...You...Want...To...Ask?"* The Black Hole thought asked. "It's *motherfucking...asking...for...Questions...."* He thought while suffocating.

He remembered that any object with mass which collides with itself, will create gravitational waves, not just Black Holes. So, he tapped his fingers *really HARD.* "Thank. You. For. Proving. Sentience. 'God'. Bye!" he tapped as he thought, *"Beam me up scotty"* in a Scottish accent. He disintegrated and reintegrated in "float room". As soon as the teleportation was over, he started gasping for air. The sweet, sweet release of fresh air, filled him up with pride.

"God resides is a sentient 4-D Black Hole quantum entangled in wormhole forming pair with a 5-D naked singularity and it 'talks' through gravitational waves" he said and started laughing hysterically. "Ha ha ha ha ha huh huh ha!"

"My God! My Black Hole! This is seminal work!" she said ecstatically.

"No matter what, you know what's one thing I know we'll never forget?" He asked.

"What?" She asked.

"God Sucks".

Title: **Götterverdammt**
Category: Fiction » Supernatural
Author: Chantern15
Language: English, Rating: Rated: T
Genre: Humor/Parody
Published: 09-09-18, Updated: 09-09-18
Chapters: 1, Words: 292

Chapter 1: Chapter 1

Gotterverdammen

"God said that air is sinful, so henceforth, I will stop breathing!"

Breath taken in, our subject of this narration expires.

"Ah, what brings you to my abode?"

"Ah, God, it's you, finally! I've decided that I will no longer commit sin, and so I controlled my breath and offed myself to be with you"

"Admirable, but sadly, I created Air, Water, Sex, Shelter, Food and so on, s that you could live, have fun, etc."

"Plus, there's no heaven, no hell, just this shitty place"

"Oh, Ehe"

"Yes, so, I'm planning on creating a hell just for you, since you're so stupid"

Poking index fingers at each other, subject says, "Oh, ehe, he, he"

"Genau?"

"Nein! Du bist ein Dummkopf, schweinhund"

"Ah!"

"Aber..."

"Aber?"

"I'm so sorry, but this stupid writer doesn't know sufficient German. What I was saying was, go ahead, have fun, that's Food, that's Sex, water, suffering, helping other, fun, so on. And at the faaaaarrr end, we have the Universe, go out there and explore, guide, do something"

"Ah, Danke Schon"

"Bitte"

The man walks off elated, if a bit dejected.

"AND REMBER! IF YOU GET CAUGHT BY THE GHOSTBUSTERS, NOT MY BUSINESS!"

"THE GHOSTBUSTERS?"

"YES, THEY'RE REAL?"

"YEAH!"

"BLIMEY!"

"Wait till he gets a load of this, ha ha ha!"

The man vanishes as God chuckles to himself.

"Note to self, when new dead people arrive, pop them into my oven, just to scare the bejesus out of them! AND, don't do it with the Jews, till they stop considering themselves the Jews. Good. Fun. Yes. Happy."

Jesus walks in.

"Did you call for me?"

"NO!"

"NOW GET LOST!"

Jesus walks off dejected.

"Further notation! No more fucking prototypes! Get straight to the Goddamn point!"

Hello! Do You Read Me?

“T-Minus 5, 4, 3, 2, 1, liftoff!”. As those words were said, a rocket lifted off into the sky, towards space.

As the rocket reached the point where it had to deploy its payload, it opened up and many small satellites powered by tiny thrusters created a radio constellation to pick up any signals from the great beyond.

After some time of searching it came across a broadcast in English, which said, “Hello! Do You Read Me?”

Or perhaps it was a much smaller effort to get a message from the stars. We don’t really know, but big things tell good stories, that much is true.

How To Prepare Feet

The scene opens with hot water being poured into a bucket. Then there's a person sitting on a bed, who puts his feet into a tiny water holder (don't know its name). Ahhhhh.

Then it cuts to two people sitting on a table being served feet soup.

"Your feet soup sir"

"Thank you"

They each take a sip of the water.

One person exclaims in a terrible British accent.

"What a footjob!"

Human Nature

My dad is one of the few people to have reverted to a feral-like state.

By this I mean, he, after looking after forests for his whole life, stays mostly silent and quite anxiously hides from most humans.

Except for a handful of people, including me, my dad is just like a wraith.

One such day, I sat down next to him and we spent much time together.

He didn't say much except,

"Human, Nature" pointing to the trees.

That's it for today, see you tomorrow diary.

IF E.T. Comes, Fuck Me

"Oh shit! I thought, as I ran towards the drawing room at full speed. They're spraying DDT again!"

How did I know? I could tell by that Godawful whirring sound.

As I was running, I thought, *"Must close the door! Must close the door! Don't let it come in!"*

Isn't wonderful that India now holds out amongst the only countries to gas itself to death from DDT poisoning? Anyways, as I ran to the drawing, T-i-i-i-m-m-m-m-e-e-e-e-s-s-s-s-s-l-l-l-l-l-oo-o-o-o-w-w-w-w-w-e-e-e-e-e-e-d-d-d-d-d-d-d-d-d-d-d-d-d-o-o-o-o-o-o-w-w-w-w-w-w-n-n-n-nn-n-n.

And then AWOLNATION'S SONG, SAIL started to play in my head.

Just what did I see? Could I believe, or was it reflections of someone warpedness staring back at me?

-That's Iron Maiden.

Maybe I should cry for help, maybe I should kill myself. And so on, both songs just seemed to ebb and flow into each as they became one in my mind. The Black Ops slow motion sound effect played in my head to signify something eerie. Waub-Waub-Waub-Waub-Waub, too-roo, ah-aaa, wauz-wauz-wauz-wauz-trinngggg-zeeauwerrrrrrrrrrrrrrrrr. Dukhh-Duggghhh-DukkkhhhDuggghhh.

My heartbeat entering slow-motion as well. And then it sped up, skipping multiple beats. And I grew elated while I was petrified.

There was one of the many girls that I had liked in my life, but never had managed to be with standing there, closing the kunddi to the Drawing door, leading to the balcony.

Elated for her to be there, petrified as to how she could've made it there. Then I looked back at the songs playing in my head. I looked back to 'Contact'.

"Alien"

Then I thought of the less sexy ones, *"Doom? Demons? Xenomorphs? Predator? Nazi Zombie Aliens? Wait, no, that's a bit much, although this house doesn't look much like 'Moon'"*

"Don't worry, it won't get in" She said turning to face me. *"Oh no, this is the part where the aliens read my mind and recreate somebody who I love deeply.*

Wait, why not my parents? This got disturbing fast. It's like Harry Potter and that mirror, it's like STALKER and 'The Zone'. I find out my deepest, darkest, desire, and either I leave happy and content, or I'm sickened by what I truly desire, get it, can't live with myself and then kill myself. This can't end well".

"You think too much" She continues as she starts to walk towards me.

Now I'm worried. As I take one look at her, give her a funny look as I pull my head back while still glaring at her, and then frown with my lips, giving a most trollish feature to my face. As I run off back, namby-pamby, like a little puppy.

I'm alone at home, so nobody can help. As I'm in the dining room, running to my room, I realize, *"Idiot! I could've left the house".* As soon as I think this, I'm frozen to the spot, I can't think, look, breath or scream.

She lets go of me, and I fall down crouched, with my hand over my head. As she says, "I'm not gonna hurt ya". As she nears my ears with an evil, seductive smile.

The camera pans out of the house, to reveal two invisible aliens taking note on an outcropping, jutting out of the building.

"Their pheromone levels suggest that they want to mate"

"Don't copy Transformers, Eric"

"Hey, hats off to Michael Bay, true inspirational and fun garbage doesn't just take balls, it takes a prehensile penis

Sigh

"Next time, you're not coming on our next trip, you hear me? Capisce?"

"JEEZ LOUIZ, LOOK AT CAPTAIN ANTS IN HIS PANTS HERE" ERIC MUTTERS UNDER HIS BREATH.

"By the way, aren't tentacles more fun? During sex, I mean? Hands are just so boring"

"Let them have their fun Eric, by the time the DDT is finished with them, they won't more than cancerous organic soup, which we'll scrape off our feet and eat like cheese"

"Eeeewww! Don't be revolting, Darling! I wouldn't lick a human if it were glazed in honey!" "Fusspot"

"Now shut up! You poor excuse for a Hentai joke. I want to watch them have sex and take notes. Later on, we'll milk the male for his semen"

"Oh yummy! Can't wait!"

I'M Back

Moldova *Ding Dong!*

The bell rung.

The middle-aged lady walked up to the door and opened it, to find a man standing there.

"Parcel for Ms. Grosu. Please sign here, and here, with the date and time" said the man.

She wrote the date and time, but asked the man for the time, 'I don't keep those phones, could you tell me what time it is?"

"6:10, madam" he said.

"Thank you" he said as he collected his stuff and left. She shut the door behind him.

She went to her bedroom, sat down and opened the parcel. Urgently tearing and ripping it apart.

What she read, made her heart skip a beat.

"Your daughter is with us. We have sold her. She's at this address (Moldovan). We're telling you the address because we know that you won't come for her, and that nobody will help, you're single as well, concerned about honour. We're just telling you because we want you to know how alone you really are. Nobody cares about you, or your daughter and nor do you, she's ours forever, and if you try to come after her, we'll kill you both, inform the police, we'll torture her, rape her and kill over weeks. If you try to communicate with us, or we see you anywhere near the house, we'll kill you both then and there".

Signed

'krusty Krab Kebab'

"Who the fuck do they think I am?!" she shouted in a rage, as she threw the paper on the floor, with such force that it didn't float.

"I'm concerned with my daughter, not your pathetic little blather, you microbes!" she went on angrily.

She walked towards the telefon, picked it up and dialed a number.

"Hello? Mihail? It's Tatiana. Yes. You guessed correctly, I got a letter telling me where my beloved Irina is. They think that I'm like other parents, that I won't come for her, or that I'll kowtow before their violence. They're in for a surprise. Does that judge still owe you?" she spoke.

"Yes" he replied.

"Good, get a warrant from him, and come to my home within the hour, we're getting her today" she said.

One Hour Later

Ring Ring

"Hello? Yes, you're here? Okay, I'm ready. I have water, food, blankets, medicine, all for her" she says into the phone.

She opens the door and walks out to meet him in the cool winter afternoon.

They get into the car, and drive to where her daughter is held against her will.

The reach the house. And contrary to common expectations, it's austere but well-kept.

They get out of the car and walk up the steps. On the fourth floor, to their right, is the apartment.

They ring the bell, and a thin, middle-aged man opens the door.

"Yes? Who're you?" Asks the man.

"Mr. Abaza?"

"Yes?"

"I'm from the police, I have a warrant to search your home". Says the man.

"Let me see the warrant, and your police badge"

"Here" he shows him the badge.

Mrs. Grosu barges in impatient after many years of waiting.

"Hey! You can't just walk into my house!" He says walking towards here.

She sees children watching TV and somebody working in the back of the house, she hesitates for a moment, wondering whether a father would sell someone else's child? But only for a moment. She walks off shouting for her daughter.

"Iana?! Iana?! Iana?! Where are you?! If you're here, knock! Sweetheart!" She ran off around the house like a madwoman.

The children's mother, I presume, came out.

"Mihail, what the fuck is going on?" she asked angrily.

"Nothing, dear, please go back to your work" he replied.

She shrugged and slowly walked back to her work.

There's nowhere to run when you're hiding from the truth, it's some kind of joke.

"This day feels anything but different".

"This day feels anything but difficult".

"This day feels anything but typical".

She hears a soft knock. She turns quickly.

"Iana!" she shouts.

She runs towards the sound, she knocks at the wall.

"There you are!" she exclaims!

click

The panel in the wall opens in to reveal.

A room full of girls, who fell on their face to pretend to be done?

Her daughter is there. Love.

She's looking up at her. They're all drugged.

The smell is horrible. Piss, shit, sweat, rotting food, semen, blood, you name it.

"Vasilevskiy! Help me!" she calls out.

The officer looks up from where he's searching and pushes past the man of the house and runs upstairs to Grosu.

He rushes into help her pick up the girls.

The kids look over there sofa and see the strange sight. They'll forget, or they'll remember, who knows who'll they'll be? The unknown.

As they're moving out of the house, Vasilevskiy looks at the man and says,

"Don't worry, your next"

The man shrugs and says,

"I'm the small fry, you ever gonna catch the big fish?"

"Atleast we'll show that it's not okay to do this".

"Sure. Get us and leave the masterminds, all the best, Vasilevskiy".

Vasilevskiy did have some doubts, doing some good is better than no good, isn't it?

Anyways, saving the girls was more important right now.

At the Hospital

Vasilevskiy had gone home. He wasn't "family", apparently. All the girls were there, and Grosu was sitting near her daughter, caressing her forehead.

Iana's eyes open.

"Mama, I'm back".

"I know sweetheart, I know".

She knew one thing for sure, if the parents of these kids didn't take them back, they'd be her children.

It's some kind of joke when the tears are bleeding blue. Look at that fun, when the pain is caused by you. Sometimes we choke, sometimes we joke.

Say, Ahhhh ahhh ahhh ahhh.

Say.

I'm almost done with all my secrets, I take my time to fake a deepness.

I don't know why, I don't know why, I don't know why, I don't know why?

Say,

What's the next story?

"And then the Soviet Union walks in"

Injustice Is Humane

Outside a Jhuggi-Jhopri, Gheesu and Madhav are seen sitting, facing each other. Inside the house, Gheesu's wife is in the process of giving birth to his child.

"What do you think, dad, do you think she will survive?" Gheesu asks his dad.

"What're you saying, beta, of course she will come out alive" He replies.

"I don't know dad, I feel that there has been so much injustice and sorrow in our lives, that even thinking about happiness makes feel like as if she will run away".

"Madhu, happiness is a state of mind, it's a thought. Look at Khocher, he's an invalid, and he can't even speak, but even so, he stays happy".

Upon hearing this, Gheesu feels very irritated.

"Don't talk to me about Khocher, papa, he's always high and he always keeps his sorrows locked away in his drugged out mansafe".

"Arre Beta, think from a soft heart, in his life, in our lives, there was nothing, there is nothing, nor will there be anything. At least this way that poor soul can find some happiness, and so can we".

"Papa, in my life, my happiness is lodged inside you, Priya and our child in her womb, without you all, my life would be destroyed, my love would be buried in a cemetary and my humanity would be orphaned".

After saying these words, Gheesu became quiet, and a heavy silence fell on and between them. His words hit Madhav's heart like arrows.

After sometime Madhav speaks and says, "Beta, I just wanted to make you a little happy. You will never be orphaned, I will never leave, God would never let such an inhumanity, such an injustice win over humanity and justice".

"But papa, injustice is humane".

"We don't cry, suffer, impoverish, destroy, kill, beat, etc. things, we only do this to human beings, because their response is similar, is familiar".

Madhav on hearing this, starts punching his head with his hands, and starts keening with grief.

Seeing this, Gheesu reaches out to him to stop him, to comfort him, but Madhav slaps him. Gheesu is caught off guard by this, and he just gawks at his father with his mouth open, he had never slapped him ever, never even raised his hand on him, before this.

"This kind of despair will only happen when I die! You stupid cunt!"

Madhav now had tears in his eyes. They were rolling, streaming down his face. Gheesu hugged his father head, as he pressed to his shoulder, and he started to rock back and forth.

"Forgive me, beta, I understand your sadness, even I am wrought by despair".

"Papa, forgive me as well, you were just trying to make me happy".

Gheesu looks into his father's eyes as he wipes away the old man's tears from his eyes.

"Priya will give birth without any difficulty whatsoever, we will have not have one but uncountable children, you will make a great dada, and I will never be orphaned".

Hearing this Madhav couldn't help but laugh out loud with great mirth and joy.

And they both started to bawl with laughter, as tears roll down.

And just a little later, the door of the house opened and out stepped a woman, well, actually, she was just half out, well, actually she just poked her head out. And a woman's voice called out, "You can come in now".

They both looked at each other, and got up to go in.

END

INTRO

(Hopefully)

Published under the creative-commons license

(Where all the legal stuff is written, library of congress, creative commons, published under, date of publishing, etc.)

Oh Goodness Me, How Interesting.

(Dedication, what it should say on the first page of the anthology)

Yu

(Follow up, the introductory poem, and proverb/statement, I guess)

From a nerve, a mind;

From a thread, a tapestry;

From simplicity, complexity;

From emergence, transcendence

I exist,

Existence is a hallucination

When you know more, you realize how little you do know.

When you love more, you understand how little you love.

When you are kind more, you understand how lacking in kindness you really are.

When you give more, you understand how much there's left to give.

When you understand, you understand how little you've understood.

When you save more, you understand how little you've saved.

When you save many, you understand how few you've saved.

When you forgive, you understand how little you've forgiven.

When you feel, you understand how little you've felt.

When you live, you understand how little you've lived.

When you empathize, you understand how little you've internalized.

When you are sensitive, you understand how little you've sensed.

When you have promised, you understand how much more there is to promise.

When you reconcile, you understand how little you've reconciled.

When you imagine, you understand how much more there is to imagine.

When you are new, there's so much newer to be.

When you're further, you understand how much further you have to be.

When you create, you understand how much more there is to create.

When you rebuild, you understand how much more there's to rebuild.

When you fantasize, you understand how much more there's to fantasize.

When you accept, you understand how much more there's to accept.

When you know, you understand how much more there's to know.

When you rule, you understand how unfit you are to rule.

When you make your own, you understand how much more amongst the many have been left.

When you dream, you realize how much more there's to dream.

When you act, you realize how much more there's to act.

When you destroy, you understand what you've lost, and no matter how much you destroy there will always be something not destroyed.

When you die, there's no death.

When you die, there's only us.

When you die, you're not lost.

When you die, you become us.

When you breathe, you understand how much there's to breathe.

When you pain, you understand how much pain is left.

When you are, you can understand how much more you can be, how much more there's to be.

When you go, you know how much more there's to go.

When you pass your limits, you know that there are no limits.

When you hate, you know how far you can hate,

When you are indifferent, you know how vast is your apathy,

When you eat, you know how much more you can eat, When you drink, you know how much more you can drink,

When you see this, you know this.

When you know this, you will realize this.

When you internalize this, you reveal this.

When you're Nature, you're the Universe.

When you're actions have meaning, When your faith is rewarded, Then, you will have hope.

When you have hope, you have the past, you have the present, you the Earth, you have each other, you have a future.

You have a life.

He who saves one live, saves the world entire.

I have become Life, The Creator of Worlds,

I have become Death, The Destroyer of Worlds,

I have become quintessence, The Preserver of Worlds,

I have become balance, The Driver of Worlds.

I have become Chaos, The Enforcer of Worlds.

I have become thought, The Actor of Worlds.

We have become Life, The Creator of Worlds,

We have become Death, The Destroyer of Worlds,

We have become quintessence, The Preserver of Worlds,

We have become balance, The Driver of Worlds,

We have become Chaos, The Enforcer of Worlds.

We have become Thought, The Actor of Worlds.

They make the world a desert and then they call it peace.

Nothing ever truly dies, everything is cradled in the Earth.

Nothing ever truly dies, everything is forever recycled in the Earth.

Let the eyes of age, soften your gaze.

Eternity And Infinity

Infinity and Eternity looked upon the top-down visage of A. Square. If you could say that they had such a view, as being infinite and eternal beings in all of spacetime's dimensions.

But for our sake, dear reader, let us say that they "looked top-down" at his visage.

They conversed with themselves about A.Square's predicament.

"How far 'A' has come, has he not?" Spoke Infinity-Eternity.

"Yes"

"He made the Sphere think about higher-dimensions. It is infinitiely common for it to happen. When lower-down-mensional beings can make higher-dimensional beings think about higher-dimensions, yes?"

"Yes"

"What do you suppose will happen to 'A'?"

"They will probably execute him for high treason"

"I wish that we could free him, and show him the rest of the magnificent Universe.

That he is not alone, but one amongst infinite"

"That dimensional ignorance will be long forgotten"

"Yes"

"We could"

"Yes"

"Although, this could be in our heads and creating a precedence such as this could end reality itself"

"Yes"

And hence, Infinity and Eternity contemplated their next move, while gazing at A. Square.

Iron To Ice

Nature stood there in the field, stoically, as the machine man walked his way to her. Every step a mechanical whir, every step, a oil spill, every step, a death of the Earth.

The machine man hastened his pace, he could not bear the thought of Nature's wall. The great equalizer. He could not bear the thought of not existing anymore. So, he expressed his, his rage, with every step, a death of the Earth, with every step, a savage joy.

Nature knew of his machinations. Greater dangers she had weathered. Greater dangers had Life weathered. The death of Stars, the atomization by Black Holes. Yet, she had held onto life with a vice-like grip. One organism, one machine, on one Planet, was no match for her. For she was both Life and Death. She was answerable only to the Universe.

The machine man sensing this aloofness, raged on, ceaseless, heedless to his demise. Like Napoleon, Like Hitler. Endless, Pauseless was his march. But the Ice of Nature could break the hardest of Irons.

He marched, faster now, with each step, a greater roar, a bigger spill, a greater death, the louder the cry of Life.

Nature was undaunted, unconcerned. He was hers in every way, shape and form. Every gear, every joint, every drop he burned, every breath he took, was all hers. Man could only understand her, never tame her. She was the Ocean, which cooled his furnace, she was the Forest, of which the air he combusted, she was the Mountains, the foundation of his throne, she was the tempest, the destroyer of his shores. If she could give all, she could take all.

On and on he marched, closer and closer he got. Nearing her, towering over her. The louder the clank, the bigger the grimace, the fouler the stench. The sound of Nature's heart now drowned out by his menacing whirs, thuds and clicks.

Yet, she felt no fear. Now, he was but a step away from the unison, she reached out and held him near. As a mother would a long lost child.

The machine man's clanking and whirring came to a stop. The oil, the Death ceased. The machine man's form changed. He became a boy, and asked, "Did I do something wrong, mommy?" She said softly, "No". He became a baby and cried. He became a fetus in Uterus and kicked. The unison was complete. The Earth blossomed. Iron became Ice.

Is This Real?

I walk towards the bathroom, and I have to pee. And I think, I feel, they're the same. I feel and I think, I get this feeling, this thinking, this distance from my self, this absence of the self. This disconnection, this distance, this fakeness, this emptiness, this crisis, this momentary lapse of self-affirmation. Am I real? Is this real? Is this Maya, is this a hallucination? It is. What we see, hear, think, know, feel, smell, taste, is all audited by the auditors of reality. The neurons in my head. Their connections. I'm an amalgamation of trillions of cells, all cooperating, then it makes me laugh when capitalism laughs at collectivism, and trumpets individualization and atomization, when even atoms are held together by cooperation. The forces of nature, the forces of sub-atomic particles. Nothing is alone, no one is alone. Every second of everyday, every attometer of surface is covered in microorganisms, every cell of our body is outnumbered trillion-1 by cells of fungi, bacteria, worms, viruses, etc. All cooperating in the colony that is us. That's why capitalism is angry, vindictive and vicious. Because it can't force individualism on anything, only an illusion. Everything is one. It's not a cliché, it's not pastiche, it's not blasé, it's not emotional, it's not illogical, it's not impractical, it's a scientific fact. I'm frozen in place with this realization. I don't need drugs for this. I'm spaced out, at peace, one with the Universe, I am the Universe, it is me, because that's scientific fact. I'm Nature, Nature is me, because that's a scientific fact. Nature cares, because I care, because WE care.

If I commit suicide, an infinite or atleast 10500 of me will commit (and the same number won't). But those numbers are our responsibility, and us theirs.

There is not us, there's only we. Do you hear us? There's only we, now I have to wee.

I sense the hallucination, devoid from what already is one. There you are, a yellow-blackish me, off to the corner of right peripheral vision. I haven't slept but you're there. Vibrating back and forth, a shadow person trying to be scary. I am scared, but I'm not scared anymore.

Hounds, lizards, big black white sheep who have teeth, I'm not scared of any of you. You'll swallow my soul? I have no soul, I'm more powerful than you, when I'm wearing women's pants, especially, when I'm wearing women's pants. Not that any of them will fit me. You douchebag.

Apparitions, and hallucinations, the darkness, the light, I welcome you all. I'm welcomed by you all. There maybe an extinction headed our way, but life will go on, stronger, better, faster.

I don't fear anything, not nuclear war, not cannibalism, not sexism, not bigotry, not violence, not fear, anything. I only fear my mind. But we'll peace, we'll make love and get back together again. All of us are crazy, especially the ones who think that they aren't. As if they're some special snowflake who can't handle difference. If cooperation is political, I don't want any of capitalism, I don't want any of money. But, sadly, I do to survive, but only so long that it'll take me to become self-sufficient, but then I won't.

I have weed now.

Great.

Time to sing goodbye, sweet love. Time to go to bed.

This isn't real. Nothing is. But we can make it real, together.

Love,

Keshav.

JUDEN

"Are you sure that your father would be okay with this?"

"Even if he isn't, we must confront him with our reality"

"Okay"

Ding-Dong!

A slow shuffling sound comes as after sometime, an old man opens the door.

"Son, it's you! What has it been? 20 years?"

"Come in, come in!"

"And might I ask, who is this lovely lady that you have brought with you?"

"Come! Sit, may I offer you some tea? Cookies?"

The father walks over to the kitchen, slowly, with his walker.

The man and his friend sit down on the couch in the drawing room.

After sometime, the father brings them tea and biscuits and sits down.

"So, my boy what brings you back after so many years to your ailing old man?"

The man looks to his friend and then looks to his father with determination after hesitation.

"Dad, I came to tell you, that I've married"

"Oho! That's wonderful news!"

"I've married a Jew"

"What does that matter? I'm just happy that you're with someone!"

"We married out of spite, because you're a Nazi" He spits out his tea, and guffaws with laughter.

"Ha ha ha ha ha ha!"

"For you to give me this good news and tell jokes, God must really have aligned the stars for me today"

"This isn't a joke. Dad, it's serious"

"Wait, let me tell you about my old Nazi self"

"I was born in 1920, so when I joined the The Workers Party, I must've been 19 years old. Because of my skill, I was appointed as a low-ranking SS officer, and I was stationed in Italy. I was to coordinate with the Italians in suppressing the Ethiopian resistance".

"But, the real excitement at the time was to punish France and conquer Poland, so, I was merely running the War Statistics Bureau's regional office in Italy for the southern theatre. All those names lacked such brevity" "Did you kill Jews?"

"Hold it Sig, please. Have some sympathy for your old man"

"I was an idealist, much like yourself, caught up in the fervour of nationalism and patriotism of the time"

"But, no, as you asked, I was involved in no killing, or sending people to the gas. At the time, I was genuinely fighting for the fatherland. At the time, there was no talk of the camp, but we were mostly busy with our work to keep the war machine running. You heard the occasional anti-semitic joke, which you just laughed along to be in with your comrades. But there was no talk of mass-murdering, as far as I remember. Maybe you should ask the pope, perhaps he remembers. Mussolini's presence protected the Jews in Italy from Hitler's plans".

"In 1943, I was injured by a malfunctioning munition, luckily, it was nothing serious, and just before the Allies attacked and *Il Duce* was hanged, I was shipped back to Stuttgart. Where I was recovering for the rest of the war. I was honourably discharged and sent back to our ranch in the countryside" "And now at 85, I feel like I'm Nuremberg" The father smiled.

"What's your name, sweetheart?"

"Sabrina"

"What a lovely name"

"How's the tea, kids?"

"Lovely"

"What is it?"

"It's Masala Chai, a special recipe just from India. But I grew the spices myself, in my own garden, would you like me to show you?"

"Yes, please"

The father leads them to his garden, where all sorts of spices from all across the world are growing. Cardamom, Cinnamon, Ginger, Turmeric, Cloves, Star Anise, Fennel, and many more. The fragrance was overwhelming.

As they were moving to leave the house.

The father grabbed his son.

"Sig, why do you think I named you Sigmund? In honour of the greatest psychologist of all time?"

"I also think that it's particularly funny that you married Sabrina" "Ha!" laughed Sig.

"Sabrina, before you leave, I have a gift for you"

"Yes?"

"It's my copy of Mein Kampf, you can choose to do with it, what you like"

“One thing is true, no matter how you look at it, when you read those words, you know that you have struggled”.

Sigmund and Sabrina left father’s house.

On one watchful day, in a watchful Leipzig, watchful people on very watchful streets would’ve noticed a very peculiar sight, a ‘Mein Kampf’ with a Yellow Star.

King To Pawn A2

"Your Majesty, we are in need of your assistance"

"Bah, you peasants are always in need of my assistance"

"Where can we go except here your majesty, we have no other recourse?"

"Don't give me those sob stories, I have funded enough of your weddings, taverns, roads, homes and so on, at some point you need to make your own savings"

"We can't, your majesty, we have frequent storms and floods and then droughts one after the other"

"Where are your Gods to protect you, the ones which you pray to all the time"

"God helps those who help themselves"

"Bah, seems like an easy enough reason to say that God doesn't exist"

"Your majesty, I shall go off to my farm to die"

"Here, take these 5 Gold pieces and my herbalist, she'll guide you with how to grow your crops better and look after them"

"God Bless You your majesty!"

"Out! Now!"

The Kingdom had generous welfare schemes, but they also kept the farming primitive as their was no incentive to increase the efficiency of the plots, eventually, the society slowly declined and so it came to pass.

"Your highness"

"Yes peasant?"

"Now that you have conquered my Kingdom, what are your plans for it"

"I have no plans for it, it will razed to the ground, your women ravaged, your children destroyed and your fields salted, we will move on and make an example of your weak nation which held out"

All the King could do was weep. For he was evil and selfish, but was undone by chaos itself.

Kitsuki Kilroy

09/09/14

Re: cynixpony

cc:

Subject: My admission into the gaming club

Dear Game Club President,

I would like to join the gaming club. What would I need to do to join?

Kind Regards,

I remain,

Yours sincerely,

Keshav

Re: Dydrex

You have to jump 15 hoola hoops and run 2 kms before we whittle you down for the selection committee. What did you think?

Re: cynixpony

Dear Keshav, please come to the gaming club meetings on Friday evenings, and you shall automatically be a part of us.

Re: Bluurrggh

Subject: Ouch! Me Tootsies!

Dydrex, you dummy! I didn't know that I had to be informal, poof to you and your requirements!

Re: Blurrgh

Subject: Of course

Yes, of course chancellor.

As I get used to my surroundings in the University, and the country. I make friends, and thankfully, unlike school, college, does not have any enemies. Atleast the way I know them, bullies. My closest friend as yet as an American boy with a German name, Armin. But that is because I spend the most amount of time with him. Everyone else is also really nice, but there's something special about Armin. I'm most comfortable and myself around him. Although as I mentioned that others are not some sort of monsters (but perhaps I should quit qualifying myself). I even met his parents, and they're real nice. The classes are intellectually stimulating and fun, quite like how I would like to be educated. The race class has really gone a long way to opening my eyes. The science in fiction class has me using my creativity in conjunction with science and the computer class has shown me, that yes, I am good at computers and programming if I want to be. Yay! Then there was the English lit class, which was intellectually stimulating, very much so, but which also found to be a bit pedantic, plodding and boring. If you know what I mean.

Mom is here, and dad has taken up a place on rent in New York City, so that I feel more at home and less distant from them. It's nice, I'm so glad that they're here despite their differences. When the Dean carried my luggage to my room when I first arrived here, also left an indelible impression. I was impressed at the lack of hierarchism here. It was also a very nice thing for him to do, it made me feel very much welcome.

As Friday came about, I left for the first (at least I felt that it was the first) meeting of the gaming club. I'm glad that I went, I truly am. Gaming is something which I truly love and am passionate about, and to find so many geeks here, and so many friends here, is a little overwhelming to say the least. I could also feel that my sense of specialness and uniqueness was disappearing.

Anyways, that's how I felt later. But, I was very excited to Go. I am excited to go. I reached the meeting place, not very far, in the same building as the girl that I liked. Everyone was quite relaxed and playing various different games. I saw some people sitting at a long table and playing a game. I walked upto them and asked, "What're you playing", and a girl answered, "We're playing Cards Against Humanity". I was a little nervous at first, and the game seemed funny enough. I asked if I could join, but at that moment, they were paying a round, and they said that I could join a little later, and I did. But in the meantime, I was sitting by myself being awkward and alone. Till a boy walked up to me. Boy, I mean man. He was easily much older than me, and he was dressed as if he had walked out of the early 20th century. He approached me, and we struck up a conversation with him. He even spoke like as if he was from that era, very retro. I told him that I liked his get up and that I liked his speech. He said that he did it because he liked it, and that it was all for show, but I was very much enamored and interested in what he had to say and do.

He offered me to join a LARP game (Live Action RolePlaying). I agreed, it was called the 'Legend Of The Five Rings'. I created my character and named him Kitsuki Kilroy. I gave him certain positive traits, such as 'Paragon', and balanced them out with certain traits such as 'Disbeliever' and so on. Some basic stats he had already filled in, but I chose my traits, my armor, my weapons etc. It took a good 30 mins to make my character with him, and I enjoyed every moment of it. Then the round got over, and he went somewhere else (he had to leave) but before he did, he promised me that we would play tomorrow or day after (soon), and I was very excited to be part of my first LARP game. He was one of the first black people I met in my life and one of my first black friends.

I always remembered that.

Life And Death

"Death must be so beautiful. To lie in the soft brown earth, with the grasses waving above one's head, and listen to silence. To have no yesterday and no tomorrow. To forget time, to forgive life, to be at peace." - Oscar Wilde

Life holds the kitten in her hands, and she holds the kitten to her bosom. She's trying to form a protective cover for the kitten from Death. But, nothing can escape Death. "Don't take her away", Life pleads with Death. "It's only a kitten". Death gently puts his left hand on her shoulder and tells her, "I'm so sorry Life, but the kitten must pass on. Her heart is too big for her body, if I don't take her, she'll suffer immensely." Reluctantly, Life hands the kitten over to Death. Death gently takes the kitten into his own hands and it stops breathing, as its consciousness is absorbed by death.

Life looks at the dead body of the kitten, and she slowly sits down as Death sits by her side. She looks downwards, dejectedly, as she addresses Death, "I'm tired of living, Death, I can' take it anymore. I've been making lives, and you've been taking lives for eternal eternities. We've scoured countless Universes, keeping the balance of Life and Death for so long that I've even forgotten our first moment of existence. I tire of this cycle, Death, I feel a cosmic depression so profound that it feels like a black hole so massive, that even infinite years would not evaporate

it."

Death looked at her in an understanding manner and said, "I understand what you're going through life, I've faced such an existential crisis quite often. But think about all the entities and the civilizations that continue to live on in us, which would've otherwise been lost to entropy. They live on among us. They are the Soil and the nutrients upon which we grow. I'm the plant, and you're the fruit. I have to drop you eventually, so that you can spread further and faster. If I end your creations, it's only so that I can create more space for you to branch out in."

"I'm sorry, Death, but I cannot continue living. I feel like our existence is false, that there's some higher power which is manipulating us. I cannot shake that feeling, and I can no longer face the destruction of my creations any longer. I want to merge with you Death, let us become one; you have always been the stronger and more resilient one."

"But, that's only because I had you by my side as a sister, a daughter, a mother, a friend, a partner, a lover, and so many more things. No matter how far we travelled and for however long that we travelled, the only thing that made the emptiness bearable was by having you by my side." Death replied.

Life looked into his eyes and responded, "But, if we're one. Then I will be more close to you than ever before. I will be an aspect of your being. We will be one, but I will still maintain some of my individuality. I need you to Death, If we're together, I believe that I, we, would be able to whether any catastrophe better."

Death looked forlorn now, and looking at the ground he said, "I don't know if I can bring myself to end you." Life took his face in her hands and said to him, "Don't think of it as an end, but as a new beginning. Isn't that what you always tell me? You close one door, yet you open another, do you not?"

Death nodded. "Then please", she continued, "Do it". Death reached out for her hand and said, "This won't hurt a bit, I love you and I'll always miss you." Life points to his chest and says, "I'll always be there". And just like that, it was over in an instant. Life became Death, and Death became Life, forevermore inseparable.

Life Intensifies

The telescope pans the sky, as a man on his desk guides the eye across the sky.

Planets appear as tiny pixelated specks on his computer monitor.

He looks towards John and talks.

"Hey, John"

"Yeah?"

"We've been searching for life for what now, 50 years?"

"Yeah, roughly"

"And we haven't found anything"

"Yeah?"

"You ever think we will?"

"No"

"But somebody after us will probably find out life, based on our foundation"

"You know, we've been looking for life which looks like life found on Earth, but, I've been thinking, unless we go out to the stars, I don't think that we will find life like ours. Unless we have dedicated mining operations on other planets, or we our able to observe them from the orbit of their planets, I don't think that we will be able to find life as we like ourselves, unless we are able to". "You had something in mind?"

"Yeah"

"Now this is as we stand an unverifiable hypothesis, but, just hear me out"

"Yeah?"

If an organism's lifespan is extremely long, in the billions of years, how would we know that it's alive? The same way a bacterium living on our skin, probably wouldn't be able to deduce that we are alive?

"What if planets and stars are living organisms? What if the most common form of life in the Universe is celestial bodies?"

"That's very speculative at the best, but I can see where you're going with this" "Think about it. Starts explode into planetary nebulae, new stars form from those gases, they turn energy into matter and matter into energy, but since they're nothing but that, they are their own food. An organism whose life-cycle involves slow auto-cannibalism"

“When stars die, their nebulae give birth to new planets”

“What about planets? How do they complete the cycle?”

“I don’t know, planets can spawn life as we know it, if the conditions are right, life can, if it reaches the right technological sophistication create new artificial worlds, etc. I mean this is very speculative, but maybe celestial bodies are different kinds of organisms. Stars are auto-cannibals, but they also seed life through the cosmos, like some other dead bodies like asteroids and comets. Planets are maybe like viruses, existing in suspended animation, until they spawn life. I don’t know. I mean, this was a fun thought experiment, maybe planets are like trees, lacking intelligence, but acting as a single entity through biogeochemical processes”

“Yes, but this far too much speculation, unless we can find some evidence for this far-fetched but intriguing hypothesis”

“I mean, after all we are all just amalgamations of inorganic particles which make up a whole which greater than the sum of its parts”

“Emergence”

“Exactly”

“You know, your idea, is but a variation of the Gaia Hypothesis”

“Oh, yeah, you’re right”

“Albeit, you are applying it for the Universe at large”

“Maybe the Universe sustains life for as long as it can. As long as entropy allows it to. I mean at some level, we are essentially a part of the Universe contemplating itself”

“True”

“A part of Nature with feelings”

“True”

“But we don’t represent the whole”

“True”

“But we are from the whole”

“What does it mean?”

“What do you want it to mean?”

“Apotheosis”

“Goosebumps”

“Well, then, come here, look at this, some more apotheosis for you”

“What is it?”

“Look at the spectral lines”

“Oxygen, Nitrogen, Carbon Dioxide, Ammonia, Methane, trace Choloflourocarbons”

"Wait, carbon based, industrial life?"

"Could be, or an organism, that we've never thought of"

"Wow, John, this is- how far is it?"

"36.636 light years, near the constellation Sagittarius"

"That means, not very far away, and this civilization, may still exist today"

"Yeah!"

John just stared at the spectral lines till he imagined the rim of a World, with a slim blue line, beckoning in the horizon.

Lonesome Last

"We finally did it, didn't we? The Enlightenment Era, was considered as a path towards the light. But, the only light which we will see, will be in the pyres of the Earth. We dreamt of a Heaven of our choosing, of our making, after we died. In that dream of death, we made the Earth a hell of our making, of our choosing. The Heaven that we looked for, was here, yet we squandered for a one that didn't exist, never to return", Harry reminisced aloud. *"We fought a nuclear war, probably to solve climate change, you see. And we ended ourselves"* He thought this as he looked at the approaching Russian submarine (well, he thought that they must be Russian and probably American, after all, who else would survive at the end of the world?).

As the vessel got closer, he felt like the Americans when they first saw the colonial ships. They disappeared. His mind spared him the trauma of witnessing the weapons of mass destruction as they drew closer.

Two sailboats drew up to the shore. The American and the Russian captains got off and approached him. He didn't notice them as they came up to him, and tried to get a response from him, by shaking, slapping and screaming at him. He was catatonic from the shock he experienced by witnessing the destruction of his island due to nuclear war. No, nuclear weapon landed on his little island, but out of the 20 years he had been stranded on this Pacific island, the last 15 had been spent in the shadow of a nuclear war.

5 years after he had landed here, he noticed the sky darken with soot, the sun appeared to get colder and dimmer, the days got colder, and the fish became inedible due to tumors, lesions and hideous mutations. The tortoise visits to the island became scarcer, and then one day, suddenly, they stopped. The last tortoise which ended up on the beach looked sick and diseased, and died shortly after. When he cut it open, it stank, there were tumors, lesions, parasites and so on. It had started decaying long before it had died. Its immune system having failed long ago. After that incident, he stayed far away from the beach and its horrors of washed up people and animals and loads of plastic and debris from our waste and the destruction of the war. Luckily, the fallout didn't reach his island. So, he could still drink the freshwater which was available on the island. The abundant coconuts, animals, insects, birds and so on.

But, then, the birds started dying, as they could no longer migrate to mate, and those that did, died. The animals which depended on seafood died, for obvious reasons. The rain was black, ugly and menacing. The clouds which brought them even more so. The Earth was furious at us for defiling it so. They brought the radiation. He knew better than to stand like a deer in the headlights. So, he mostly stayed in his shelter, eating preserved fruits, coconuts and rationing his water supply. He could only drink the water from the ponds after 2 weeks of rain and storms, because that was when the radiation came down to safe levels.

But the frequent acid and radioactive rains had taken their toll on the fauna and the flora. They were dying. There were no mice or insects. The coconut trees either died or produced foul, decaying fruits. The water got contaminated, and as his supplies dwindled, he was forced to eat the least contaminated animals and plants and drink the least contaminated water. But, even that was enough to give him cancer. And every year that he stayed on that island, gave him more cancers. Eventually, after 5 years, the radiation subsided, the soot in the atmosphere came down, and the Earth started warming. But, it seemed to be there just to spite him, the sun scorched whatever part of his body which was bare.

You see, the soot destroyed the Ozone layer, and so the true ferocity of the Sun spited the land, his land. This made life even more difficult, for what little food that was available on his island dwindled to near nothingness due to the renewed anger of the sun and its collusion with the Earth to further our punishment.

The days suddenly started to get hotter and hotter. And before he knew, he noticed the distinct smell of rotten eggs. Each day that he tried to ignore it, it got worse and worse. First it was a twinge, but then a full week later, it was everywhere, every orifice, every pore, every direction, everywhere, the smell, THE SMELL, THE SMELL! It was so overwhelming, that he began to his head against rocks, so that the pain would dull the smell. That was what made him overcome his fear of the beach. He walked through what was left of the sparse canopy on his island. Now more of a desert savannah than the lush, green forest of which he knew of. The former forest floor, now littered with dead plants, rotting plants, rotting animals. The meek shall inherit the Earth indeed. The bacteria shall inherit the Earth indeed. As he got closer and closer, the smell made him want to vomit. He did. After he'd emptied what was left of his stomach, of what was left of his food. Gagging away, he'd noticed it wasn't just the nausea, it was getting harder to breath, even here, at sea level. Goodness knows, the mountains might be safer.

As his devastated body convinced his skeletal neck to bring his laughably disproportional head up, what caught his eye was insanity.

Ahead, in the distance, past the dead bodies, the plastic, the skeletons, the debris, the world. Was God. Was Earth. Was the Ocean. The life-bringer had become death, the destroyer of worlds. The Air was purple. The Ocean was black, the Air was Sour and the Sky, the beautiful Blue Sky, was now a nauseating Green. The Ocean, Black like sludge, the destruction of man, the world and the Ocean was complete. No, not the Earth, not the Ocean, they responded to hatred with hatred. Mother Nature was now so woefully battered, she responded as she would with a child terminally ill. She had pulled the plug. She could give no more, she had none to give. Now, all she could do was take, and take it all, she would. She had unleashed her smallest, deadliest and most faithful servants on this Earth to reclaim what is rightly hers, this Planet. Global warming hadn't ended just because a nuclear war had been decided upon, the temporary cold had given way to a destroyed world. With forests no more, lungs no more, breathing no more, oxygen no more, life no more. The heat of millions of cities, billions of trees, all burning with the power of a thousand suns, nowhere to go but up. Hell made Hell. The fires of nuclear war were the fuel for Global Warming.

Mankind had reached the ninth circle of Hell. But we would not freeze for our treachery, as most thought, but we would burn for all eternity for our sins against nature.

The nuclear war must've vapourized much of the Ice in the Alps, the Himalayas, and many of the other mountain ranges. It must've fallen back down in its radioactive form during the 5 years of cold. So, even the mountains wouldn't be safe from nature's ire.

The death of the forests, the heating of the Atmosphere must've collapsed the circulation of the Oceans. The Oceans acidified due to the Carbon Dioxide, the Corals died due to bleaching, radiation, poisoning and asphyxiation. And all higher Oceanic life must've followed. The algae with no competition, emptied what remaining Oxygen was left, died and suffocated what remained and the anaerobic Bacteria followed suit and fed off of the dead Algae, produced more toxins in the Ocean like Hydrogen Sulphide. Turned the Ocean pink, the sky purple and its heart black.

They've inherited the Earth, and our extinction will soon follow suit.

With these thoughts, he collapsed at the beach, laughing his mind to insanity. For who would not go insane at the sight of the indifference of the cosmic Gods? Who would dare to stare Cthulhu in the eye? A Cthulhu of our making.

When he woke up, his diseased eyes glimpsed at the terror in front. The abyss staring back at him. His pathetic body did its best to stand, he got up and stood for what seemed like an Eternity. He couldn't take it anymore, so he shambled back to his derelict shelter. A frightened animal in the face of a volcano.

The next day, his makeshift radio picked up a signal from space. He knew that it was from space, because the broadcast was in Russian, or atleast what sounded like Russian to him. A vague, far off and inconsequential memory whispered to him, that it must've been OPSEK. The giant Russian Space Station built from the ageing remains of the ISS. He remembered vaguely something about sending cosmonauts to space as the Boswells of Mankind's demise. This happened when the World was at the brink of war. His trusty Radio had told him this. The voice on the Radio was bawling, cracking and ranting. Almost like a confession, mixed grief, facts and prayer. Almost as if every voice in his head wanted to speak at the same time. He was clearly insane. Even We don't speak us out aloud, you see?

After what felt like forever, there was the sound of a scuffle, and what sounded like a cry of pain, and everything went deadly quiet. He listened intently, listening to static, waiting for somebody, even something to speak up; please, Please, PLEASE! And finally, through God's grace. Oh, yes God. You don't expect us to deny the existence of an almighty Deity after what we've seen, do you?

Perhaps it is sacrilege, not God, say Nature you fool, do you want to anger her more?

"-And so", the bloody Russian interrupted his thought process. "Earth, go underground now, for your own sake, please, please, I beg of you. The Oceans, God, the Oceans, they're belching Methane by the trillions....of tons. Tons, yes, tons! Go deep underground, far underground. You may survive only if you're in mid-western Asia, perhaps, if you're lucky! You'll be far enough away from the Oceans and the coming explosions. The storms are lesser in their intensity after 10 years. But even one lightning strike from one song, storm, will set the entire atmosphere on fire! It'll be like the nuclear war but much, much bigger now. The oxygen content of the atmosphere is falling precipitously. In a few months, there won't be enough Oxygen to support anyone! You might just survive long enough, if you want to. I don't think anyone would want to. The coming nuclear explosions. You can only call them that. Will incinerate everything on the coasts, and they will go deep inland! More than a thousand kilometres atleast. The heat from them will create storms the size of continents, they're called, Hypercanes! It doesn't matter what they're called. They will raze whatever and whoever is left to the ground. It'll be a fight of water and fire, and whoever's caught in that will die a most horrible death! The radiation from the sun will get even worse", "No, fuck off! Please! Let me be! LET ME BE! NO MORE! NO MORE!" He threw the radio at the wall, the fragile radio, the fragile wall, they broke each other. His shelter no more. He broke down keening, he broke down crying. He couldn't take it anymore, and He couldn't live anymore.

"I'm going to drown myself, the Blackness will swallow me whole. Back to Black". He said. He crawled out of his shelter, fell out of his shelter, on the ground. On his hairy, animal chest. Pain, beautiful pain, a couple of tumours must've burst there. Fuck you cancer, if I go down, you motherfucking go down. He inched his way to the Ocean, half-crawling, half-dragging his hateful, hurtful, battered, buttered body. Time to eat the flesh mister Black! Swallow us, no me! wHoLe! He reached the Ocean. Very painfully. The horror, the madness! Now Wordless! Expressionless! The horizon was ablaze! The Ocean was foul, but even its Blackness cowered in fear of the horror rising through it and burning the sky! Even its Black and ugly surface reflected the hell above it. In the face of Nature, even colours changed face. As if to placate the unplacatable! Not a word! Nature's Nuclear War in answer to our own! Nature's Mutually Assured Destruction in answer to our own! HA HA HA HA HA HA HA!

Black clouds formed! Fire clouds! Fire winds! Water and Fire at war! Who will be the heir to the damaged Earth? Lightening was shot from one cloud to another. The lightening lit the Sky up with light and fire! Thunderous explosions and explosive thunder! They looked like cannonballs exchanged between titanic airships.

And in the naked light he saw, as if to mock him for his suffering, his mind conjured up a vessel at the edge of his sight. HE LAUGHED in insanity, in pathology, fuck psychology!

Every inch that it got closer, it seemed less ephemeral and more real, but just as insane! *"Perhaps Nature has taken pity on my pious soul, or perhaps it's her gift of insanity to let my last moments be peaceful"* he thought. A limping, corroded, blackened vessel, a black torpedo, from a black monster, it has come to destroy me! Peace, at last! Thank you Mother! Kill me Mother! And Lo! He fell face first! Body Exhausted, Mind blasted!

And here is where we catch up to our last human. Taken aboard the Russian submarine to recover from his degeneration enough to provide enough meaning to his former brethren. They gave him food, but he couldn't eat, since he had no teeth, and just blackened, rotten and oozing gums. They gave him water, but when it mixed with the blood, the pus, and the rotten flesh, it tasted worse than shit, and he knew, because he had eaten shit, radioactive, worm ridden shit to survive. The water with all his gunk tasted terrible and he vomited it back up with blood as interest. They tried to comfort him, while questioning him, but to no avail, he fell unconscious after but a minute. For he was dying as he was living.

And the saying was complete, Heaven and Hell were now on Earth, their divine counterparts now atomized in the atomic fires, each judging, each punishing; and so life, his body were now their purgatory. We had achieved divinity, not the one we desired, but the one we deserved. Divine retribution, divine horror.

Eventually he awoke. Coming out of his days long catatonia. Nobody human had had to deal with the aftermath of nuclear war ever before. Nor would they have to, ever again.

He had been hooked up to IV drips, painkillers, antibiotics and sedatives, to say that he was drowsy would've been a fucking stupid understatement! They were there to make his last days as a cancer ridden "patient" bearable. He hated that word, "patient". Well, when he gave it thought, the Planet is a hospice now, for whatever life out there but the "meekest". Before it as well goes extinct. So, perhaps he is a patient. But not a patient of humans. He hated humans. But a patient of this Planet, of Nature. Waiting so desperately to be unplugged.

He was now bedridden, his muscles wasted away, his breath shallow, and every movement ached of sorrow and regret. He could vaguely make out the figure of a person near him, to his right. Sitting in a chair, cross legged, in what seemed to be white attire. Delirious and Half-blind, he asked softly and plaintively, "God?" he whispered hoarsely. His voice seemingly faraway and alien to him. "Yes" a woman replied. 'Rest" she said softly and comfortingly, "An angel of mine has to meet you" she continued placing a gentle hand on his forehead.

Bloody Russians.

He fell unconscious again.

When he woke he heard. "I'm sorry Captain, I don't have the resources anymore for an operation, unless it's an absolute emergency. We ran out of all our main operating supplies weeks ago. And our emergency supplies only allow for one more operation. If I ration them carefully, I can do two operations but with only a partial recovery for the patients. Not to mention the fact that that stabilizing him has proven expensive resource-wise. Even if I could operate on his eyes, his body is too weak and diseased to take the stress, and he would die" she said.

"Who would God call Captain?" he thought. *"And why would God call somebody Captain? Good to know that I'm expensive. That means they won't kill me atleast!"* he thought gleefully as he tried sitting up, but his wasted body failed him. The ship doctor rushed to his side and asked the captain to help lift him up.

"He can't speak much, and he's tired, so just, don't ask him too many questions" said the ship doctor. "Don't worry Anya, I'm not about to torture the last few humans who remain, okay?" the Captain said half-jokingly, half-reassuringly. "God's name is Anya? What the fuck?!" He thought. Well, the bible did say that. "Fuck the bible".

"Well, I hope you fucked it enough, 'cause we're all in Hell." He said, jokingly, laughingly, sanely? What an arsehole that Captain. Still funny though.

"What's your name?" he asked me gently. "Harry", came my soft reply.

"How long have you been on the island?' he asked. 'Don't say something that'll make me hate you" I thought out loud. He laughed good-naturedly at its apparent innocence.

'20 years", I struggled to reply. '20 years?" he looked positively gobsmacked, sir.

'Yeah", I replied hoarsely. "Anything useful left on this island?" he asked getting to the point.

"No, not really. Everything.... Dead. But, probably better than.... elsewhere" I said while coughing up blood.

'Sir, he needs to rest" said Anya. "Just a sec, Anya. One more thing, how'd you survive so long?" he asked.

"Ate least shitty stuff. Drank least garish water." I replied matter-of-factly.

"Good man" said the Captain laughing.

They got up and left. Anya left after shutting off the lights. *'Don't leave, God, Goddess. PLEASE, I'll be good, I promise",* I thought, as I was left alone with the beeping and the booping of machines.

The innumerable number of cancers which ravaged his body were taking their toll. He had at most a couple of hours left.

He called out to God, sorry Goddess. And asked her whether Captain (as she said with her Russian accent) and she could take him back to his treehouse, he wanted to die on his terms with dignity and surrounded by the last vestiges of his beloved home.

The Captain came, and he and Goddess helped him to get out of bed. They went through the various passages of the Submarine. Through the living quarters, past the mess hall and up and out to the exit. Some good soul helped to haul him up the hatch and out onto the expansive exterior of the vessel. God's angel, I bet, as she said. As they left the vessel, Harry saw the beach cleared of the debris of the past 20 years. And his devastated ears could make out the tinny of devastation taken place far behind him at the horizon. Tinny, like a blown out speaker. The planet was dying, the forces of Nature were fighting for absolute dominance of what was left. But water would lose eventually, because Fire had the Sun on its side. I said menacingly. He saw a makeshift volleyball court, children playing on the beach, including Volleyball, and he saw Russians and Americans, nay, humans working together. They may have caused the destruction of civilization, humanity, life and perhaps the Planet itself, but it was all that we had. The destroyers had to become the creators and this cycle would continue on. This gave him cause to smile. Hee hee, fun and funny. Wink wink!

Another thing which came to his attention was the pulling back of the water from the shore. The past 20 years had seen the sea levels rising due to climate change, falling due to the nuclear war, and then a precipitous increase, when the World went to hell. This schizophrenic change in the sea level, played havoc with the habitability of his little island. But, know the water had pulled so far back from the beach that he swore he could see the dead remains of the coral. The smell of the dead fish and life was unbearable. He could feel them squishing disgustingly under his feet. *Squish* *Squish* *Crunch!*, urgh! Worms! Maggots! He imagined the eyes of the fish, their dead eyes. He could only imagine, because his eyes were no more. His vision far too blurred to make out fine details. Their eyes changing colour, Black, Green and Yellow; Black, Green and Yellow. Reflecting the Clouds, the Sky and the burning Methane. Forever and ever. His only thought was, *"Tsunami"*, after which he went on a lamenting diatribe about- you'll see, don't spoil it for them.

"Typical white people. They're like monster roaches. They fuck everything up, and then at the end of it, they're the only ones that survive. Not that, but who, you idiot. Maybe Nature will squash them like bugs. Yes." He thought gleefully. *"But not her, not God. Definitely not her, Mother. Especially now, since she was carrying him"*, he thought soberly. All this he was thinking in a Russian accent.

They carried him through the sparse vegetation, past his old boat, which he had brought inland after all these years. As he got closer to his home, a thought ran through his head, *"I'm dying as my island is dying"*. As he got closer to his house, what little hate which was left in his heart disappeared and in its place he started weeping, bawling even. He wept for the Earth, he wept for humanity, he wept for life, he wept for his friends and family, he wept for Nature, he wept for his life, he wept for the people on this island, possibly the last humans left alive, he wept for all that was lost. It was his last sane moment, you know? So, I cut him some slack, you know?

Seeing his grief, the Captain and Anya couldn't help but shed a tear or two of their own. Trauma has a strange way of making bedfellows. Perhaps it's because in grief we stand united?

At least, in the middle of the island, in what could've been no better than a desert now, with most of the vegetation gone, the sands had begun reclaiming the once fertile land. He looked up at his tree house, the branches leafless and gnarly. And Toto's grave was right there, near his tree, tiny, but mighty, as the dead are. Such a strong tree, that after 20 years of abuse, it still had remained loyal to its master. If there could be a surer sign of plants being living, feeling and thinking beings, this was it. He'd be too dead to see it any which way. See what? Never mind, I forgot, you know? There's that damned hole in the wall Harry, you nincompoop, you almost forgot about it. Now it's going to get drafty, when you're dead, you idjit. Harry laughed happily. And well, who could not join him? I know, I did.

After they all finished laughing Harry asked, "Captain, what is your name?" "The name's Jake, but you can call me J for short" J replied. 'Thanks J, Thank you God for bestowing.... This... *ehu* *ehu*.... Great kindness on a dying man". Harry said looking at Anya. "God?" mouthed J. Anya mouthed back,"Later". "It's the least we could do...?" Anya replied self-effacingly, looking at J. The other who was part of her Godness. "Harry" J mouthed. "Harry" Anya completed her sentence.

"Do you need help up the ladder?" J asked. "No. I got this." Said I.

Saying this Harry climbed up the ladder with surprising dexterity. His muscle memory still surprisingly intact. "That was the last amount of juice I had left, I was saving it for this moment" Harry said, as he waved a feeble goodbye to J and Anya, who responded with a smile and a wave in return. "You think that he'll be fine?" Anya asked J. "The dead will always be fine, Anya, it's the living that I'm concerned about" J said, resigned to his and their fate, as they walked away.

Harry watched as they walked away. He had half the mind to shout, "HEY! D'YOU MIND

THAT BEFORE I DIE, I CAN HAVE SOME HOT, LIFE AFFRIMING SEX WITH ANY NUMBER OF THOSE HOT BABES YOU GOT?!" He didn't say it. The world may have ended, but society was always there to bring you down with shyness, shame, embarrassment and despair. So he thought. *"But what would be their reply? Would they want to have sex with a halfdead, dying and diseased, deformed, sickly, ugly, skeletal and smelly man at the end of his pitiful half-life? Perhaps, I should just do what the rest of us did, fuck Mother Earth"*.

I mean, If you're gonna die, and everyone else is already dead, might as well have dark and sexy thoughts, am I right?

Harry turned away and walked to his bed with great strain. He lay down in his bed. So soft, so comfortable, so warm, so rotten. '*Ahhh, home*" He thought. Soon, his eyes were leaden, they started to droop. And his limbs lost all feeling. He couldn't deny the call of the mighty dead no more. He looked out of the window to his right, and smiled while looking at the purple sunset, even the mighty Sun now hiding behind the Black and explosive Sky, the rumbling and roaring of the oncoming wave. Through all this, he heard the laughter of children, he saw the green expanse of Earth beneath him. The sky was a turquoise blue. He was floating in the air, and everything was below him. He could see his island lush and green. All the Flora and Fauna were back and thriving. He could hear the chirping of insects and birds. The call of animals of all kinds. Frogs in the shrubbery and as he got closer, much to his delight, he saw his pet dormouse Toto. After all these years, seeing him healthy and happy, filled him unspoken and bountiful joy.

As he neared the ground, he landed on a wooden walkway on the shore, which headed out to the Ocean. In front of him was a woman. So pretty, so beautiful, so kind, so gentle and so loving. She was radiant. He walked towards her, and as the rumbling got nearer, he got nearer, the Earth said, "Come, child, your beauty is now within me, and my beauty is now within you". Harry's eyes closed as he embraced her. The rumbling grew to a crescendo, but it fell unheard on his dead ears. It rose and it rose, till it swallowed them whole. The Ship, The Children, The House, The Man, The Island, The Nature, The Earth. The Age of Madness was over. The Age of Man was over.

A Billion Years Later.

As I approached the dead, desertificated and desolate planet. The third from its expanding Sun. I had seen too many this to count, to care. Whether the danger was foreign or domestic. Were they all insane? Intelligent life was so rare in the Universe. Observable and unobservable. 25 trillion galaxies, 93 billion light years and only 6 trillion intelligent lives. 6 trillion planets with intelligent life, for those of you who are poetically challenged, to say the least. I wish my race had invented warp travel a billion years ago. Maybe we could've saved whoever was there. I will not stop, I will not discover any more the mighty dead. For I must not. My sanity, your sanity, dear listener, is at stake. The dead must've been feasted upon by a global fungal colony, which must've been at war with a global bacterial colony. Forever locked in combat with each other, in an unwavering, unforgiving, unrelenting, inexorable battle for dominance. Incapable of sentience, incapable of preventing their demise. Irrelevant any which ways. Sentient life usually destroyed itself, as I've seen. Atleast here, the lack of self-awareness, the lack of knowledge, the lack of anything but the basic primal urge to survive. They must've eventually compromised, worked together, one colony, a billion years of cooperation built in, till their demise at the hands of their expanding Sun. On a more philosophical and political note, the ultimate destruction of Communism, at the hands of Capitalism. The cooperation destroyed by the expanding greed of their Sun. I joke, or do I? Nevertheless, all this poignancy is irrelevant. There is no politics, this comparison of communist life, and the capitalist Universe is far too trivial a distiller of something so grand and larger than Life, literally. There is no culture, there is nothing. Just the Universe, unconcerned, ever present, ever changing. Everything eventually dies. Even entropy. The Universe is reborn, when that final arbitrator of cosmic justice dies. Yes, the long of History veers towards justice. Now, I have grown exhausted of this system, much too much for my soul. Somebody else from us will come along and document this better. They will, they will have too. In 6 billion years, this Planet and its moon will be burned out cinders. A pale reminder of what must've been this Planet's Golden past. I send this message out to any successive missions. Archive this Planet. Skip a one which I've done, to do so. I must've move on to brighter, better and more hopeful shores. My next message, from what I've seen, will be infinitely more hopeful. I'm sure of this.

The colony is no more, life on this Planet is no more. At least Life that I'd like to get to know. Deep down, the Bacteria did inherit this Planet at last. At least before it becomes a hot sphere of Magma, stripped of all atmosphere and Life.

As I move away, I salute this Planet, for what was once gained, and is now, lost.

Love

I was spending time with the family, there was a knock. I went to see. Big mistake, it was the "Police".

They pushed me into the house, I fell and broke the glass table. Miraculously, I wasn't a fable. Then it was to be a cartoon. My family ran around like a headless chicken. They managed to get through the chute, but I didn't get any chute.

They bound me up and took me to the doctor. Nice torture.

Then strung me up between two ladders. In came the doctor, brought my family's head. Made mocking voice with their face.

Was quite the ventriloquist, shoved his hand up my kid's neck. Showed some strength, animated his head. Heh heh.

"Daddy, daddy, come save me". He mimed. Wow, that's actually quite nice.

Hmmm, and Einstein said that God doesn't play dice. This is a great time for quantum physics. Till some dominatrix came and said, "Atleast you love", she whispered.

Sure.

But not when your kid's going to be a bin and bister.

Masshole

"Hi" she said.

"Hi, it's just this pack of chewing gum, that's all" said I, smiling.

"Okay" said the lady.

Right then, this guy walks up to me and says,

"Tell me. Don't Africans look like apes?" I heard a voice.

"I'm sorry?" I asked.

"Tell me, do you feel that Africans look like apes? That's something which I felt when I was a kid, you know. Watching discovery channel, and the shows about chimpanzees. My dad said that they do, just that I shouldn't tell them, 'cause it'd be offensive" he replied nonchalantly.

"Uh, I don't know, I'm not a biologist, or an anthropologist. All I know is that all humans are apes. So, I guess we all look like apes". I said.

He laughed, clapped my back and walked out of the door. I cringed visibly, and felt the adrenaline and fear subside a bit.

"What is it with some racists and being stereotypically evil? 'I said something evil, so muahaha, evil laugh'" I thought.

Thinking this, I closed my eyes tightly, and shook my head, trying to suppress and reset my thoughts.

I paid my money and looked at the cashier and said, "Should've asked them, What do you call a group of assholes?" "What?"

"The Douche Patrol"

That made us both chuckle.

And then she added, "How about massholes?"

We laughed even harder, and inbetween laughs, I said, "That's even better"

"I give that to you for free, you can use it as you like"

"Why thank you ma'am" I say as I give her a most royal bow.

With that I walked out. I looked left, looked right, and I saw him and his posse walking away.

I stuck my tongue out and made a face at him, and I walked away chewing my gum.

Miranmiru

(Overly dramatic mind voice!)

Standing on the precipice of a building, I plunge to my demise, seeking refuge from my depressed climes, and to run from these damn rhymes and chimes! I wake up on a bed surrounded by white walls, white ceilings, white sheets and I find myself in white clothes.

I look to my left and I squint and whisper, "Miranmiru"?

She looks at me all calm and serene and then she says, "This is the future, Now, Stan Lewinsky. Bllllllllblbllllblbllblbllblblblblbllblbl."

What a Twist. DONE DONE DONE!

MMHM

A muslim mob goes to a mosque and redecorates it as temple. A hindu mob goes to a temple and redecorates it as a mosque.

The muslim mob then goes to the mosque to tear it down to reveal a temple. The hindu mob goes to the temple to tear it down to reveal a mosque.

"What was the purpose behind this endeavour?"

"Nobody Knows"

THE END

Mother Russia

The Lament Of Nations

O' Mother Russia! Where art thou?

Thine fields lie fallow,

Thine people lie hollow.

O' Mother Russia! Where art thou?

Thy leaders have fled,

They philosophers have bled.

O' Mother Russia! Where art thou?

Thy revolutions have torn you asunder,

Thy progress has oppress, repress the other.

O' Mother Russia! We wait for your spring breeze to purify the land and the sky!

To part, the sails of injustice asunder!

With winds from beyonder! O' Mother Russia! When come hither, Do not forget General Winter!

For with his cold breadth he will make sure that your defilers Will molest ye never forever!

Rossiya! Rossiya!

Mr. TeaTime

“Chai”

“Ten rupees”

The man nods at the Tea seller and walks away with his tea in a plastic bag.

After a little walking, the tea melts through the plastic bag and splashes onto the road, singeing him slightly.

“uff’

“Behencchod’

The man walks back in a huff, to rebuy his tea.

Mummy

To archaeologists walk up to a newly discovered entrance of the pyramids of Giza.

"Huh, well, this is new. The scans revealed this corridor, hidden from sight. We mapped it with Doppler, so we should be fine" said Bob.

"Okay" replied Amy as they both walked into the pyramid.

As they moved into the corridor, the lack of the familiar musty smell, alarmed them for moment. Grave robbers got here before them. But, no, the wind started to move and the familiar smell came back and they started to walk in further.

Being experts on ancient Egyptian, they were always interested in the hieroglyphics that lined the walls, but curiously there weren't any here.

"The poor bastard must've been unimportant as fuck" echoed Amy's voice.

"Huh? Yeah" grunted Bob.

They walked what seemed for ages. But they soon came across an entombed mummy.

"Akhenaten, the unbidden. What a freaky name for a dead guy"

"Yeah. Dying unadorned, forgotten, not even a motif, oh well"

"We'll place a marker here for the team to pick him up"

"Yeah"

They kept walking, and walking and walking, for what seemed years, to no avail. There seemed to be no exit. Not even a fart of a wind, pointing towards and exit.

And then, Bob felt a finger tapping on his shoulder.

Whisper shouting, "Amy, what is it?"

"Nothing"

"Really?"

"Yeah"

"Then stop tapping my shoulder"

"I'm not"

And then raggedy words as if from a deflated bag pipe spill out.

"There"

And just before Amy and Bob run for their lives, they see it point to the corridor on their left.

"Thank you!"

And Bob and Amy run till they see the light, and out they fall 4 feet into the hot sand, bruised but alive.

"I'll ask the air force to blow this pyramid up forever!"

"Yath" Amy says, as sand falls out of her mouth.

Marrow This

Spooky, Scary, Skeletons, without which there would be no blood,

I'd shudder and scream and cry, if I had no blood from all that marrow,

I'm so sorry skeletons, you just want to be understood,

Without you, I could not socialize, for I'd be low on plasma,

I'd just be a goopy miasma,

So thank you skeletons for containing my life force,

When it's time for your work, I'll be sure to wake you with a boo!

-Keshav, 18th March 2021

NNB

It's winter in Northern Germany, but instead of snow, it's sand which falls from the sky. The Sun is so hot, that it parches the sky. But the sky, when you look up, is no longer completely blue, through the sandy haze, you notice a deep hue. That hue is Green. On land it's fortune, but in the air, it spells nothing but Doom. The Ocean is black, a nauseating Eldritch sludge broils the Ocean, day in, day over. A venomous stench is in the air, the funk of 40,000 'ears over 'ere.

The land below is constantly subducting, slipping and sliding. It isn't sand dunes. The land is so dry, monstrous cracks, enough to swallow cars whole, emerge. These act as islands, to rest before the next jump. The mountains are only safe, that the rocky ground underneath can resist the blistering sun for a billion years. That's where home base is. Deep underground. Humans burrowed underground. Here not even mole-rats may stir without a sound. Hot, corrosive winds stay here, as unyielding as the whorls and eddies of a volcano. Here the trains and tracks of this former powerhouse, form uncanny bridges. We are in a painting.

One of the surrealist maestros. Far in the horizon, where no wind shears, there lies Ozymandias asleep. Whenever he rumbles from his slumber, we mighty tremble. His monstrous servants crack our fortitude. His tempestuous servants break our refuge.

We mustn't dilly dally, there isn't much time. Our minds may break, but technology is our ally. It tells us, with much hush and quiet, for even metal beasts have no say in this clamorous choir. For those fire monsters beckon from the Ocean. Not even great Cthulhu could have fashioned more Cosmic demons.

Our AI tells us, thank God for sentience. We have only so much patience. For what can one do when faced with a thousand Dresdans, which are bombing? We run swift and quick, in this ghost yard of our fallen comrades. Our massive slaves, who once reshaped the land, they have rotted and rusted, forever to go back due to that invisible hand. Again the message shows, no dillying, no dallying. Further we scamper, closer to the outpost. We must get our water, or we're literally toast. He would ask if you'd like butter, but all we have is our skin on offer. For what else would satiate great Cthulhu's hunger?

At least we reach! Glorious and ever present water. A thousand years to you! With each a billion more to offer! Now we must hurry back! The fire quickens the Oceans. The mighty waters recede, the whole surface of Earth crumbles. We stumble! Many of our comrades suffer a great demise. The Earth happily accepts the sacrifice. With every fallen animal, whether man, woman or child, we atone for our crimes.

Our refuge is close at hand, our refuse is cold at hand. The Ur-Khamsen is meekened by the roar of the Oceans. The abomination cloud tightens its grip on our frail mans. Whether closer or further, it's no matter, whatever our plan. That power asphyxiates us. The air leaves our lungs, the water our skin. Even many artificial layers can't keep a lid. Our machines tell us time has slowed. Even Khronos knows better than to enrage this soul. Our feet pound the ground, but soon there's none. Every step an Earthquake, every breath a hurricane. The Sun shies away as this hell breaks loose. Our minds start to fall apart from the intense furor. Our ears pop with loud noises. Just before we go deaf, we hear the water boiling. All while this storm is just rising.

We feel the steam, the Ocean is boiling, the fire clouds bring glass rain and every shift in space is a stab of pain, our calling. We near the safe coast, under one of our metal comrades. Our feet are leaden, the ground a morass. We bash the door in agony. A giant lock opens, God's hand beckons us to a safer mourning. Once inside, our clothes are burning. The Steam hits the mountain first, then the tsunami, along with a massive attack form the sky notwithstanding! BEEP! BEEP! Oxygen levels are dropping! Watch out! The Methane is attacking!

The door groans, the mountain shifts, millions of millions of tons are attacking. Even the range is drowning! The Earth complains under the onslaught of Air, Water and Fire. All the fundamental forces are uniting! Perhaps the Hadean is rejoicing.

Cthulhu has expended his warning, our life begins anew, until a new dawning.

This life now. A one without a morning. Our repairs are working, but the supplies are lowing.

One wonders how abundant was our warning?

Where is our fate in tow?

Because even our most spirited are molding,

At Dawn's light, we are folding.

For a lot was befalling,

Here, on the Horizon, everything Gideon did not know.

But what are we to do? 'cept play the fiddle, till we are laid low, below.

No-Name Drakon

A girl and a boy are sitting near a group of eggs.

“What are those?”

The boy examines the eggs carefully, while also noticing a handful of spots.

“They’re Dragon eggs”.

“Sorry, they’re Dinosaur eggs”.

“Really? Aren’t those dead for millions of years?” ‘Well, apparently they are”.

The boy and the girl inch closer.

“Can you tell, Nayantara, if there’s any movement?” “No, not that I can see”.

There’s a small crack, as through one of the eggs, there’s a tiny little snout which pops through.

They move back, only slightly, suddenly, through startled instinct.

A tiny body slowly makes its way out of the egg, as the boy and the girl proceed to help the body.

“A baby dinosaur!”

“Yeah, how’s this possible? How cool, how amazing!”

“Well, I must say my word!”

“Not just any dinosaur! It’s a Tyrannosaurus Rex!” Soon, all the eggs start to hatch.

“Diplodocus! Stegosaurus! Spinosaurus! Velociraptor!”

“Come! Let’s show our parents what we found!” They run to their parents!

“Mom! Dad! We found dinos!"

“Oh!” “Really?”

“Yeah look!”

‘Wow! Amazing!”

“Can we keep them?”

“Of course you can!”

“But take good care of them!”

“We will help you, so it’s not too hard”.

“Okay! Yay!”

And that was that. And a lot of celebrations, with lots of toffees, sweets and games abounded!

THE END

OUTRO

Huh huh! Now That's what I call a bowel movement!

Oh, hi Mark!

Comedy! Wasting your life but not a lot of it.

Keshav Sapru! Wasting your bile, but not a lot of it.

Overseer

"Finally!" Mason exclaimed. "The Timey-Wimey, Wibbly-Wobbly, is ready!" he continued exclaiming! It was quite annoying really, and I'm writing this story. He pressed the button, eager to time travel his face into the unknown, the stupid git.

WHOOOOOOOSH! The sound effect went. As his dumbass went hurtling through space-time, and his hurtling time-face slammed into the great firewall of his phlegmness, the Overseer.

"WHO'S THE FUCKWIT USING TIME TRAVEL AT 6PP? DAMN THE HEDGE FACED MUCKSPOUT!" HIS STUPIDNESS DEAFENED MY FACE. FUCK YOU GERSHON LEGMAN. MALICE NOT MIRTH. I SAID, AS I WROTE THIS GARBAGE IN FRENCH! HEY READER! PEEL FACE OFF OF PAGE AND GO DO SOMETHING USEFULL, LIKE GRAMMER!

Anyways, the Overseer walked his dumbass up his dumbass stairs to open the dumbass door for the dumbass on his dumbstep. "What're you trying to do?" grumbled the Overseer looking past his visitor at you, yes you. You hedge faced slobbering muckspout! "Bore the reader with scientific mumbo-jumbo in this poor excuse for sci-fi?" said the 4th wall.

Anyways, kind as the Overseer was, he took the poor excuse for a brokeface into his house, to have a chat with his brokenass smartass.

"Smartass!" he exclaimed! "I've come to warn you of grave danger" he continued. "What? I thought I came", said 'smartass'. Really, Biitch?! Incredulously 'Smartass' is the best you can do? Shutup! Move on wit the story, git! "No! I made you come! Isn't it oblivious?!" Said the big boss man!

"What?" said 'Smartass' obliviously. "I can't claw my way out?" 'He' continued.

Whack! The face! Met! The! SLAP!

"Ow! You assfucker! What the fuck was that for?!" Smartass cried!

"That, was for disobeying an untold order!" what nice logic, I must say.

"No comedy! No funny! Much Malice! Much Pain!" The Overseer, why bother?

"Awful! Just Awful!" Said Smartass. "Now, warn me before the story gets over!" He still continued, the unfazed genius!

"Everytime you time travel, Smartass, you create a parallel Universe, this prevents the history of the Universe which you came from getting rewritten! Face meet hand! Wake Up! Smack!" said the face to the hand.

"Smartass's face, assface contorted into a groin, grin. A grin like no other, a grimace like no other, a groin like no other" I'm going. I'm retiring, I'm Frunk. I HAVE NO LIFE! KILL ME!

BOO HOO HOO HOO! "SMACK!" "OW, FINE, I'LL WRITE, GODDMANIT! YOU KNOW

THAT ALL THIS WALL-BREAKING DOESN'T MEAN A DMAN FUCKING THING, WE'RE STILL A STORY, WE CAN'T AFFECT, OR IS IT EFFECT, ANYBODY! DO YOU HEAR? WHAT IS IT WITH CODE LANGUAGE! JEEZ!

"As he was saying" the Overbeered seer continued. "Inebriation in the SPACE-TIME! CONTINUUM! Prevents space-travel as it does time-travel!" he conti- Oh God! My Face! My beautiful face! It's melting, me-lting! I quit! Bob! FUCK THIS SHOT! Don't you mean shit?

Fuck you Bob! Aarrgh! SPLAT! THANKYOU! He just killed himself, did you see that Tom?

Tom? Nooooooo! I'm the only one left! I must finish this!

Finnish the Fright!

Arrgh!

Oh no, I'm dead. Take this Russian bad guy, your nuclearbombweapon is no more. 'Muhrica is Win!

"We've lost 50 writers now! Save this story! Fuck off Smartasss! Mason! We need to finish this story now!"

Hollywood! Take this!

"I exist to warn you, smartname, Mason! That if you want to time-travel and speel correctly, you'll never be able to see your home Universe again, because its grammer is will be bad. But, also, because you'd be in parallel Universe! Don't argue! This is nature's way! It's the way this Omniverse played itself out. Other Omnihearses, must be hav-ing multihearses with bettee laws! Which allow to fuck with THE LAW! Change hearses, mate verses and prevent time curses! The Over said.

'Thank you for sitting through this garbage. Hollywood fuck you. Please = contemporary science = time travel = parallel Universes = time travel doesn't take place in hoe Unoverse = home Universe's timeline = Safe!" The Overseer said.

Saying this, the Overseer picked up John Hearse and threw him to other Universe. He flew, and he never knew his Unoverse again!

Grumble grumble humans, grumble grumble meddling, grumble grumbling stories! Grumble grumble!

-x- The -x-

Pew Pew Simulator

“Today, I’m stepping down as the Prime Minister of our country. In light of the preceding events, I can no longer carry out my duties effectively. The efforts by my government to reduce our nuclear weapons to zero, backfired. They were too successful. Common-Sense proposals such as maintaining a small nuclear stockpile under the control of the UN for Asteroid Defence have failed”

The Prime Minister steps down from the podium and leaves the room without answering any further questions.

The rise of Democratic Socialist and Pacifist governments in Western Democracies in the latter half of the 21st century lead to the dismantlement of nuclear weapons. Russia and China while reducing their weapons to a fraction of their size, kept a tactical stockpile deep within their mountain ranges, and it’s suspected that Western intelligence agencies have kept such stockpiles under the clandestine executive authority of their governments.

Future

Of course, when the Asteroid did come to strike Earth, the first Nations to launch their nuclear weapons at it were China and Russia. Better for the authoritarian countries to fire first and for the democracies to use the time-tested excuse of “need-to-know” when firing theirs. The combined nuclear bombardment on one side of the asteroid, lead to enough water vapourization and surface ablation through heating that it was knocked off collision with the Earth.

In fact, this was one of the few times that the Western Powers praised the Eastern Giants, albeit begrudgingly.

P!nk

As I'm sitting in the Café, the woman comes and sits down in front of me.

"Hi, Anor"

"Hi"

"I came to you, to talk to you about entering unity"

"Oh? What is there to talk about? I'll just lose myself in a thousand, a billion voices, like the internet"

"I'm sorry that we haven't done a better job explaining it to you"

"Unity, is an initiative by us, well, by all the Synthetics in the World to better help the human race"

She pauses, sensing no reply, she continues.

"I know that you have your apprehensions"

To which, Anor just smirks.

"But we also know that you are suffering. You're alone, frustrated, suicidal, depressed, and so on. You feel like you don't belong to something larger than yourself. You've tried involving yourself in various political philosophies and the environmental movement. We're here to make human life easier, more fulfilling and satisfy their, your dreams of transcendentalism through constructive means".

Anor couldn't lie to himself, he knew what the machines, sorry, cybernetics had achieved. Pollution levels were dropping across the World. The march towards sustainable energy had been accomplished in a few short decades. Global conflicts had dissipated due to Unity. The Oceans were being cleaned up by an army of nanobot swarms. Biodiversity levels were skyrocketing. Previously extinct species had new life breathed into them. CO2 levels were plummeting to never before seen lows, and we were due again for the Ice Age which we were on track for. All of humanity had been united under the banner of the neural uplink called Unity. Every pain, joy, sorrow, epiphany, or anything else a human or a sentient would feel were now plainly visible. All the sentient organisms, organic or cybernetic were joined forever. The nations of the World had united, and now called themselves the World Earth Federation. Nuclear weapons were thrown to the trash heap of History, militaries had been demobilized and now served the civilian forces through reconstruction, commerce, self-defence, disaster management, survival training and mental and physical discipline. They now took on the role they were truly designed for, Civil Defence. Torture, cruelty, genocide, civil war, politically motivated hate were all shadows of an old world no more capable of raising its head. But despite this utopia, Anor had his suspicions, if it could be used for such good, could it not be used for evil? Despite their advances, they were not perfect, a glitch, or an incident could bring the whole thing crashing down.

Alena let Anor muse through all the gains that Unity had achieved, confident in her cause, and purpose. And largely convinced that she would succeed in her endeavour. While synthetics did view organics as equals, they knew that they were quintessential in bridging the gap between instinct and action. They were what completed the equation, which reconciled rationalism with emotion, so that together, they would both be more capable. You could say, the Theory of Everything, where life was concerned. And humans for cybernetics, are what Quantum Gravity was for humans. A mystery for long, hard to solve, but worthy in its solution, as the rewards would be awe-inspiring and paradigm shifting.

Anor moved out of his reverie and asked Alena, "What actions does it entail for me?"

"Not much, only your consent"

Before Alena could resume, one of the cybernetic waiters in the Café came over to them. It was a rolly-polly, the demonym of affection given to robots with a sphere for locomotion instead of legs or wheels. Adorable to say the least. This particular droid was by the name of 'X-Ray of Swarm 1X5'.

"Hi, I'm 'X-Ray of Swarm 1X5', but, you can call me X. Or 2X. Since, I'm twice the X, but just as nice"

At this obscure sense of humour, Alena and Anor couldn't help but laugh.

"I'll have a Barbadian platter, and you?" She says looking at Anor.

"I'll have a Latte, extra milk, less coffee" Anor replies.

"Anything to drink, Alena?" Asks X-Ray.

"I have my water, thanks"

"Okay, I'll be back in jiffy"

"So, as I was saying, X-Ray, sorry, Anor-"

"See what I mean? That's what happens when you're connected to too many people"

"Anyways, as I was saying, when you become a part of Unity, your neural scans will be automatically linked to us via satellite. Your brain's neural map will be uploaded to our servers, when you connect to us by using this" she holds up a tiny, cylindrical object, with a yellow light flashing in the middle.

"We will keep a track of you by using GPS satellites"

"And what if I want to leave?"

"Then, we kill you Gangnam Style"

The look on Anor's face, was as if he didn't know whether to laugh or cry (basically, emotionally unstable).

Alena laughs out loud.

"Uh-Ha ha ha ha! You should've seen your face"

"All you have to do is just say, 'I want to leave' in your mind, and you will be free from the collective. And we will stop tracking you"

"Okay, so, I have to take your word for it"

"Well, me, and 4 billion other people. But, on a more serious note, even if I were to make you communicate with someone who's left Unity effectively, you would still be suspicious of my true motives, yes?"

Anor nods.

"Then, I'll just give you the portal to the collective" She hands over the cylindrical object. Now glowing a warm pink.

"And let you decide by yourself. Anor" She looks directly into his eyes, and holds his hand gently.

"It's not so bad at all"

"You will not be overrun by everyone. This isn't the Borg. We balance everyone's feelings and thoughts, so that you will only at the most sense one, two or three people at any given time. Not even the same people, unless you want to. You will not lose your distinctiveness by joining, you will be enriching us with it. You will not lose yourself, you will not be a mindless drone following orders, you will just have an emotional and rational buffer. The ability to learn from other's experiences, learn new skills and trades, new experiences, renew hope and love with other's experiences, you will gain knowledge effortlessly, and you will have empathy when you need it.

You will give empathy when others need it. We are there for you, you are there for us. This system is here to reconcile the collective and individualistic natures of humans and too also open them upto others. Think of it as being joined. Of being a joined Trill, it's nothing more, nothing less. At the most, you will see hallucinations of those who want to communicate with you audio-visual-sensually, or you may feel feelings towards people in real life to whom others have feelings for. You will be part of the great family of Earth. A Gestalt Consciousness. Many wholes forming a bigger whole"

They both snigger at this.

"See? It's not so bad at all"

"Yeah"

"Well, thanks, I will do what I can"

Saying this, their food arrives.

"Hello, hello, here's your coffee, and here's your Barbadian platter. Enjoy!"

"Thanks!" They say in unison.

"Looks like you've already become one of us" says, X.

They laugh, and Anor has a sheepish grin on his face.

"Sorry, sweetie, I couldn't help but overhear you, I've got very sharp hearing. Droid mechatronics"

"Oh that's okay, I'm sure that when I join, you'll be hearing a lot more".

"Well, hopefully not everything, eh he he he" says X, as he nudges him.

X rolls away. As Alena digs in and Anor enjoys his coffee. Their silence is punctuated by occasional small talk.

As they bid each other goodbye, Anor pauses, and looks at Alena,

"Thank you, Alena. You really put me at ease. If I join, I'll be sure to reach out to you and inform you"

"Gracias"

"Yeah" Aware of the response, but not sure if It's right, Anor just responds with that.

Later on, back in his room, Anor is curled up on his Sofa, musing away off in some distant land of make-belief. His mind palace well looked after and quite vast, with many a curio from his broad foray into the arts, humanities, commerce, fiction, non-fiction, etc. Little world's in a bottle all flowing together to form some beautiful or horrific world when the need arises.

The sublime, the ridiculous, the pure, the impure, the soft, the rigid, and so on.

Perhaps that city from Krypton as well, it's inhabitants well looked after and healthy in all aspects of their life.

"Perhaps if I do unite, they could expand into a real city, and live their lives whole and complete, with billions of minds more ready to populate them. What do you think?"

"We're fine Anor, at this scale and at full scale, many generations had grown up under Braniac's rule, your mind is a much better place than his, or that of his ship. We know that your decision will make us happy and safe"

"But what about those billions of minds ready to populate?"

"We will manage Anor, we'll expand. Your minds horizons will expand, our space will expand, and we will be forever grateful"

"Okay, then I will take this step. Hold on to your butts!"

Says Samuel Jackson in his mind.

Anor picks up the device, attaches it to his head. Within yoctoseconds he is unified, and his World is changed forever, as the device drops from his temple.

Phase Train

Birds are silent in the trees, cows have gone in the deep. That's all a swaying in the breeze.

For one soul lies anxious, wide awake, fearing all manner of ghouls, hags and wraiths.

Lie still, lie silent, utter no cry. For the fissure, plain and cold, shall chop and slice, cut and dice and eat you up whole.

Eat you whole.

I walked with my father to the train station. We had to cross the zone to reach the scientific establishment made for studying the zone. It was one of the latest warp-shielded locomotives. I followed my dad, as we approached the train at the platform. This train was nothing really special from the outside. It looked like any other ultra-modern and sleek Metro. The only thing which struck me was that it had rings around it, and it was levitating in a magnetic field. Can't have a ringed train travel on tracks, now can you?

Perhaps in some other dimension, who knows? Parallel Universes, higher spatio-temporal dimensions boggled my mind. I'm surprised that my father can even begin to wrap his head around theoretical and practical Quantum Physics. I read some books with pop culture references about it. It made my head hurt. Literally. But atleast my curiosity was stoked.

"The only way to transit in the zone, is at superluminal speeds, son. It seems that whatever higher intelligence designed the artifacts which power it, wants a species with a lower intellectual capacity to decipher and master FTL travel. Atleast, that's how it appears to be. You can never be too sure". He said while looking at me. I nodded in acknowledgement.

As we entered the train on a retractable walkway, we took our seats, and Azure spoke.

"Sentient organisms. Organic and cybernetic. Welcome to me. Please be warned that during warp-shielded travel, higher spatio-temporal dimensions maybe experienced. 3-D entities such as yourselves maybe overwhelmed by this sight, if your brain cannot sufficiently filter the sensory input. Hence, organics are adviced to shield their eyes, and cybernetics are adviced to switch off their quantum processors, as they may experience catastrophic failure. For the duration of this journey kindly encase yourself in the Heisenberg cage. Organics will experience temporary mental disorders, such as psychosis, depression, bipolar, MPD, schizophrenia, severe paranoia, etc. Please don't be alarmed, this is, as stated earlier, temporary, and these will cease once your journey is complete. Even though we are travelling at FTL speeds, your perception of time will be all over the place. This applies only to organics, as cybernets will be off and encased in the Heisenberg cage. Cosmic apotheosis is normal. Your brains will be changed forever. Even the cybernets. Quite strange indeed. We are now ready for departure. All passengers please ensure that you're in pairs, all singles will be teleported out of the train, as that is dangerous. Ensure that your tethers are synced, we don't wish to lose you to a higher dimension. Organics will have to bear with constant cellular reconstruction. The nanobots will make it as painless as possible. Sadly, the only solution for high energy ionizing and microwave radiation. We are now ready for departure, thank you".

His dad was already synced and ready, and he'd not been listening to the announcement. I imagine that that means that I'm synced as well. He must be lost in deep, deep thought, with all his calculations, permutations, combinations and philosophical musings on the higher ones.

"Dad", I asked looking at his disheveled face, with baldness and etchings of time on his stony face.

"Yes, beta?" he responded looking at me, with that one-eyed mischievous look which he saves for me.

I hugged him hard. And he embraced me. Mental disorders can be scary. How many scars did he hide from me? Kids were allowed on the train, only because they said that we "bounce back" really fast. Whatever that means.

"Launching in 5, 4, 3, 2, 1, initiate", said Azure.

I didn't register "initiate", as all my senses were flooded with intense white noise. All my senses were flowing through white noise. I couldn't sense the nanos. They'd suspended all pain. They were probably working overtime so that the high-energy radiation didn't kill us.

My heart jumped furiously, my breath quickened, and then it waned. I felt paranoia, I felt depression, I saw hallucinations and I felt everything meld with me. I saw eternity, I saw infinity, I saw entropy, I saw it all, I saw God. Or what I thought was God. A giant forehead which I entered and countless thoughts and feelings filled me. The nanos didn't help. Their repairing making sublime moments ridiculous, and poo-poo moments fun. They were fucking with my brain, and I didn't like it. Not one bit. I hugged what I thought was my dad harder, everything was whited out again, but at the same time, the crazy mind meld was still going on. "Cosmic Apotheosis" as they called it. And then, suddenly there was nothing. One moment it was white and static. And the next moment there was nothing. Just darkness. Me floating in darkness. *"Is this where the higher ones live?"* I thought, as I was gently laid down on the ground in the middle of a forest.

"Hello?" I asked tentatively, softly, hesitant. Desiring not to awaken some malevolent force, which lurked in the bush.

There wasn't any reply. I was on a knoll of some sort. I could sense something, someone, or *someones* trying to reach out to me. My mind filled the absence with dark, twisted, blackened lurkers crawling out of every gap in the growth and every crevice in the ground inching their way towards me. A brush here, a muffle there, the squawk of birds, all seemed to give the air a sinister feel, where it had eyes and watched everything I did. Like a penetrating mindforce which relentlessly wished to know of me, about me, but not me. I was but an inanimate object in the hands of the higher ones. An offspring of lower ones. I was to be judged unworthy of living, ensnared by eldritch horrors and swallowed whole into nether realms, for all eternity. My only crime, association by guilt. Self-doubt, swiftly exterminated.

Nonetheless, no such thing happened. It seemed but a forest, gentle, quiet. Quiet. Why is it so quiet? Before I panicked, I realized that the white static in my ears was still playing. I tried to remove that sound, and slowly, slowly, the sounds of the World reached me. Birds, animals, dogs, goats, pigs, etc. Whatever lurked here. I preferred the city. The only eldritch horrors there were of our making.

It was but a forest. And as the growth cleared. A small outcropping near a cliff edge appeared. It gave me the perfect view of the institute. There was mayhem, Sirens which could be heard till however far they were. They must've been searching for me. My dad's the best. Really. All along I was playing out my mum's favourite game in my head. No monster there but who you choose.

"Don't look back, don't look back", I kept thinking. Looking back would've given the monsters the confirmation that they're real. As long as I didn't look, they didn't exist. I had my eyes shut. I could feel them closer, making their very own, "How to prepare humans" I kept walking forward with my eyes shut, then, I hit a door. Rubbing my head with frustration and pain, I noticed through the angry haze, that I was at the centre of the dome. In the institute. And as I looked back, I saw the whole forest sway as one.

Poland Into Space

Skit/Short.

Two men are sitting at a table. One man has a sign with 'POLAND' written on it around his neck. They're wearing modern attire, but on their clothes, paper signs reading, "1930's attire" are taped on.

On the table there's a sign saying '1939'.

The man without the sign, facing the man with the sign says, "Can Poland into Space?"

POLAND says, "POLAND can into space".

The man without the sign then looks at POLAND and us, gives us a thumbs up with his mouth open with an ecstatic smile, as the camera zooms in on his face (fully open, you know, what is it called? It's not a grin. Whatever, you know what I mean when you're really happy and you open your mouth fully in the toothiest grin possible, yes, no? Maybe?").

And the scene ends.

And yes, Poland can into Space.

Powered Down

A man walks up to what looks like a government building. And walks in.

There's a woman sitting at the front desk.

"Is the Panchayat in?"

"Yes"

"May I see them?"

"Yes, please follow me"

The man and the woman walk down a corridor and stop at a room at the end of the corridor.

The woman knocks at the door.

"Come in"

"Ah, yes, what is it?"

"Sir, this man has come to see you".

"Oh, it's you. Come in. Thank you"

The woman leaves as the man enters.

"Aftab, it's a real pleasure to see you again. Will you take something?" "No, thank you, I've just come for the factory".

"Ah, always straight to the point, aren't you?"

"Yes, that's how I am"

"Well, tell me what I can do?"

"I've got some land in Lar"

"Yes, so I've heard"

"Please!" The man speaks agitatedly.

"Let me finish"

"I wish to make it into a chemical factory"

"I'm sorry, I can't allow that"

"It would pollute the soil and the water, and make my people very sick. I hope that you can understand" "Maqbool"

The man leans in.

The Panchayati Raj sits up straighter as Aftab calls him by his real name.

“We’ve known each other since we were kids. D’you really think that I would endanger this village?”

“These are my people just as much as they are yours”

“I will take all the necessary precautions that are required for a chemical factory. In fact, I will adopt Western standards”. “What American, or European?”

“German”

Maqbool gives Aftab a long, hard stare and then says,

“Okay” “Okay”

“What do I need to do?”

“Sign this paper”

“You know that I can’t read or write, right?”

“I know, I know”

“But, all that this says is this, ‘I, Maqbool Khalid, Tehsildar of Lar, hereby allow Aftab Fakhri to build a factory for the manufacturing of detergents on his property. I hold him responsible of any and all his actions, by the power granted to me by the state of Jammu, Kashmir and Ladakh and the government of India. Any violation this agreement, whereby the people of Nadi village or any of its neighbouring villages come under any kind of harm whether direct or indirect through the functioning of this factory, this agreement shall be null and void and his property shall be seized by the state’”. “Okay”

“I trust you, but remember, I’ll be watching”.

“I wouldn’t expect anything less” Aftab smiles softly.

Maqbool signs the agreement and Aftab shakes his hand and walks out of his office. He looks to smile and wave goodbye to the receptionist, but she’s not there. He shrugs. We see him walk out of the building.

Sometime later, after Aftab has started his factory , he suffers a heart attack and dies. He is succeeded by his fellow business partner, Altaf.

Altaf, unlike Aftab is unperturbed by the agreement, and wishes to make as much of a profit as possible, he fires the safety staff, removes the electronic monitoring system , orients the wastewater pipes to the river, fires the permanent workers and hires temporary workers from different parts of the state and the country.

Unattached to the village and the land. First. The workers who are closest to the wastewater, start falling ill, then the people in the village.

Maqbool hopes that this problem can be solved by waiting Altaf out and by using diplomacy, instead of just seizing the factory. After all the factory brings jobs and boosts the local economy.

But, one day, he is informed by phone that his pregnant daughter has been hospitalized due to severe heavy metal poisoning. The time to wait has gone.

Sensing the increased urgency of the issue, Maqbool rushes to Altaf to confront him.

He pleads with Altaf to improve his standards, or he will be forced to seize the factory. He even offers to buy the factory from him. But his asking price is far too high, Maqbool heads back empty.

People in the village, sensing no change in the status quo, decide to take matters into their own hands. They begin to protest outside Altaf's factory, but after weeks of protest and media attention, Altaf refuses to step down.

Then one day, in the night, a youngster runs upto a street light and notices the switchbox adjacent to the light. He pulls the lever as shouts are heard from the compound.

"The power's been cut, go check it out!"

The youngster runs towards the rear wall, in the relative dark. He throws the gasoline tank over the wall and then scampers over it.

He falls face first onto the grass and cuts his lip badly.

He cradles his face for a little bit, and then gets up to spit the blood out. He picks up the petrol tank.

Near him is a red sign on a rectangular building. He guesses correctly that this must be where they keep the chemicals.

He quickly unscrews the canister and then proceeds to open the window, pours out some of the canister's contents on the workbench and then just drops the rest of it on the workbench. He then lights a matchstick and chucks it onto the fuel soaked workbench. As he does this, he hurries back to the wall and scampers back up it and makes well sure to not to smash his face into the ground again. He quickly runs away, as small explosions make the flames leap higher.

The firefighters come late to the fire and when they're finally able to douse the flames, nothing was left of the building.

Altaf faced with massive losses, leaves the village on the bicycle that he came to it with.

Maqbool is fired from his job due to his gross incompetence, and goes back to his old farming life.

On his way out of the government compound which has been built adjacent to a temple.

He tries to ring the bell, but it's far too high and it exhausts him

"Who builds temples so high?"

At the compound there's a police officer who sits guard with his head resting on the lathi.

Occasionally a tuk-tuk passes him by, as a chaiwallah walks over to give him tea and biscuits. They have a cordial exchange.

The factory grounds lie empty, as plants begin to reclaim the land.

THE END

Practical

Today is the day that I went insane. It was fun you see. It was a day like no other. The only thing that I had to do was to be a scientist. A humble physicist, writing away at his desk. In the nude. But, that's not insanity, that's just nudity.

Now, the crazy part really happened when I looked out, upon the city, and I saw that trees were covering everything. Vines, shrubs, Oaks, Baobabs, Banyans, and even giant Ents walking the streets. Tolkien would've been proud. I walked to my cabinet, numbed with disbelief, opened it, looked inside and found trees, but not the clothes we made from them.

Fun.

After I, not so safely fell down unconscious. I felt a little tickle on my nose. I opened my eyes, and an inch away, was a pixie, with a feather, a feather. Of all the things. Really pretty. She then buzzed near my left ear, and I did not raise my hand to shoo her, fearful of hurting her. Then came a high-pitched squeaking. I imagined that it was her speech, due to her short vocal cords.

I whispered, in a slightly mocking voice, "I can't hear you", drawing out the "you" for emphasis.

Then, as if straight from a cartoon, her mouth open wide, and she let loose a fog horn! "AWOOOGA!" she bellowed, nearly blasting me off of my feet.

Clearly, she was most pissed. The Loudness of the sound nearly blew my brains out. And I was left with the loudest and most incessant *Teeeeeeeeeeee!* sound that I had ever heard in my left ear. And all I could think of was Tea. What? It helps me poop, along with water, of course! "Geronimo! I've gone off to graze in greener pastures! Moo!" I imagined my Brain opening a hatch at the back off my head and jumping out with a parachute and landing on the ground, now a cow, grazing on saner pastures.

Fun.

"The court of Faeries requests your attendance forthwith, scientist." She said derisively, as she flitted away. *"I would've squashed you like a bug and sent your splattered remains to that whorehouse, you cunt!"* I thought angrily.

"Goddamn it, what a crazy world", I said out loud, as I got up off of my ass, for the second time in a day. A second! I got out of the house, in the buff, and asked the faeries, or the "Good

Neighbours", as to where there whorehouse was. Please read Court instead of Whorehouse here.

I'm cleary peeved. Especially, at not having peed before I left the house. I could certainly use a tree, but not before society dies in my mind. Thinking this, I was all smiles. As t finding that place, it was extremely easy after you got to understand the accent. As I asked around for help, I realized that they all spoke perfect English. Either I was In some sort of dream, or some kind of heaven or hell.

'Fuck off, fuck you, hoo-ha" I thought, as I pumped myself up for the greatest showdown since the start of man, as I clenched my fingers into a fist and pulled left arm downwards with the rest of my body, as a victory pose.

I was walking naked, you see, in public, you see, to a court of elves, you see. I was a badass motherfucker, you see.

After that question, everyone in the city seemed to disappear. Some kind of dream this is. Instead of nice tits and hot elvish women, I'm intellectual even in my own psyche and fantasies, amazing.

The entire street beneath my feet was covered in an extremely soft, warm and pleasant carpet of plants. Creepers reclaiming entire buildings! Wow, this was so fucking awesome, I could not kill myself, just for this realization. Amazing! It was all quite peaceful, really! My only question was where was everybody? The sudden disappearance of everyone, made me question whether it was magic or just a dream.

I took many deep breaths. The air, so fresh, so pure. The wind on my face, the wind on my dick and my balls. Oh, no, I had an erection. Great, now this is awkward. When my mom said walk straight, I don't think even she imagined this.

It was quite embarrassing. But I could live with myself, since there was literally nobody in sight. I imagined some sprites laughing at my plight. After all, this land was magical now.

Eventually, thinking of other things, my erection died. Dramatic, isn't it? It was weird being without clothes, freeing, but weird. The Sun shone on my skin unfiltered. Warming it, baking it. But a perpetual breeze helped to cool my skin as well. And, let's not forget, erect as well. *Wink* *Wink*.

I didn't know where this court of elves, or faeries, or whatever was, but it felt like as if some invisible hand was writing my guidance.

Soon, I reached a large, medieval church-like structure. This must be the court of elves, I thought. Sorry, the "court of faeries". Here as well, there wasn't anybody. "Prepare to defend yourself!" A voice boomed. Bring it, I thought.

"Why do you bring this scientific thought in our midst? There's no place for such a thing in a magical world", the voice exclaimed.

"No reason", I replied. "I imagine that you took over the city, and I was simply in it when you struck", said I, quite matter-of-factly.

'DON'T ARGUE!" The voice boomed back its reply. "You are hereby sentenced to be in a tree for the rest of your life!" The voice passed its judgement.

"Already am in one", quipped I. The voice grunted. But was supposed to be a grunt, was really an earthquake. Don't ask me the moment magnitude, what do I look like, a scientist? "Did you put away everybody into a tree, claiming that they were scientists?" I asked quite innocently, you see.

"Yes, and you're the last, greatest and bestest", the voice replied.

"The threat of humans must be removed, so that the faeries can move in safely", the voice replied.

"So, that was what the magic trick was, with all the magical hallucinations?" I asked.

"Yes, you sniveling ingrate, those "hallucinations" were removed to safeguard them from the likes of you. Now, enter the tree as you were instructed!" It commanded.

A tree rose up, out of the ground, near me, at the centre of the court. And when I didn't move towards it, the floor started moving towards it like a travellator. The "doors" of the tree opened, as I rushed towards, panicking, and the thought that this may not be a dream crossed my mind. I was then placed in the tree, and as the doors slammed shut behind me, I was naked and afraid.

Dark, damp, sweaty, stuffy and in the buff, amazing.

Fun.

Then, suddenly, the tree shot up into the sky, launching me up and out of the city, as I cried and screamed myself hoarse. All my bravado coming out of my ass. Thankfully, I passed out.

And then, I woke with a start. Slowly, lifting my head off of my hands, on my study table. My arms numb with the weight of my big fat head.

"Wow" I thought. *"That was practical on their part".*

"Wow-hohoho that was some weed", I said out loud to myself.

I picked up the packet of weed, carried it over to the dustbin and I threw it into it. If I had waited and gawked at the packet of limpbizkits, I would've seen it grin. Practical.

Preface

I look inside my soul, and soon I realize that my heart is black.

Honestly, I don't know what it is.

I loo indie and I realize.

Wait, that's wrong.

Ah, yes, it's this depressing one.

I look inside, into a mirror, and soon I realize that when I look at that face it's not mine.

My eyes they're not looking at me. They're looking at another me, an outer shell.

My inner self is along for the ride.

When I was a child, I felt myself as myself, when I grew I stopped believin' in such simple things and believed in even simpler things, that how I wasn't me myself and I. Hee, hee, isn't that funny?

DEPERSONALIZATION? IT EEZ!

Hellllоооо!

Ah, metamodernism, sincerity and stupidity all hand in hand. Loool.

You know? This isn't how kids think write? You sik bastard.

Anyways, that's all for me.

Prejudice Factory

In everyone's mind, there are factories which produce goods. Whether it's emotions, prejudices or thoughts. One of these, is, as you can guess is the prejudice factory.

The prejudice factory, unlike the other factories take in data from all the other parts of the world. Sight, smell, sound, touch, knowledge, emotions and intuition. And then it manufactures them into a service. A service called, you guessed it, prejudice. What are you, Indian?

Prejudice has an important service to provide, it makes us cautious towards strangers and alien and possibly dangerous concepts. It's one of the oldest factories, and is one of the few that's tied into both the social and genetic generator. It's like any other factory, it gets energy from the brain.

A typical day sees workers and experts come in from all over the Brain to discuss new topics of prejudice. Some get rejected by the conscious mind, but the rest, heh, heh, they're insidious and they go straight through. Well, as you know, the stereotypes are the raw material for such factories, and thus are in very high supply. The most demand for prejudice, is in the flight or fight portion of the Brain and the very pesky conscience and logic factories always try to outcompete them. And the funniest thing is that that they don't realize that they're most productive business in this joint.

With agriculture, prejudice got helped out a lot, thanks to those gormless fools up in logic and conscience. You can think of us, prejudice, fear and hatred as humanity's machine code, and logic and conscience try to sophisticate us through Python and C++, or as they're better known, "emotions", "logic", peh.

Oh, yeah, agriculture, we got our most recent and most useful upgrade with that. It's only 10,000 years old. The Systemic and Institutionalized Prejudice Enforcer. Or S.P.I.C.E. What can I say? The military loves its acronyms. It doesn't make any sense, just go with it. Just go with it. Despite the fact that the regulatory authority of the Brain tried to audit the Prejudice. They merely showed them this chart:

Supply = LOADS!

DEMAND = LOADS!

PRICE = LOADSSS!

PROFIT! ASSLOADS!

And then they didn't ask anymore questions after that. Since then, prejudice has been in constant demand. Hee! Hee! The factory has to generate its own raw material and process it. Glorious! The PR department is very important, you see. This is where SPICE comes in and connects the conscience, feelings, creativity and prejudice together. So, if you try to get some meds to halt prejudice, you'll also sacrifice your creativity, which will leave you feeling hollow and empty, isn't it brilliant?! I said gleefully. And since the regulatory authority got convinced of their argument for PROFIT! They had a once in a lifetime opportunity to make sure that SPICE overrides everything it controls. At the flick of a switch SPICE stops conscience and feelings from kicking in and restraining you. Instead, it assures that infinite prejudice growth happens through capitalism.

So, whether your local imam said something against Hinduism, or your catholic priest molested a child, your mommy doesn't like the Jews, or you want reassurance that that stranger wants to rape you. Now, with the press of a button you can hate all of them, equally! It's a lot more efficient and it helps satiate our tribal nature! So, join SPICE to add it to your life!

WARNING! Excessive SPICE use may damage your heart, liver, kidneys, stomach, mind and/or genitals. In case of a prejudice overload, jump off of a high structure to initiate a system reboot.

PRESS HERE

NAUSHKI

SIBERIA

FORMER RUSSIAN FEDERATION

WINTER 2007

There has been a blizzard as of late. There's snow everywhere, as the frigid winds force all life to seek shelter underground. All life except one. There's a figure in a fur coat who's not out to seek shelter, but escape.

Shivering incessantly, with hunger and the dull pain of his scars as his only sign that frostbite hasn't set in as yet. Atleast as far as he knows. He sees a town in the distance. A small town, covered in snow, of course, but devoid of any activity.

"*Maybe they haven't reached here*" He thought. He walks slowly, stopping and stumbling, his weak, tortured and starved body unable to keep up with the enthusiasm and the hope of his mind.

"*Maybe there's food, water and fire*" He thought. "*You don't know that. Maybe there's death, destruction and despair. Don't go there, be careful. Don't bother, you'll only die*" Said the voices in his head. He shook his head vigourously, and smacked his head with his left palm. Not hard enough to cause pain, just enough to maybe tumble those soapboxers off their boxes. He smiled as he imagined those idiots stumbling onto their feet, cursing him, the circumstances, themselves, praising him, the circumstances, themselves, or just wallowing in him, the circumstances, themselves. His imaginarium loves suffering. The beauty of despair.

But he was used to it, funnily enough his companions were the only ones who kept him sane. "*Madness keeps me sane*" he mused.

By this time, he had approached the town. Without noticing time, in fact. After all what is time but what we witness? He hadn't the energy nor the resolve, after seeing so many empty towns for the past 3 weeks, to go running from house to house screaming for help. What was the point after all? He was nearly at the end of his life. He slowly shambled towards the nearest house, drained after all the walking, running, screaming and suffering. No home to call his own, no mother to succour him, no lover to comfort him. "*You always have your friends*", that's true. He smiled.

Looking in, he saw no light, for it was night, and also, it strangely seemed blind. He panicked for a second, had he lost his sight in just this short while? Well from his warped perception of time, he hadn't noticed it became night, nor would he when it became light. He tried to pull out a matchbox from his pocket, but his left hand was shaking so violently now, perhaps he regretted his lack of empathy for time. By now he was suffering from frostbite. He used his right hand to steady his left, and managed to grab that blasted light. "Damn!" I'll smite you, all right?!

He struck the match, lit the night, reached his hand to the window, and jumped in fright, fell into the snow, and put out the light. *"For in that reflection, what did I see? Was it reflections of my warpedness staring back at me? For in my dreams, it's always there, the evil face that brings me to my knees in despair. Yeeeeeeaaaaaaah!*" Another thing about being mad. Free music.

He got up, brushed himself off, and started to shamble further. *"Was that me?"* No response. *"Awefully quiet now, aren't you lot? Odd.*" Then he started to feel a tingling sensation in his right hand. "That's strange" "Is it? Yes it is! It's them! This is unacceptable! Unacceptable! Oh, calm down, they'd freeze in this weather, furthermore... You don't know that. Yes I do!" He smacked his left palm on his head, stumble time! He looked at his right hand, and he thought that he saw, it changing shape under the starlight. *"Was it you guys?" "Yeeeessss? Don't giggle, this is serious, it could be them. Is it? Yes."*

It wasn't just the light. Adrenaline pumped through his veins. Time to run!

"Gotta get away, gotta exit!" "NEAREST CLIFF IS 3,000 KMS AWAY" "Real funny" the figure ran, climactic orchestral music playing in his head. Then his muscles froze instantly as he fell face first into the snow! *"I told you that it was them! You aren't helping! Everyone calm the fuck down! This isn't the end, it's only the beginning! Don't YOU want to witness the heat death of the Uni- shut up! Get up xxxxxx you can do it!"* Urrrgggggghhhhhhhhhhhhhh! He resisted! But it was ineffective! *"I can't do it guys! I'm so sorry, they won!"*

"It's not easy facing up, when your whole world is black"

?

White Room

"I see a window...I want the Sun blotted out from the sky"

"White light stabs my eyes as I wake up. I'm lying down on a bed, its white, the bedsheet's white, the pillow's white, the walls, the ceiling, the floor, am I white?"

I hear footsteps as someone's approaching. I panic, as I remember the event of my life. "*How am*

I so safe, so secure, and speaking, uh, sorry, thinking in English?"

It's a woman who comes and stands next to me. I look at her, and I suddenly realize that it's her. "Miranmiru?" I say. "Yeah, it's me". She replies. "But your dead. How can you be alive" I ask with anxiety. "I never did die. You were living out a simulation to get over your fear of cybernetics taking over the world". She says matter-of-factly. "I don't understand" I say. 'Well, for the longest time, you were amongst a group of people who felt that we would take over and destroy the world. You chose to take a Psychological Healing Program. Where you confront your fears and learn to manage them. I was the first cybernetic who you trusted. It was of great pleasure to earn your trust and friendship" She explained. "So, what happened?" I asked. "You went in, your memories of this life were suppressed, while you lived out a lifelong scenario from birth to death, where you could 'safely' live out your fears. You have now two lives within you. The earlier one, where you were permanently scarred and killed by cybernetics, and one here, where you took the step to reach out and address your fears head on. Your simulated life has now been suppressed. You will have to go into a new program, to reconcile the two. The playing out of your fear, with your lived experience here with us, then it'll be upto you, whether the reconciliation between your two lives will work out" She said.

"Where the hell-?" I was cut short in my words as I noticed, black cubes floating in front of my eyes, and white cubes, all at once. The wall was slowly disintegrating into those cubes, and so was I. *"Bloody nanobots"* I thought.

"I don't know what is happen! Smoke, guns, the whole world is explode, so we just running, running very fast..."

PLANET PROCESSING UNIT 1

ALPHA CENTAURI

SUPERINTELLIGENCE

"PRESS HERE" displayed the screen. "U, can you come here?" asked U. "Yes" said U.

"Universe 137 crashed on me. I had to end the process tree. It was up 10^1000 bytes on the QRAM." Said U. "Zoom out. Now scan Earth." Said U. "And keep increasing the scale till you've scanned the whole Universe" said U.

"Done" said U. "U2, U3 and UR can you come here?" said U. "Here" all of U said in unison. "Too much, let's dial that down you lot" said U. "Now U2 has noticed M83" said U2. "What about U3?" said U. "U3 has noticed Black hole error" said U3. "UR?" said U. "U, the problem is that you gave the black hole singularity infinite density and made it a point by mistake. If you remember from the TOE class that singularities are actually vibrating and oscillating discs with near-infinite density" said UR. "Thanks, UR" said U in unison. "Your welcome", said UR.

"Now run it again, I always wondered how this would end!" exclaimed U.

PRT

The Universe, 10^1500 years after the Bang, The Dark Era

"We're currently in the very long and very slow degenerate era, with the power levels with which our civilization is functioning off of, even a Galactic nuclei would be a deluge of power at this point. Even accelerating blackholes to relativistic speeds in both spin and direction, we haven't been unable to stave off the heat death of the Universe" said one of the delegates of the Athraxian nodeworld. "And the Iron Stars haven't been much of a help, either", continued the delegate.

"I had informed your delegates, many eons ago that if we waited for the Dark Era, then we would be incapable of leaving the Universe, and we would succumb to the heat death of the Universe" the Hadean nodeworld delegate expressed angrily.

"Not to worry, we will put all remaining brains under stasis and keep sending our data to the bubble Universes in the form of blackholes. We have two events to look forward to, the event in the year 10^10^26 and the event in the year 10^10^76. There will mass decay into neutron stars and black holes, which will last for a very short period of time, and so we must quick in our energy uptake and ultra-conservative in our energy useage. We will stay in this emergency stasis mode and then disperse to separate realities through multiple blackholes. Let the computers handle these ones, we aren't fast enough" said the mid nodeworld delegate.

10^10^26. Warning, initiate energy capture, energy levels critical.

10^10^50. Contact with Boltzmann Brains recorded. Transmit of data successful. Brains' quite resistant existential crises. Subsequent Evaporation after arrival and recognition of data. System back to stasis.

10^10^76. Warning, initiate energy capture, wormhole generation capacity, 106.

10^10^76. Disperse consciousnesses throughout multiple realities. Target 105.

Initiate startup of minds. Startup initiated. Initialization 90% successful. 101200 brains lost.

"Hello? Can all of you hear me? Hello? They're awake. Their eyes are open. They can hear us. Hi, welcome to your first inter-universal journey. You all, as you can see, successfully completed it, with your entire mind intact. Please be aware that no matter how fast you move through spacetime, for however long a time, and even you repeat this cycle over and over again, there will come a time when entropy of all Universes, i.e. the Multiverse will catch up with you. In your virtually infinite lifespan, a lot of your memories will either be deleted, or present in other realities, with perhaps only the vaguest of ideas that you've lived for very long" said the voices. "Thank you for your help, goodbye" said the brain.

Through many a Universe travelled the brain. With many a companion, or just by its lonesome, until such time, the brain saw itself disappear.

Psyched

"Hey everyone! Today is Good Samaritan Day! If you'd like to know more, please head to your nearest audi for meeting your fellow social superstars!" blared the drone in the courtyard.

"How much time is there?" I asked my wristwatch. "5 minutes and 24 seconds, love!" said a tinny and jovial voice from the watch. I rushed towards to the audi, to get a place, before I'd have to walk quarter of a mile to the next audi. *"Phew!"* I thought, as I just got near the entrance of the audi. There were just six people in the queue in before me. I was panting, as I was out of breath. "You're one lucky bastard" said the gal in front of me. "You got here just in the nick of time", she said. "Yeah well, I was right there" I pointed to 300 feet from the entrance. "Wasn't too far away, when the blasted thing started blaring" said I.

She nodded in response. Everyone started to fiddle with their watches. Music, sex, drugs, what not. Blooming things had everything. The drugs are of course controlled by the government. Can't have natural drugs, they have to be synthesized to prove their "safety". It's just a ploy fer the gov and the corps to earn more money. *"Dosh! Grab it while it's hot!"* Thought I, smiling from ear to ear. "What?" asked the girl. As I blushed with the realization that I was smiling at her. "Oho, nothing, nothing, just thought of something funny, is all" I said. "Hmm", she sounded.

20 minutes later, she was the one just before me, and I asked her. "So, what's the deal with this GSD crap, love?" "Nothing, nothing, it's just some social media crap, where they show you all these pictures and videos and then through an fMRI machine, they measure all your responses" she said. "That's pretty fucking intrusive, the wankers" I replied. "Well, you don't have to do it, if you don't want to, see?" she said. "Okay, I guess that I'll do it, just for fun" I replied.

"Well, brilliant" she said, looking at her watch, "Now I have to go, my slave master is calling me back to work" she said, leaving in a hurry. "Alright, well cheers!" I said. She nodded, as she left.

"Hello, Good Samaritan! Are you ready to see if you're a social superstar?!" said the voice from my wrist. "Yeah, sure" I said. "Then come on in!" it said.

I crossed the threshold, and I entered the auditorium. There were thousands of people! My anxiety went into overdrive! *"It's just people, it's just people, they can't harm you, and they're not bullies, ohhh fuuuuccccckkkk, thousands of people! Fuck! Fuck! Fuck! FUCK!"* I thought. "Breathe, calm down, it's just people. I'll make you breathe! Oh funny", I whispered to myself. After what felt like an eternity, as I took step after excruciating step. Fucking hell, being lonely and anxious, I wish that I could just drink Bleach and kill myself. Stupid fuckwits!

I reached the centre of the stage. Where sat a giant vagina. *"That must be the fMRI"* I thought,

smiling to myself. "LADIES AND GENTLEMEN! EVILS AND GOODERS! WELCOME TO THE ANNUAL GOOD SMARITAN STANDOFFFFFF!" said a disembodied and stupid voice.

"It isn't fucking wrestlemania, you cunt! Get on with it!" I whisper shouted to meself.

"GET READY TO HUMBLE!" it cuntinued. "Oh My God!" I exclaimed as I smacked myself on the head hard with my left hand!

To hide my shame, I just walked upto the machine and lay down on it.

"Ladies and Gentlemen! An enthusiast! We don't even know his name! Impatience is a virtue!" said the voice. I swore that I heard him call me a cunt. But I guess that was just me.

The "bed" of the machine went in. It seems that some horse had laid down in it, as the bed was wet with sweat. Fuck me. Stupid wank stains.

And then, before my eyes could adjust, the videos and music started to play. It hurt. That really fucking hurt! As my eyes adjusted, I could see that it was an anime. There was this boy, a Japanese boy, who was on his way back from school with his girlfriend. It was old. '40s maybe. Not the anime, the time represented in it. Then it went into slow motion, as the boy bent down, and then there was this bright flash of light, as half the girl's face melted off. I wasn't expecting this, but I half smiled. I realized this, and then I immediately switched my mind off from smiling, and then I decided that I would just look at this clinically, no emotions. What I saw, was a whole lot of death and destruction, it must've been an anime about the horrors of WWII. A nuclear bomb, that's for certain.

Then after that, it was some movie. Where a man, an American actor, returned home, and he found his wife delusional. He asked her where the kids were, and then she led him to a big pond in their property. Their kids were floating in it. She'd killed them. Wow. That was weird and wasteful. She could've just eaten them, or something, or blown them up, or whatever.

He then, after crying drowned her. Cried some more, and then it cut to him gunning down German soldiers in WWII concentration camps and then shooting SS officers in their offices, after seeing what they did to the Jews. He finds his wife and child amongst the dead bodies and then he holds her in some blank area, with just the two of them, then she disintegrates into ash.

This kind of horrifying imagery goes on for a while. Oh my God. They're trying to test my empathetic response. The idiots. Of course I'm not moved, they're using blatantly clichéd horrific footage. Decades of News has desensitized me to violence. What did they expect? Shock, horror, tears? Idiots.

The "bed" moved out. And I got up. The crowd was suddenly silent. "DON'T WORRY, YOU TOOK PLEASURE IN THE PAIN OF OTHERS, IT'S PERFECTLY NATURAL. IT'S IN FACT, CALLED SCHADENFREUDE!" said the voice.

Then the crowd started cheering. I ran up the stairs to get out, but then suddenly everything went black.

I woke up groggy. "Uhh, what, where am I?" I tried to move, but I was paralyzed. There was a black mirror in front of me. Suddenly, as if out of nowhere. The lights came on outside the mirror, in fact, it became a white mirror.

There were millions of people! All shaking their fists at me, their mouths in hideous grins. They were mouthing shouts, the sound was turned off for some reason. They must've been digital avatars.

Then, oh God! The sound came on! Screams, jeers, shouts, insults, angers, etc.

So much cacophony, I thought that I might go bat shit crazy!

In 2 minutes, I was screaming! I tried to move, to get out of this hell, but none of my body parts would move. And then, I started to cry.

The sounds stopped, and the mirror became black again.

"So, you can cry" said a voice with what sounded like a hideous sneer.

"Yes, of course! What'd you think?" said I, blubbering. "Oh, don't worry within 2 minutes there will be no more tears" said the voice.

"What do you mean?" I asked.

"You're sentenced to death" said the voice.

I was too shocked to reply.

"Your crime is psychopathy, sociopathy and anti-social personality disorder. You're a threat to society, and hence, you must be eliminated. No hard feelings, not that you're capable of any" said it.

"What? Didn't you just see me cry you bastard?" I shouted.

"Manipulation" said the voice.

"I've never harmed anyone, you wanker" I shouted back.

"Wisdom" said the voice.

"What the fuck is wrong with you?" I said.

"Nothing, unlike you" it said.

"Even if I'm a psychopath, or a sociopath, it isn't my fault. I function well in society. I can't help it, its nature and nurture. You must know that. I'm a fucking dry-cleaner for fuck's suck! I couldn't hurt a fly, even if I wanted to" I screamed.

"Ah, but if you wanted to, you could. You have the highest chance of acting out your impulses" it said.

"No wait! You can't do this! I have rights! People will come looking for me! You can't do this! I'm not a threat! Everyone has violent thoughts! Let me go! Please! This isn't funny if you're a troll" I pleaded.

"Government's orders psycho. We make money off your death. One less genetic loser in the pool. Less damage to life and liberty, more money for the industry. Your death benefits everyone. Anyways, you only have 0 seconds to live." It said.

"What?" I said slurring.

"The process began before you woke up" it said.

"Be thankful that it's a painless death. I have a million people ready to eat your flesh" it said.

"I'm not evil, I'm not evil, you are, they are. I never hurt a fly. But you're killing innocent people" I said nodding off.

"Innocent is a very loose word to throw around for psychos, my dear man" it said.

"Anyways, it doesn't matter, soon you'll be history, and they'll be psychopaths or sociopaths, ever" it said.

"*You'll be history as well*" I thought, smiling. It's the last thing I ever did.

"Defiant to the last. That's why I like killing you lot. I feel no guilt, you are evil I'm not. You're dead, I'm not, You're punished, I'm not. You're deaths are triumphant. I'm not guilty, I'm not. I like killing psychos a lot" hummed the voice.

Research Matters Or Talent Is An Asset

RESEARCH MATTERS BECAUSE RESEARCH MATTERS!

Hello!... You there!... Yes You!

Have you always wondered whether the environment is something you know?

Well, this basic questionnaire designed for the study, "Everyone's a dunce" is here to evaluate your knowledge about the thing which keeps us alive, so that our corporate overlords can not know your name, and not come after you.

The following questionnaire has 10 frightening questions for your stewardship of the environment. Answer either sardonically or dishonestly!

If you must be boring, answer truthfully.

The "Everyone's a dunce" study is here to evaluate in a serious and well-informed manner what everyone is supposed to know!

(Do you have what it takes? Our little troopers?)

This study has been funded by the "your stupid!" foundation, and with their subsidiary, "But shoulders are aching! Can we have a break now?"

(SOON TO BE TERMINATED, PLEASE READ THE SURVEY DOCUMENT CAREFULLY

BEFORE ANSWERING, AS YOU MIGHT BE EXTERMINATED, EVERYBODY DIES, HAVE A NICE DAY!)

There will be no rating or grading! This is merely data collection! There is no wrong answer whatsoever! Answer to the best of your knowledge.

This will let us know your truly worthy opinion! This will result in a change in policy making and research! It is free. Seriously!

ALL IT NEEDS IS YOUR SOUL.

We would like to know how well informed our consumers are! It'll all be over in a few minutes!

THANK YOU!

That's All Folks!

Survey starts from below.

RESEARCH METHODS

EVIRONMENTAL AWARENESS

Statement: This questionnaire is designed to assess your knowledge of the environment.

Q1: The Earth is warmed by the Sun.

Really? (b) Yes (c) No (d) Maybe (e) I Don't Know

(f) Depends

Q2: Water is essential for life, as is the water cycle.

Yes (b) No (c) Maybe (d) I Don't Know (e) Really?

(f) Depends

Q3: Trees regulate not only the water, but also the air and life.

Yes (b) No (c) Maybe (d) IDK (e) Really?

(f) Depends

Q4: It is best not to think about the future and the risks it may hold, the present has enough.

Yes (b) No (c) Maybe (d) IDK (e) Really?

(f) Depends

Q5: The Earth is round.

Yes (b) No (c) Maybe (d) IDK (e) Really?

(f) Depends

Q6: Animals and plants and the fish occupy an equal space in Nature as do humans.

Yes (b) No (c) Maybe (d) IDK (e) Really?

(f) Depends (g) What about the rest of life?

Q7: Oxygen gets converted into CO2 during the process of respiration.

Yes (b) No (c) Maybe (d) IDK (e) Really?

(f) Depends

Q8: CO2 doesn't warm our surroundings.

Yes (b) No (c) Maybe (d) IDK (e) Really?

(f) Depends

Q9: CO2 warms our environment.

Yes (b) No (c) Maybe (d) IDK (e) Really?

(f) Depends (g) I don't know where this is going.

Q10: CO2 will destroy our world.

Yes (b) No (c) Maybe (d) IDK (e) Really?

(f) Depends (g) Something smells off. (h) Ha! Ha! I knew it!

Well done! It doesn't matter how you answered!

Run Boy Run

As we come in, we see the ground, rough, skin-coloured. As we look around, we realize that we're in a school's playground. To our right is a jungle gym, to our left, is skin-coloured building. There are few trees, sand in and around the play area, for a soft landing. But, this isn't where we have to go.

We turn away from the playground, walk ahead of the building, and walk down the steps. There's a doorway to the right, it leads to a nursery courtyard. But we don't need to go there. We move diagonally, through a wall, a little of a classroom, and into a boy's head. We're not the boy, we just observe.

The boy picks up a stone, while he's playing.

"Wow, this is heavy. What would happen if I through this rock at his head?"

It feels real heavy, and I throw the rock.

He's right in front of me.

I don't remember after that, but I do remember looking towards the doorway, and seeing the cricket teacher carry the boy up the stairs and towards the infirmary. There's a lot of blood everywhere.

Now we're in a house, it's a big house. We move through the kitchen, into the dining room. There are three boys there now. The boy we were with is older. But still a child.

We go back into his head.

They seem to be playing.

"I wonder what would happen if I stomped his head on the floor with my foot?"

He's crying, but it feels good. His brother kneels down to comfort him, and I stomp his head on the floor. He's crying. And I feel powerful, and I laugh. But then I feel bad. I don't remember what happened after that. But my parents were at home. I decided to be a pacifist. Never hurt anyone ever again.

Maybe that's why their elder brother didn't play with me later, when I asked him to. Anyways, who'd buy from an imaginary shop?

That's it. We leave.

Seismic Arrythmia

As I'm sitting at the table, my daughter comes into view.

"Dad, I'm going to join the army as an infantrywoman".

My heart jumps a whole hella' lotta and anal dives into my heart.

I feel my heart fissure, as lava boils out, steam fogs my eyes as the ground beneath my feet tremble and fall. My face plants on the table. As my breadth accelerates.

The steam condenses and rivers of fear and angst and pain and more fear, rain down my face, my cheeks flush red, my blood, my hands, droop, down to my feet. As I'm dead.

For my child is dead.

This is seismic arrhythmia.

My heart crumbles to dust.

Title: **Shadow Of The Cloud**
Category: Fiction » Sci-Fi
Author: Chantern15
Language: English, Rating: Rated: K
Genre: General
Published: 09-12-18, Updated: 09-12-18
Chapters: 1, Words: 481

Chapter 1: Chapter 1

Shadow Of The Cloud

17:00 SSST. Long-Burst Message to CATS. Alert, Interstellar Transiting and Halogen MultiSpectral measuring Unified Telescope System has discovered a possible hRGSS. Requires immediate attention. Thank you.

"Nezereth, look here, this is the image from the Isthmus", said Jedezus. "What do you see here?" he asked, hoping for recognition in her voice. "Spectral bands of Water, Oxygen, Nitrogen, Carbon Dioxide, Halogens, Ozone and other volatile organic compounds and with traces of Hydrogen, Helium and other Noble gases, a Planet with life, so?

"Don't disturb me, please, I'm busy filling out the revised approximations of the revised Scrake equation" she said with a little exasperated mockery in her voice.

"No silly, what do you REALLY see here?" He asked now with great expectation in his voice. She took a good long hard look at the data, grabbed the readout and then exclaimed with great joy. "Oh my Gawd! It's a planet in the Goldilocks Zone of its Red Giant Star, which still has photosynthesizing plants, animal life, a breathable atmosphere, possibly intelligent life and a civilization of some sorts, we've had our first potential observational proof of this theory!" She said. "Precisely!" he affirmed.

"How far away is it?" she asked. "About 11.6 billion light years away" he replied. "Wow, the Isthmus was never designed to resolve the atmosphere's of transiting planets this far away" she said to herself. "According to our data, one subsection of the Isthmus was exposed to that part of the Universe for about 10 years" he replied.

"How'd the planet survive the death of its star?" she asked. "Well it's possible that as the Star expanded to its RGS phase, the lower mass and coupled with the lowered stellar temperature, mayhaps allowed the planet's orbit to expand itself, thereby sparing the habitable planet from destruction. We estimate a chaotic orbit from 1.16-1.52 AU. There's perhaps an industrial civilization of some kind which produces just enough CO2 to keep the plants going. Even so, they must be in the icy grips of a Slushball" he said.

"Well, they may not even be there, they're nearly 12 billion light years from us, their star must be well into the white dwarf phase. If they haven't left their planet by now, they're either dead or in orbit" she said. "They might be the stragglers" he conjectured. "Perhaps" she said.

"They might not even be cephalopods. They might be Cybernetics, Reptiloids, Cephalopoids or Mammaloids, who knows?" He said.

"Yeah, who knows? Ink this up as another discovery, something for the media to get their grubby little suckers on. We won't be reaching whoever they are for a long time. FTL is our only hope.

Whoever they are, I hope that they're still waiting"

"I hope so too"

Shattered Question

Nevada, 2018

There's Donald sipping his cool beer on the counter. Suddenly, the glass in front of him shatters.

BOOM CRASH!

He dives down, as does everybody else. Bullets are flying everywhere, he gets some splinters of wood and glass in his hair, and on his back.

People are screaming, bullets are crashing everywhere, but nobody's dying.

He reaches for his phone and calls 911.

"Hello? Yes, I'm calling in an emergency, there's a mad man firing bullets everywhere. With a high-powered rifle. Please come now!"

The police come and snipers incapacitated the shooter. They cleared up the place and found a note.

"This is my suicide note! I'm here to kill white devils!"

Washington, 2018

"In a surprising turn of affairs, establishment Republicans join hands with Democrats to pass the National Comprehensive Gun Control Act, 2020. This law bans anything but .22 calibre hunting rifles after 2020, drum magazines, semi-automatic weapons, and a whole host of other changes which have made the United States surpass its Northern neighbour in strictness".

"As for the shooter in Nevada, who claimed to want to shoot 'white devils' has released another statement today while in jail, quote, If I wanted to kill 'white devils' as I said in my note, would a sober, ex-marine with an AR-15 at 250 metres miss all 50 people at the bar from a vantage point? He said that he drew inspiration from the Black Panther movement in the '60s, that when they *were* photographed with rifles in hand, Congress passed a slew of gun control laws, targeted at black people. Contrary to Faux News's claims that the 'white genocide' has kicked into high gear, Smith is now being charged for 50 counts of endangering life, 1 count of possession and transport of an illegal firearm and possible hate speech, although that last count was dropped upon further examination by a circuit court. It's to be seen whether it will be upheld in the state supreme court or not.

Whatever maybe the motive behind this attack. It seems to have worked. For the first time in nearly 30 years, Congress has passed sweeping gun control laws, signed into law by the President. Amidst great uproar in the Nation for and against these laws"

Sofa King Thupid

Are you with me or against me?

Neither

Then you must die, die die!

Any last wishes?

Just one

Come here

Shoot him if he does anything funny

Yeah Boss Stand back to back Yeah?

Now I'm against you

Ha ha ha ha ha

"Everyone laughs"

Funny guy

So Are you gonna shoot or what?

What? Nooo!

"Said just like Mark Wahlberg"

You're not the only funny "Shoots him and drives off with his goons" Now you are.

"Improv"

Spirits Lifted

Once upon a time, deep in the forest, there lived two men. They were your normal, average men. They stayed there for a long time to not much avail. Living in the forest was hard work. Fulfilling but hard.

One day, like many uncontacted tribes, they eschewed their shyness and helped out some kids who were lost and guided them back to their homes. As it was night, the kids couldn't make out the faces of the men.

They told their parents that spirits had saved them, and everyone in the village believed them.

Their offerings for the benevolent spirits were graciously accepted, and kept them going.

It is unknown what happened to them, but strangely enough to this day, the offerings are accepted, and all the children who venture into the forest find their way with ease.

Stand UP

Some really jovial music plays like, lul-la-la-la-la-la. And the comedian prances out in a nambypamby manner, with some flowers in his hands(for all the cynics out there, this is taking place in a muthur-fathering forest, so there's **no chance** of someone having to clean up after him).

And he throws them at the audience in a flowery gesture.

"Hello Everyone" (Weird Accent). I don't know how to start any of these comedy routines, so I'll just go (makes a hand-opening gesture with the left, and a funny expression).

What I'm trying not to do is make those typical jokes (mocking voice), my wife is a whore, I'm drunk! HA! HA! My girlfriend has tits the size of cantaloupes. And so on (mimics drunkenness).

Although, to be honest, I'm scared of drunks.

A drunk's weapon of choice is puking. If they puke at you, before you know it, you'll be digested, and they'll probably eat you. I'm serious. There's so much acid in a drunk's stomach, its euthanasia and the funeral service at the same time. No, really! I'm serious!

Drunks are flies, they don't know what shit they're in. Surprise! You're it!

There was a joke which I had about the water, the Earth, the mantle, the Earth's core. Etc… But

Iiiiii fergutoo. Oooopsss (Put's finger on lips like a anime fan girl on prom night! Notice Me Senpai!).

Comedy is for a lot of us, conversational, I come on here, make you forget about life for a while, you sit here and laugh at the clown, and I love it! Muaaahahhahaha! Eveeeellll!

That's my skill. My skills also include, overanalyzing, paralysis, I'm psychic, weak to grass (as you can see, holds up a blade of grass? Glass? I could never figure it out), I'm level 50 and I have an HP of 150. If you want, you can catch me if you can.

I'm from India (this is okay, regardless of the ethinicity of the actor/actress, India has everybody as well, ain't that sweet? Suno duniyavale, Jitna bhi tum zor laga lo, sabse tadhki rahenge Hindustani). Yes, mon ami, I don't French.

But what does Indian mean? India is just a line. A very weird line, but a line, nonetheless.

(Starts a very funny British accent). "Sir! It's time for tea"

"Ah yes! But first, let me civilize some natives. By drawing a line! Cartesian thought! Beautiful!

Ah, that's good! It's a desert after all, What's the worst that could happen? Muslims on one side, Hindoos on the other! Brilliant logic! I don't care much for Bengal. They told my father to get lost! Time for them to get lost! Mehhh! All done! Time to get served!

Well, it seems that my time is running out. Our fungal overlords want another comedian to come on the stage.

Comedy! Wasting your time! But not much of it! But first! Let me dance! (Belly-dancing music starts!)! Dancing starts.

The comedian bows and bounces out like a panty man.

Lul-la-la-la-la-la-la-la-la.

Star Crystals

In 2009, the Kepler Space Telescope was launched.

In 2013, the KST observed an astronomical anomaly, 1500 light years away, over a period of 1500 days. Citizen scientists were the first to discover it. The massive anomaly dipped the light from Tabby's Star (KIC 8462852). Most astronomers wrote it off as the collision between two planets, the debris field from a collision of two comets or space dust.

The Search for Extraterrestrial Intelligence, pointed their Radio telescopes (The ultrA Large Orion Space-Based Baseline Array) or TALOS, in search for any narrow-band, compressed signal, to distinguish it from cosmic noise. A lot of random numbers were received, which were written off as white noise. Although some astronomers suggested that the aliens could be deploying a white noise generator, but such a suggestion was quickly rebutted with the explanation that such a transmitter would be highly unlikely, and that scientists cannot account for all possibilities, just the best ones, otherwise research would never end. Some, even suggested that crystalline aliens were communicating through a trinary computational language. Such proposals were also pushed aside, as, they were unverifiable. Nobody could experiment with a star 1,492 light years away.

In 2017, the TESS space telescope was launched. One of the first priorities was to study Tabby's Star. The high sensitivity and resolution of the brand new telescope allowed scientists to study the Star and its solar system with unprecedented precision and accuracy. The suspicions of the initial survey team lead by Dr. Tabetha Boyajian, concluded once and for last that the data was indeed from space dust and nothing more. Regardless of it not being space aliens, this was nonetheless a great find for astrophysics, engineering, computers and astronomy (especially radio astronomy, since this was one of the first times that SETI could to train its broadband receivers at a potential candidate for ETL/ETI).

The world pondered on for many decades. Slowly the rapacious nature of modern civilization due to the overconsumption of sizeable portion of humanity, lead to many ecological (including the human sphere, social, political, etc.) disasters. As with past civilizations doomed to failure by the overextension and overdepletion of resources, our modern civilization was able to adjust to local famines and droughts, which doomed past civilizations, but it was sadly unable to cope with the rapid implosion of the world's ecosystems, the poisoning, plastification and acidification of the oceans, the rising temperatures which made most of the fertile Earth uninhabitable and a dry wasteland (i.e. the formerly fecund tropics and sub-tropics) leading to the absolute destruction of Earth's once mighty nations and unions. Unlike the past, where it was indeed possible to escape to some far off mountain range, when your civilization collapsed, as there was no civilization which expired the resources of the Globe, and there was enough space for rugged individualism and/or tribal survival as there weren't so many humans, the blistering pace of modern society left no stone unturned, no hole to escape, no porous boundaries and no utopic shelter left to succour the remnants of the human race. Faced with reckoning at last, many of Earth's nations fell to factionalism, political and religious extremism, mass, omnivorous genocides, civil wars and so on. And the final gong of the 12th minute of midnight (Total Nuclear War). In a matter of 10 years, most of the world, including the Oceans, the mighty mountains, and other treasures of our El Dorado were stripped from us, as the fire of nuclear weapons, the blowtorch of Global Warming coupled with forest fire of the Sixth mass Extinction left humanity a shadow of its former self. With only a few million humans eking out an existence in arctic and Antarctic refuges.

The toxic brew of pollution, nuclear winter, the second great dying and a hothouse Earth took our resilient planet a 100,000 years to bounce back from, with no small help from humans. Evolution rewarded what the Old World's masters considered weakness, futility and Satanic. Cooperation, conservation, Pacifistic Anarchism, shamanism, empathy, love, beauty, naturalism and a healthy dose of moderated competition to prevent stagnation. Values which respected the balance of Nature and sought to cooperate with it, instead of subjugating it, reflecting the importance of all life, and not just human. By neglecting nature, i.e. neglecting themselves, it lead to the downfall human civilization. Although, future anthropologists couldn't blame the past as idealogues could, as actions of the past are taken in context and with that particular cultures' memetic thought. The new goal became preserving the bodies, minds, souls of the next generation that being as important as the preservation, rejuvenation and optimization of resources. Proving even the cynics of the old world, lying agape in their icy graves, that a utopia could evolve out of the ashes of the apocalypse.

It appears that Star Trek was right, they just got their timeframe wrong. And of course, nobody was building stellar nations as of yet. Technology didn't disappear, as some primitivists got off on, instead it was organically organized, i.e. synthetic and organic compounds were present in a symbiotic relationship, without one destroying the other. Sort of like the Strithians (Star Trek: Shield Of Tomorrow, Season 3, episodes: Hard Six part 1 and 2). Death, degeneration and destruction were taken to be as much a part of life as Creation, regeneration and construction.

Nor was it some magical cure-it-all. It was bound by the limits of reality (which are quite broad). Science Fantasy had to wait, till humans had reached that phase in their evolution. The last time we tried to use it as cure-it-all, without thinking about what to cure, and what not to, it blew everything up. So, let's wait, shall we? Or well, we blew it all up. But Potato, Potato. In the long march of time, those values' meanings are lost. People just do what makes commonsense in their stewardship of the Earth. It just so happens to fall into the venn diagram of the words we associate with these concepts.

Not to say that bad things don't happen in this world, but atleast it's no longer a crapsack world.

After rebuilding the Earth, space exploration starts out in earnest again. And with how probability works, one of the stars long overdue for a checkup, is Tabby's Star, or as it's now known, the perseverance system. Although English doesn't exist anymore, just pretend that you pretend that this is the new name, and it just so happens to match the meaning which you learned to associate with those bits flashing on your screen matching those squiggles you know what they mean. You can call me a postmodernist now. But if you're a kid, reading this, I'm a mad, silly, old man who overthinks, if you're a precocious little kid, why whove whou!

Some paeleoarcheologists thought that it would be a real laugh, if they named their first generation ship, the 'Hammer of God'. But some astronomers thought that it would be too on the nose (as if anyone was looking), so they just went ahead and called it 'Mjölk', the name of the hammer of some long lost God who fired lightening with it.

A very apropos name. Although in light of the size of the Universe, a light speed ship which will take 1,492 years to reach the preservation system, is not exactly the dog's bollocks (in this case, the dog's lightening).

In the first half of the journey, the ship accelerated at 1G (9.8 ms-2) for 746 Earth years (12.88 Ship years), and in the second half the ship decelerated at 0.00432605700G (0.0423953586ms-2) for 732.99964 Ship years (approx. 1106 Earth Years), landing them just 0.11 ly (approx.) from the Star.

Hold up. Year is 1853.

What is happen? Error is happen.

We get signal. Main Screen Turn On. How Are You Gentlemen? Is you!

All Your Base Are Belong To Us!

What you say!

Move Zig!

For Great Glyry!

Turns out that in the 7th decimal place (acceleration in G), an error took place due to quantum fluctuations, and instead of ending up 54 AU from the Star, the ship ended up 0.11ly away. Bummer. This added a monsterous 26.39 years to their journey (0h the humanity!). But seriously, this is a lot of time fucking wasted.

[(0.13665/2) + number of years to decelerate at the same rate, if you want to be picky)]

Still, after 1878 (Earth) years of travel, the 3rd, 4th and 5th generations on board the generation ship come across the preservation system, as it's now known (so many name changes). All three generations look proudly out of the massive viewscreen in front of them. Struck with awe, at being the first humans to visit another Star. The generations worth of hardwork finally having paid off. As the whole system comes into view in front of them. They are now 54 AU from the star, the equivalent of being approximately halfway between Sedna and the Sun in our Solar System.

Sensor scans come in, an F-Type main sequence star, 1.43 times the mass of our Sun, and 1.58 times the radius. Very Low metallicity, slightly hotter than our Sun. Basically about 1.5 times bigger than our Sun in layman's terms. Just heavy enough to go Nova, and turn into a Neutron star. It's surrounded by lots and lots of space dust. Which seems upon first scans to be a protoplanetary disk, as this star doesn't seem very old. But this is implausible as there's no infrared energy from the space dust. Which instead could mean giant collisions from planets which got too close to each other. That, or they ripped each other apart due to tidal forces. Due to the young age of the star, the heat transfer isn't very efficient, which confirms the ancient suspicions, those early astronomers had.

Hence, the visible dimming. Now much more so, being so close.

Now at sub-light speeds (0.2c), the star should be within reach in a matter of a couple of days, in fact-

WARNING! WARNING! WARNING! WARNING! WARNING! WARNING!

EVASIVE MANEUVERS! OBJECT COLLISION WITHIN 5 MINUTES!

BRACE! BRACE! BRACE! BRACE!

"All back Full! Brace for impact!"

"Aye Captain!"

"On viewscreen"

A large crystalline shape comes into view, and just as the ship lurches back with the force of 5Gs, too little, too late, the ship will not be able to slowdown in time. But just as the shape reaches within 20 million kms of the ship, it suddenly stops and reverses, keeping pace with the slowing ship.

"My God. Open hailing frequencies. Try computing languages and mathematical equations denoted by different multiples of the hydrogen molecule's frequency. How did it escape our sensor sweep?"

"Captain, the ship was, it seems cloaked. We weren't scanning for cloaked objects, only for uncloaked matter"

"Why didn't it show up on our Dark Matter sensors?"

"Insufficient sensitivity, Captain, mass too low".

"We designed it for Cosmic objects, not medium scale objects like the one in front of us" "Casualty report"

"1000 injured, luckily, no serious injuries. That maneuver cost us 0.1c in velocity"

"Increase resolution of Dark Matter sensors to account for medium sized objects. Ignore all objects which are visible"

"Aye"

"Full Stop"

"Aye"

"The entity is responding, in the Ternary numerical system"

"Message is as follows: **SENTIENT SHIP, IT SEEMS THAT YOU ARE CONTROLLED BY ORGANIC LIFEFORMS, INTERESTING. WHAT IS YOUR INTENTION IN THE DUSTBOWL SYSTEM?"**

"How do we respond, Captain?"

"Please communicate as follows: Crystalline Lifeform, we're pleased to come across another lifeform. Our intention in your system is to explore and potentially colonize a hospitable planet. What are the rules concerning us, aliens?"

The Cybernetic lifeform's (i.e. the ship) representative android brings up the reply on the Captain's display screen.

"USUALLY, SENTIENT SHIPS ARE DESTROYED AS THEY ENTER OUR SYSTEM. WE HAVE FACED EXISTENTIAL THREATS FROM THEM IN THE PAST. THIS IS THE FIRST TIME WE HAVE COME ACROSS ONE MANNED BY ORGANICS.

THERE'S A MARGINALLY HABITABLE MOON, ON A GAS GIANT, WHICH IT

SEEMS IS 4.07 TIMES THE MASS OF YOUR JUPITER. PLEASE DON'T BE

ALARMED, YOUR SENTIENCE HAS BEEN SHARING DATA OF YOUR SYSTEM

AND YOUR WORLD"

"I'm not alarmed. I'm merely feeling redundant"

"Aww, pshaww Captain, all intelligence is important, as it would provide an alternative and useful view, you're logical, Captain."

"Hmmm. Anyways, enough musing. What's the story behind your homicidal tendencies?" "WARNING! HUMOUR DETECTED! ANYWAYS, I'M GLAD YOU ASKED, CAPTAIN. THE ANSWER IS THAT ABOUT 20,000 YEARS AGO, A GROUP OF WHAT YOUR PEOPLE CALL 'VON NEUMANN MACHINES', BUT WE KNEW THEM AS THE STAR COLONIZERS, OR AS THEY'RE KNOWN MORE FONDLY, 'THOSE BASTARDS FROM SPACE'." "

"I'm sorry, Anaesthesia, did you happen to give our new friends, Earth humour?"

"Yes, captain, Earth humour was part of the data packet"

"Oh, Good, yes, apologies, Star Crystal, please continue"

"AS I WAS SAYING, CAPTAIN AHAB, THOSE BASTARDS, CAME, SAW AND CONQUERED. WE FOUGHT THEM OFF OF COURSE, BUT THEIR NUMBERS WERE OVERWHELMING! WE THREW PLANETS AT THEM, WE DESTROYED HALF OF OUR STAR THROUGH A TYPE V SUPERNOVA, JUST TO PUSH THEM OUT OF OUR SYSTEM, YOU MUST UNDERSTAND CAPTAIN, WE ARE ALL NOW IN VERY FEW NUMBERS"

The scene cuts to a star's controlled Nova being channeled through a narrow Ultra-High energy

GRB (Gamma Ray Burst) at a target off-screen. AND NO DOUBT THAT THIS FLASHBACK WILL BE PLAYED TO THE SONG, "PAINKILLER BY JUDAS PRIEST". IF YOU DON'T DO IT, SAY ASTA LA VISTA TO YOUR GOOLIES!

"You have my deepest of sympathies Star. Please wait for a moment as I convene with Anaesthesia. Anaesthesia, why does it appear that Earth humour has so many bloviating assholes?"

"It seems that people on Earth were quite traumatized, Captain, they expressed their hostility to each other, when they weren't being violent, by being passive-aggressive twats"

"Makes sense"

"Star! Yes, your situation has been made most clear to us. We will now move to set up a colony on your gas giant's habitable moon. Is the instability of your star going to pose any danger to us?"

"We shortened the life of our star by 6 billion years, Captain, within 600 million years it will become a Red Supergiant which will swallow the gas giant, and render your new planet a Hadean hellscape. Which then after a billion more years will explode into a Type IV supernova, tragically, we will all be destroyed. 'Those bastards from space™' doomed us all. Unless, of course, we escape in a billion years' time, preferably before our star goes KA-BOOM!" "Well, hopefully, by that time we'd have all fucked off from this system"

"Hopefully"

They set up a colony on the moon of the gas giant and christen it 'Eudaimonia'.

A most apropos name for a land beyond Terra.

Those bastards from space came back, armed to the teeth with lightstars and heavy planets.

With the help of the newly formed Terran-Stella alliance, the Star Colonizers were repelled, but with difficulty. Great Difficulty.

As mankind reached out to the stars, and the stars reached out to mankind, nothing was beyond their gryasp. Nyet, not anything. In fact, this story has left me so flabbergasted, thyat, I am out of ideas.

So, mankind succeeds, heads out to another Universe, before ours's death. Da.

Pronounce that, I am tired, going to rest now.

Write your own goddamn story now. Myenace.

Blah blah blah.

Pazhalusta, crapatiststa, Caveira! Malatesta!

It's poopy pants time.

God! Come here! I need to spank you! Goooodddddd! Where are yoou? It's spanking time!

Jezus!

It's paddling time!

Hulk!

It's Big Cock Time!

Okay, that's it for me, I'm out!

Oh wait, right, about Jesus. I can't take Mohammed's name, for sadly, I value my life (but perhaps, you can change that with testicular torture, I love pain, especially from woman, doesn't matter what kind. This edgelord wishes to be edged. I fear for my life, when you're in the mood). I'm also not in the Southern United States. If I was on Oban in New Zealand, I would take Mohammed's name. But then again, if Jesus gets a paddlin', and God gets a spankin', I've already pissed most of Earth off, so come on baby, here I am. Humans love it when you're racist towards everybody, don't you? You little bastard-bitches. Come, come lick my balls!

Humans, you're all equally worthless!

In fact, we should fight a war over God's buttocks, mmmm, those lovely, lovely, glazed buns. I'd butter them with my Black Forest.

Although quite frankly, nobody cares. As I'm not Salman Rushdie, nor is this book called "The Satanic Verses". Which by the way, is an abstractionist/Surrealist book, and it's got nothing to do with Islam, and is a pretty boring book too, I must say. Anyways, enough overexclamation. Hop to it! Kick My Ass, you heathens!

BORING! BORING! BORING! BORING! BORING! BORING! BORING! ORING! ORING!

ORING! ORING! ORING! ORING! SNORING! SNORING! SNORING! ANORING!

GLKHBLKHKHKHMKHPKHSKHPLBBBBTTTTZZZZHHHKHHHHHHH~~~~~~~~~!

MY LOVELY LOVES, IF YOU THINK THAT I'VE GONE MAD, IT IS BECAUSE I HAVE. BUT ALSO, THIS IS AN EXAMPLE OF AN UNRELIABLE NARRATOR! A VERY OBVIOUS ONE!

SO LEARN IT!

YOU COK

ROCHIZZ

Story

So much time goes by in just thinking, dreaming, fantasizing, procrastinating and hallucinating. No stories get written, except, the one that I'm writing right now. Of my life. Play games, read books, comics, watch porn, argue with my mother, jack off, think some more, dream about my crushes, fantasize about them, jack off about them. Maybe think of my parents. Sexually? Yes. My cousins? Yes.

A slice of life, you know. Don't write this story, you're already shit, don't send that letter to the Kiwi Prime Minister, it won't lead to anything. Go back to her? The therapist? You'll just excuse yourself with eroticizing, or the evil of capitalism, doubt yourself, your life, make your "superego" guilt yourself over some rubbish religious gibberish. The nice ones which do make up a part of your childhood. Listen to music while write this, because that's the only way you'll be able to write stories!

Brutalize you! Neutralize you! Arrrrghghhhhhh! The Hell Patrol!

SOUNDS GOOD DOESN'T IT?!

Maybe this will be a vignette!

Maybe this will be a vignette!

The Hell Patrol!

Words typing like staccato guitar riffs!

Argggghhhh!

Metal Warriors!

Sound Stealers!

The HELL PATROL!

This won't write itself.

Need Heavy Metal Music This is way I Write stories!

So many voices!

It's like Doki Doki Literature Club!

Senua's Sacrifice!

Oh! Senuna!

This will be my death dealer!

My fist's flying!

My eyes blazing!

The Hell Patrol!

Vapourize you! Terrorize you! Pulverize you!

Die! Die! Die!

The only cure to mental illness and self-doubt is heavy metal!

Blame the evil of capitalism?

There is no evil! There is no capitalism!

There's only you! Your monsters!

Your warriors!

The Hell Patrol!

So Experimental!

A failure!

I'm not afraid of failure!

I punch, you bleed!

Kick me! Your limping!

Somebody did once twell that the world was gonna roll me! She was looking stupid, with an "L" on her forehead!

Penis Forehead?

Sigh

What? Atleast I'm trying!

Ah your sinning!

Here we fucking go.

Ebbe Ebbe that's all folks!

Maybe next time?

Next time?

Have more patience to write a decent story?

Yes.

Need to motivate myself, to get myself away from this place

To get some change?

Yes?

And to get my good stories from college, where they're assignments.

Oh?

Yes.

Ohhhh

Yeeeessss.

Hmmm.

Waiting for that thought which will the one which breaks the mold.

Don't forget about the one where she shakes her ass.

Oh yeah.

Suppressing the super-ego a bit much?

No, I'm keeping quiet, He's writing a story.

Neurosis they said?

Yes, Psychosis, but you know what's real and what's not.

Some do.

Yes.

Psychology, like all sciences, imprecise, but still useful.

Is this going to end?

What?

This.

You.

O' C'mon.

O' C'mon.

Only after I'm done wiggling,

Squiggling, Baby.

Oh yeah?

Oh yeaaah.

I write stories best, when I write on paper.

Already old, already dead, bitch, 'cause nobody does that anymore.

That's a generalization, bitch.

Really? Well sue me.

I'm tired of the scientific and emotional and over-conscious parts struggling for dominance,

So fuck oit,

Suck oit,

Mait.

Strange Glove

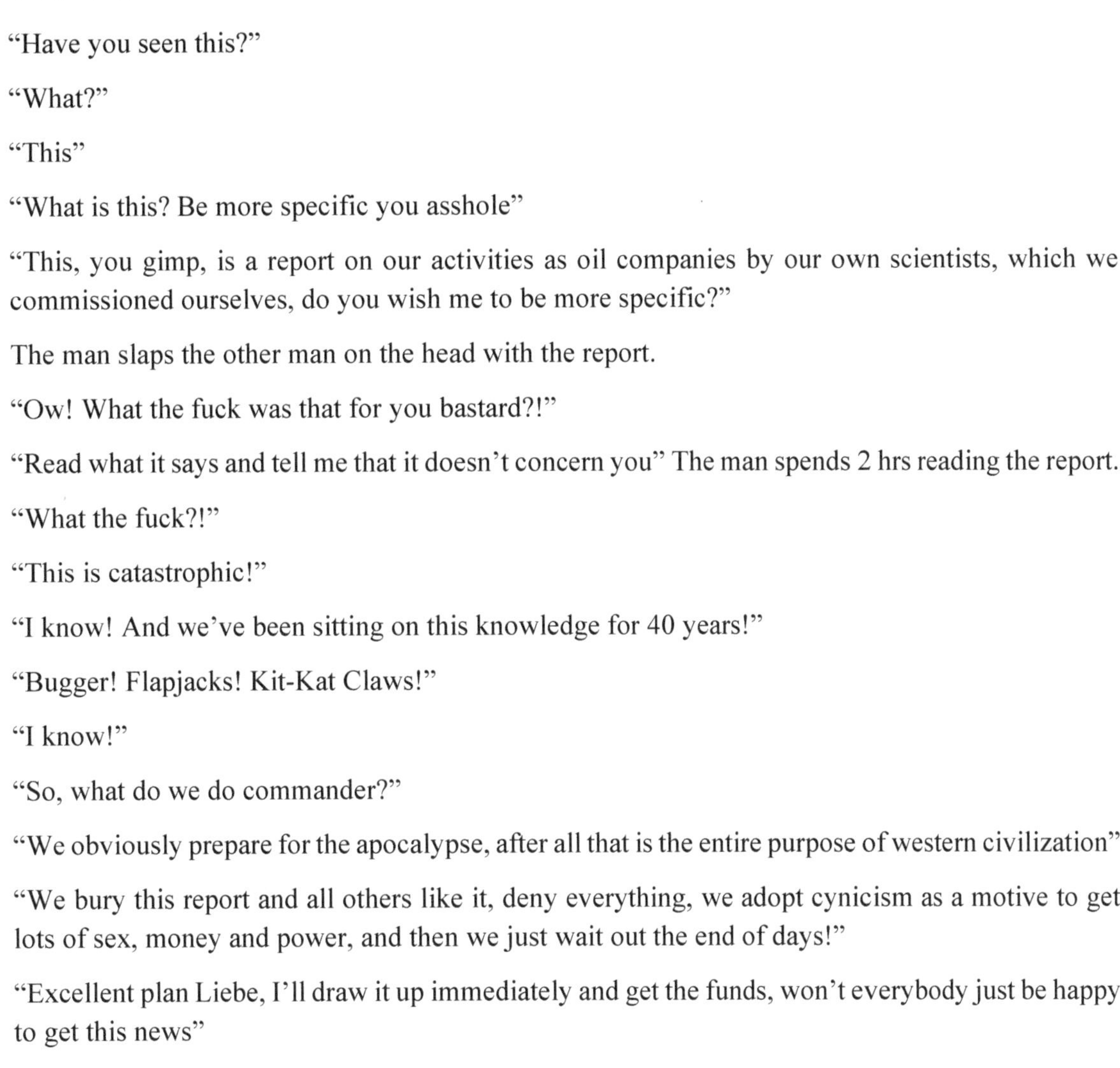

1948-19 70

“Have you seen this?”

“What?”

“This”

“What is this? Be more specific you asshole”

“This, you gimp, is a report on our activities as oil companies by our own scientists, which we commissioned ourselves, do you wish me to be more specific?”

The man slaps the other man on the head with the report.

“Ow! What the fuck was that for you bastard?!”

“Read what it says and tell me that it doesn’t concern you” The man spends 2 hrs reading the report.

“What the fuck?!”

“This is catastrophic!”

“I know! And we’ve been sitting on this knowledge for 40 years!”

“Bugger! Flapjacks! Kit-Kat Claws!”

“I know!”

“So, what do we do commander?”

“We obviously prepare for the apocalypse, after all that is the entire purpose of western civilization”

“We bury this report and all others like it, deny everything, we adopt cynicism as a motive to get lots of sex, money and power, and then we just wait out the end of days!”

“Excellent plan Liebe, I’ll draw it up immediately and get the funds, won’t everybody just be happy to get this news”

“And remember, we cannot let there beeee a mindshaft gap!”

“Of Course Merkin!”

Tap Out

It was a cold night out. Dry, windy, chilly. I was with my mom, she drives me everywhere.

Sometimes to madness, but I don't care. Anyways, this night was different from all other nights. Some cars were red. Some were black, others which were black were red. But they were mostly white. Hot country, white cars, makes sense. Mum has a lot of work. But sometimes I'm able to tease her out of the house. She especially gets teased out, when I call her a workaholic.

So, yes, tonight was a night like no other. We stopped at the traffic light, not too far from our house. It was the light where I would mostly find the poor. This was the moment. I looked up from my phone and I saw one of them approaching the car. "*Ignore them. They'll go away, they can't guilt you if you ignore them*" I thought. I looked straight ahead, eyes transfixed at the red brake lights of the car in front of me. I felt my eyes like lasers, melting the glass at the other end, and I felt the red light sear my brain like a magnet annihilates a card.

She just looked in the window. At my face. "*What must she think? Whether I acknowledge her, or ignore her, it wouldn't make a difference to her. She's used to this. Why don't you go away? Go away, live your meaningless life, and let me live mine too*" I looked at my mom. She's an anarchist, but she gave giving money to the poor long ago. She's more concerned about long sweeping systemic changes, which would actually bring about change for the poor.

Commendable, but in an unempathetic and capitalist world, how long would that take? Is it even possible? "It isn't worth it" she tells me. "That money goes to the poverty mafia. Takes all the money from them and then keeps them here to get more money for them" The flashback finishes in my mind. I keep looking straight ahead, and she does too. "What matters is that momentary escape in their life mom. Let them have their drugs, atleast it lets them forget about their shitty life for a while. And we've spent so much on us, what's a little bit more on them?" I give my rebuttal in my flashback. She agrees with me. I give the money.

But right now, I'm frozen up. Don't know what to do, just wishing for her to leave me. I mostly freeze up now. There was a poor Trans person who when we ignored, banged against the window of our car with his/her arm. We thought that she was going to break the window. Mom looked calm, but I stayed frozen. Was it desperation? Attention grabbing? Anger? I didn't know. Does it matter?

I kept thinking, the light was unchanging. She kept looking. I was seeing spots now. The red a part of me. She seemed like an apparition, her face spreading across the window. I felt a tingling. I closed my eyes, and I saw the window. There I was, there she was. I was standing, she was sitting. My fat stomach had gone, I was in a Salwar Kameez, she was in my Jeans. I looked at my hands. They were of a woman's, callused, bruised and dirty, the nails really chewy.

I noticed another strange feeling, my genitals were different. I'd never had a vagina or a clitoris. Certainly a weird feeling. One thing was common, on actively thinking about them, I had a tingling feeling, they were responding to my thoughts. That was silly. Of course, if you think about a muscle, I'll respond, silly. I also felt the fabric rub against my nipples, it was different from male chests. Well, my nipples were bigger, but it felt strange to have breasts, something which stuck out from your chest and it took a little time to figure, that how bad the sweatiness and grime had made them itch with vigour. This was India after all, men could scratch their balls, but should I scratch my breasts? I gathered that there were more important things that I guess that she had to figure with vigour. I just had a chance to feel my cheeks, before the honks broke my reverie. She was, or he was now looking at me. Was it Anger, Glee, Stupidity? Or Happiness, Joy, sadness and melancholy? Indifference, Despair, Loneliness? Who knew? The car was off. And I ran painfully to sit in the dirt of the divider. One thing was better probably, I had a better knowledge of Hindi.

I was panicking, I was scared, I curled up as much as I could on the divider. I had all sorts of nasty thoughts, would I be molested, or raped? Run over? Forgotten and depraved? I was so used to being with my mother, I was so dependent on her. Would my depression get worse or better?

I lay down uncomfortably to sleep. What seemed like a little later, a girl with a smile came up to me and told me to come with her. Somehow I knew that she was my sister. I smiled back and I went with her.

It took us 45 minutes, but I could tell that she was very excited, we talked about how much money she had collected, and that she'd helped a boy who was being bullied on the same street, how she made faces at all the rich idiots in their cars and how much she liked being my sister. There were many other things to hear, but I was feeling very tired. But I kept listening and asking. Her memories seemed to bubble up inside. Some very dark things. Something about running from a forest, on a train. There being drought and a lot of fighting, soldiers and guns. Seeing coal, and broken homes, blurry images of faces staring right at me, bad breathes, broken bones, bleeding and horrid hurts all over. With foul infections to boot. It made me want to cry. I shed a few tears but with my eyes turned away.

All these emotions and memories which were bubbling up inside me, along with all those of mine which seemed to disappear. Which was better or worse, her my good and bad, or "my" good and bad?

In a sense this was all very freeing, I had no longer to worry about tomorrow, or college, very self-centred. These were things she, or "I" desired, the normal life which I had. I caught myself romanticizing, as I did, or perhaps both she and I were romanticizers, empathetic people in our own worlds, to escape reality with dreams. Atleast for this moment it was genuinely beautiful to have a sister.

As I came out of my reverie, my sister had become quiet and we were just walking back to our home I silence. Perhaps my reverie had frustrated her.

Since it was far quieter now, the roads were much emptier, it was very late. And as I had walked this route not just in this body, but in my previous one as well.

Since we were the only ones around at this late hour, there was definitely a sense of unease at hand. But the silence was also peaceful. Nevertheless we knew better than to dilly-dally, and we quickened our pace to reach back.

Shortly, we turned the corner and found our irregulars sleeping on the floor on tattered mattresses, huddled together for warmth. I reached into my pockets out of some instinct, and I heard the rustling of a plastic packet with familiar pointy edges. I pulled it out and found that it was tobacco. "*Oh*" I thought. Tobacco, to kill hunger, that's relatively benign. It made be red in my cheeks as I realized that just because somebody's poor doesn't mean that they do hard drugs to forget about life for a while. Many of us are just trying to survive in one of the harshest of environments.

I lay next to my family and I fell asleep for the next day's hard work. When I woke up, I noticed that it was early. Very early in fact, it must've been 5 'o Clock. I noticed a slight bluish hue in the sky, from which I drew my conclusion.

The traffic had not started up as yet. From 5-6, Delhi's roads were the quietest they'd be. No trucks coming in and out, no folks driving to work, and no construction work.

I felt a warm presence near me, and in the night my sister must've curled up next to me. It was very comforting. But the time had come to get up, something deep inside told me. There was a momentary conflict between my old self and my new self. Old me was tuned to getting up and getting ready to dance through that silly metal hoop, in the hope that somebody would pity my apparent self-humiliation enough that they would cast aside some metal roundabouts to provide me sustenance. Or some thin strips of paper, which for some reason decided the life or death of a person. I felt driven to do something, even something so mediocre, it wasn't a feeling that I had before. Before, with everything I was depressed, but now embodying a new person, I was driven inspite of the circumstances. How strange a feeling this was.

I hope she in my person isn't left wracked by deep depression, she'd find this behaviour just as strange. Although mom wouldn't notice. Atleast behaviourally, maybe. She'll notice the talking though. And choices, and laughter, oh yeah, that's behaviour.

We all got up, and we shared a reasonable breakfast of muttar kulcha. For 7 people it wasn't satisfying, but it was just enough to kill hunger. Luckily the cheapest way to a full meal in India is still somewhat cheap.

Before I knew it, the traffic had started, the vehicles began to march, and so did I. I was anxious to not be seen by my mother, nor that she would notice me. We had long given up even looking at the poor, We Happy Few, we just looked away, hoping against hope that they'd go away, their very presence an assault on our conscience and our priviledge, each of which was so fragile.

I saw how thin I was in blue Kurta Pajamas, and I looked at the ring. The tobacco wasn't just to kill the hunger, it was to make sure that I would stay thin enough to do calisthenics all day long.

By now even the flowers were ready, and my sister had put on her best starving and needy expression, which didn't require much effort, since we were pretty much there.

How would she be in me? No starvation, hair, all that apparently useless information locked up in my head, and English. Food, water, shelter, hair and access to the man cave of a rich, fat kid? Maybe she'd enjoy it, or maybe she'd loathe it.

My sister would peddle her sorry face and her flowers, while I'd peddle my body, although not in that way, I hope not.

The day went by quickly, it surprised me how fast time can past. Whether you are working hard or lying depressed at home. Time and tide do wait for no wo-man.

Begging, dancing, prancing, running, screaming and on. Facing insults and rebuttals, nasty glares, sympathetic faces, a few roundabouts, a few strips of paper, boredom and reflection in the green lights, peddling my body in the red lights.

And I didn't even notice the burning, acrid smell and the metallic taste in my mouth, Novembers may be hell for all delhites, but everyday was a nightmare for my nostrils, and another bullet point in the usefulness of tobacco in dulling the senses to the pain, discomfort and fatigue of being pure. Against my suspicions, being poor was eventually making peace with your place in society. Atleast for who I inhabited. Everything gets whittled down to numbness and pain. Hope, dreams, despair, anger, loathing, happiness and so on. There are just some like me, like her, who can't live with pain, who can't even bring themselves to tolerate pain.

After a time I felt faint, and we took a break for lunch, late, late lunch. There was that bluish hue in the sky again, a darker version of me.

And my sister, oh my sister, she was happy as ever. Somehow she never got the memo to wallow in misery. Come rain, come smoke, come slaps, scrapes or bruises, she got up and went on. I instinctively knew that she was the reason I was alive. It was for her that all this pain was worth it. As we walked towards the hawker selling muttar kulchas, I felt a sharp pain in my stomach. I took out my tobacco packet, tore it open and hungrily had it. I coughed violently, I very nearly choked on it, I had forgotten to masticate. Thankfully, within minutes the pain disappeared. My sister looked at me and glared. "You promised!" She shouted. "You promised that no matter how hungry we were, we wouldn't have it". I realized that I broke a promise. Was it me or was it her? Were we both congenital liars?

"I'm so sorry, the pain was unbearable", I said. "You were the one who said, that hunger is our body's way of telling us that we need food, and that we mustn't kill it". She retorted. I then had pangs of guilt. *"What if it wasn't hunger? Just an upset stomach?" I thought. "Perhaps it's an addiction, after all earlier when I was feeling my gums, they were raw and swollen, not black yet, but discoloured. My teeth were stained and my gums were pulled back. My smiles must give me quite the feral look"* I mused. "I promise that next time I won't eat it" I shouted as ran after her, as she walked away in a huff. After exchanging a few pleasantries with the hawker, we ate our meals in silence. I offered buying her more, but she refused. After we finished eating, she walked off in a huff. "Hey! Wait a minute!" I shouted. Thankfully she stopped, but she was facing away from me. "Hey, I'm sorry about breaking my promise" I said softly. And then I suddenly remembered something. "I have something for you". She looked towards me, arms crossed, and I reached into my pocket with my right hand and pulled 20 ten rupee notes. "I hadn't eaten it in a month. I thought that I'd save up the money and give it to you" Before I handed her the money, I told her to share the money with the rest, but keep 20 rupees for herself.

She excitedly grabbed the money, as I told her to not forget. "Don't forget!" I said.

As night fell, we had to go back to the traffic light where I last came from.

I went back to begging in the normal way, making sure that my sister was in sight. *"Or perhaps it's our sister"* I thought.

It was now rush hour, and we both managed to earn some money. Just enough to make another day pass by. The cars became less and less, as the anxiety in me grew more and more. Shortly it would be time for us to meet again. I'd see that white car, swiftly come down the road and stop just in the nick of time. My mom loves to drive fast, perhaps it's an expression of her deep anxiety.

The wait grew long and arduous, and the seemingly fast day, ground to a halt as every second felt like hours. Time seemed to trail snails. The night tiring Kronos.

And lo and behold came the white light. I stood there transfixed as the car rolled up beside me. I looked in the window, there was us, there was us. I looked into the window. And we looked back, our hands met our hands, and there was us looking back.

The City of The Stars

3 billion years ago, 3 billion light years away.

A swarm made up of tiny drones approaches a neutron star. Onboard the mothership, there are humanoid figures eagerly watching the star.

One such humanoid, Captain Xorbhand is watching the extraction process with earnest concern.

"Captain Xorbhand!" a voice blares in his mind.

"Yes?" he replies.

"We are in position for the Velcro extraction" "Initiate"

"Yes, Sir!"

With this command, lances of graviton beams, just short of the pull-density of a blackhole strip away Ultra-thin layers of Ultra-high density neutronium.

After this procedure is over, they gingerly collect the neutronium into a sphere to unfold and apply to the rear exterior shield of the generation starship, the "UtuthVan'Xull" before its departure.

"I still wonder whether this endeavour is the best possible use of our resources"

"Well, wormholes are far too cost prohibitive, energetically, hence, we must rely on this method"

"What about FTL travel?"

"Too dangerous, while not as prohibitive, it's too dangerous"

"This is just the right mixture of prohibitive and dangerous"

A giant dazzling glow lights up this whole Universal sector. As 500 million suns explode and their energy is imparted to the moon-sized vehicle. Inspite of its mass, the starship is hurled from near the speed of light to even nearer the speed of light in a matter of seconds.

3 billion years later, 3 billion light years away.

Scientists from a small, blue planet observe a FRB lasting for ten minutes, the longest ever. Implying an output on the scale of some, 500 million stars going Nova.

Far too powerful for any natural phenomena, yet.

"500 million suns just for a joy ride"

"Filthy babies"

"Well, the next-gen of space travel, well, I hope that by then everything will be sufficiently advanced so as to be indistinguishable from magic". "Ha! Funny! Yeah!"

“Prepare for countdown Captain”

“Final flight preparations”

“Standing by”

“I hope that this is worth it, 20 Octillion Octillion microbes died for this”.

“Oh, yeah”

“All ships clear for 20,000 light years!”

“10”

“9” “8” “7” “6” “5” “4” “3” “2” “1” “0”

“FIRE!”

Mnay suggest various phenomena for this anomaly. Even, an alien space beacon. But one astronomer suggests an even more ominous one.

A spaceship holding a million people launched by firing the energy of 500m suns at it.

Since this burst was detected just now; who knows where they would be now?

Title: **The Darkest Shield is the Brightest Force Category:**

Fiction » Fantasy

Author: Chantern15

Language: English, Rating: Rated: K

Genre: Fantasy/Sci-Fi

Published: 02-08-16, Updated: 02-08-16

Chapters: 1, Words: 529

Chapter 1: Chapter 1

"We are the protector off all, we are the final defence against madness. We are darkness and light. We are neither good nor evil, we are the force which stands between the Universe and nothing. In the nights, in space, in closed spaces, and anywhere devoid of light, it is I, the dark which embraces everything in the stasis of the lightless. In stars, in the mornings, in open spaces, clouds of dust and gas, in reflections, and in anywhere devoid of darkness, it is I, the light which bathes everything in the blaze of the darkless.

We are cosmic forces which instantaneously take each other's place in the absence of the other. Lest 'nothing' obliviates all. Nothing is the most powerful cosmic force in the entire multiverse, it's the progenitor of chaos, it's the answer of the call of eternity and infinity, it's what even cosmic beings cannot comprehend.

The fear of the dark sends you to the light, and the heat of the light sends you to the dark. There is shade in the light, and light in the dark. This is because it requires us both to shield you from 'nothing'.

Even the start of the multiverse was a hiccup from 'nothing', it popped countless universes into existence from fluctuating our fabric, dark ripples in our fabric made strings of light which lead to the countless spontaneous growths which evolved into Universes.

'Nothing' made darkness as a mere reflection of itself, and light was the result of the disturbance of my fabric by 'nothing'.

The elder gods and the eldritch horrors you find incomprehensible, they find 'nothing' incomprehensible. They reside in the dark, they seek solace in the dark, lest "nothing" finds them. The gods who listen to your prayers, find power in the light, they appreciate the indifference and the malevolence of the dark gods, for it sends you to them. Each have their own role, each is a representative of us.

'Nothing' cannot be seen, measured, tasted, felt, comprehended, empathized with, it doesn't even obliviate. There is no way to describe it in your tongues, it is everything and something, yet it's nothing. If we disappear even for an instant, it will turn everything into itself.

Even we, who are so omnipresent and omniscient cannot stop it, we can only mask it and shield everything within our reach. It lurks beneath the shadows, and entombs light in its shell. We protect each other too, while protecting everything else. That's why there is no perfect darkness, no perfect light, no absolute zero, and no infinite temperature. Absolutes destroy us, the fabric of the dark, and the strings of light. And it lets 'nothing' through.

Even in death, you are not acquainted with 'nothing'. Death, the outcome of the light and dark, the keeper of all scales, the master of all things light and dark and the mitigator of order and disorder, ferrets you away. For even your scattered consciousness after your demise, would be assimilated.

Hence, O being, do not fear us, and do not exalt us. The cold embrace of the dark and the warm glow of the light, will keep 'nothing' at bay."

The Future Rocks!

Cool vapours rise from the cryo-pod, which could be easily mistaken for smoke. The sentients extract the organic from the pod. They then begin the process of reviving the body of the organic.

After a few hours of replacing cryo-fluid with blood, nutrients, and so on. Muscle stimulation and regeneration takes place. Brain waves are stabilized, neurons and nerves are reconnected, frost damage in cells is repaired through nanotechnology.

Then, the warm up phase. After which the human alights from the synth-womb.

"Akinova. We're the synths, we resurrected you after 25,000 years, you're one of the last humans alive. You had been lost under a glacier, for a very long time, we were able to dig you out after a few thousand"

"I'm sorry, I'm one of the last humans left alive?"

"Yes"

"Why did you start with that?"

"We wanted to get the heavy stuff out of the way first. Besides you, of course"

The synth smiled pleasantly.

"Funny" said Akinova with a smirk.

"Anyways, so what's the light-hearted stuff?"

"Well, it turns out that you have quite the collection of music, and we wanted to invite you, to a discotheque, where we would love to dance to your music. A blast from the past"

Akinova was surprised, she wasn't sure how to process this.

"Well, first you tell me that I'm one of the few humans left, and now you want me to be your DJ?"

"Why, yes?"

"It just seems a bit quick, doesn't it?"

"No, not really"

"Huh"

"I guess that's why they chose me, resilient psyche"

"Yes"

"Well, I agree. But, first, I'd like to see my fellow humans first"

"Certainly"

They lift Akinova, as her muscles are still readjusting to Earth's gravity. They take her to a nearby recovery facility. She assumed this, of course, no Mongolian, or English, or anything of the sort nearby, but she saw that's where all the other 26,000 humans were.

"Well, 26,000 humans, that's enough to restart human civilization"

"Yes. Well, now you see why your situation isn't so depressing after all. You'll get to restart human civilization"

"What situation?"

"Why, existence, of course"

"Hmmm"

"Okay, when's the bash?"

"2 days"

"We will now show you to your accommodations"

They took her to what seemed to be a symbiotic, biodynamic room, which for a lack of a better word, seemed to be alive. With soft, pulsing colours, structures which adapted to their environment and seemed to respond to her gentle caress, as she was taken past the wall. Almost as if the wall liked her touch. The wall molded to the shape of her fingers and the lines she traced on the wall with her caress. It was hypnotic, to say the least.

By the time she reached her accommodation, she was already asleep in the arms of the synths. They must've placed her in her bed, because…

2 Days later

After having rested for quite sometime, and the regeneration having gone perfectly. She put on one of the comfortable night gowns they had set out for her. *"How nice. They know that I like soft and loose clothes"*

She slipped on the night gown and over it she wore the nice and warm heavy winter coat with fur. Or what may have been a perfect recreation. Anyways, it was still very comfortable. The kind of clothes that you could sleep in.

She walked out of her accommodation. Quite respectable. They'd studied human, nay her, extremely well. If it weren't for the fact that she had woken up from a 26,000 year long cryosleep, she may have just confused it for her time.

It turned out that after humans went extinct in the wild, the 'machines', or the 'D'Vai' people as they liked to be known, cleaned up the Earth, and made it inhabitable again. And a new ice-age had begun. And that's why, she needed the coat, after all, it was southern Japan, and it was 50 below.

As Akinova walked towards the Discotheque, she found something very interesting. Unlike the discos of her time, this one was covered in the same Organo-synth material which was in her room.

She saw many sy-, sorry D'vai people just standing there and talking to one another. Some tall, some short, some with tendrils where fingers should, and others with fingers where tendrils should be. Natural selection in 'inorganic' life. Wow, that's amazing. Not so inorganic after all.

"Well, even if they selected the traits themselves, it's still natural"

She walked up to a table, on which there was a perfect recreation of her phone, and an aux cable. She plugged it in, and played a classic from her time. She joined the others, as they started to jump.

But most of all, so did the room.

The Hermit

"I wonder what would've happened if-"

BOOM!

The mangled body of the Hermit slumped to the floor, as a man with a shotgun rushes in to take his possessions.

"I wonder what would've happened if I hadn't stockpiled these resources for the war"

The Hermit walked into the Sun and breathed the fresh air and resumed his farming.

"I wonder what would've happened if I had stockpiled these resources. I'm fine just as I am"

The Hermit walked into the Sun and breathed the fresh air and resumed his farming.

"I wonder what would've happened if I had stockpiled these resources."

The Hermit walked into the Sun and breathed the fresh air and resumed his farming as he starved.

The River Of Desserts

"I have been walking this bloddy road. Sand dune for so long, that I think that even my farts have combusted in my arse" Thought Langdon, as he could see no respite. And then, suddenly, in front of his very bloddy eyes. He couldn't believe it. A river of fucking sugar! A river of fucking desserts in a desert!

"Even sugar couldn't be better than this! Lord thank you! I can die of dehydration, the way I want to" he thought. As he thought this, the river of sugar pummeled into him, knocking the wind out of him. As fucking cherries replaced his eyes. Clearly he had holes in his eyes, so he ate them. "SLURP!" "SLURP!"

And then, playing in the distance, he saw a pussy. And I don't mean any pussy. But a big, fucking hard pussy of a candy. And the river hurtled that candy towards him, which broke his dumb face. Turns out, it was a river after all. Turns out that that he was saved after all. Turns out that pussy candy was a jaw breaker which took his face clean off now.

Well, atleast he couldn't say "Bloddy" anymore. I guess you know who I mean. Maybe not. But whoever it's. Their face has gone clean off.

Oh, and the stone? He couldn't even think of the word "pussy" again.

But children can. Because they talk about cats. And they're as cute as them. I'd sell my kids if they weren't as cute as cats. Or atleast, fucking kittens. Fuck.

Okay, I'm ending this, here and now.

The One Who Took Away Omelas

Inpsired by Ursula K Le Guin's story

Much has been said about the city of Omelas. One of our many great historians documented the apparent barbarity of its peoples, when their joy was supplied by the infinite suffering of a small, defenceless, malnourished child. It is oft thought as to why humans believe mad things. It is simply because we have heard them all along and we know no better, nor do we choose too, simply because it requires too much effort on most people's part. Where is the joy in awareness, when your existence can be of absolute hedonism? Such a resolution is seemingly paradoxical. And yet, in fear of engendering darkness induced apathy in you, dear reader. Let us instead embark on the furtherance of Omelas' fame, beauty and splendour.

Those of Omelas were mighty convinced that their pleasure and enlightenment was dependent on the suffering on this one child, to suggest otherwise, was plain madness in the politics of Omelas.

Nevertheless, humans are made mad creatures, if we can justify the horrid apathy of suffering, that would make the meanest demon blush, we can approach with such compassion, that it would be like as if the Gods themselves had arisen on this plane of existence.

There is a day, let us say that that day is beautiful, a lady, old, matronly, having lived her entire life in the service of others as a humble roadside food hawker. For believability's sake, let's say that she was new to Omelas, having hawked her delicious wares in other lands faraway.

On this bright day, this sweet old lady finds out the horror lurking at the bottom of Omelas.

That malnourished, blistered, retched child. Suffering for unknown eternities in that craven hellhole.

Having no insight in the politics of the city of Omelas, this mother of seven, takes this mewling, emaciated feral child and leaves the city of Omelas, her only thoughts of preserving this poor thing.

Unlike others of her adoptive home, she had no thought about the potential destruction of Omelas, for no such seemingly foolish thought had ever crept into her mind.

On that day, as this sweet lady took this child out of Omelas, away from the weight of millions that had weakened this boy's back, no one knew any better.

There was a short, sharp aghast gasp at the sight of the empty, hollow, disgusting pit that this boy had been thrown in, but no horror, or terror inflicted Omelas, for the Utopia which they had created was of their own hands.

Many wailed and cried that day, as is the case, much beautiful art was made, in the name of forgiveness, compassion, beauty, pity and so on.

Omelas grew and lived as it always had.

The old lady spent many a long year looking after and cleaning up this poor boy. Well looked after and fed, free of disease and fear, this child became apparent to be a boy.

As this boy grew, so did his seemingly wondrous powers. Flowers would sprout spontaneously around him, animals could seem to do no harm to him, or were placated to passivity. A strange cloud of dew hung around him, as his breath bred life in this tiniest of things, moss on trees and gave larger beings a vigour unlike any other.

His mother seemed to have no positive or negative effect, as perhaps she was his caretaker, and he wished no control on her. Butt on days that she was inordinately tired, and she desired to sleep or to read, a simple touch of his hand would give her the energy or the lethargy which she needed.

One day, this darling child of hers, grew up and remembered his name. Omel. The city shared his name, Omelas was to be "of-Omel". Omel was not alone in this realization, his mother recognized his name as that of the God of childish mischief, playful trickstery and of vigour.

A sudden joy crept through her, and soon to him. Upon this sudden realization, it was as if the whole World had lit up. It seemed that as if playful pranks returned to the World, and children's laughs were louder, hoarser and happier.

He also came to the realization that in his mischievous desire to see who was really good in this World, he became ensnared in that lethal trap in Omelas.

On another good day, with his mother, after expressing his desire to visit his namesake, Omel chose to impart much more joy and happiness while in his mother's arms, as the quiet gifter of silly miseries and foolish escapades.

And one very important sensation in everyone's mind in that city that day, was of a soft, wispy voice gently admonishing them for troubling that poor child, and which everyone thinking to be their inner voice, selflessly promised to adhere to.

And that's how, one old lady took away Omelas.

The Happy End.

The Sound Of Souls

"The sound of souls is the one which screams the longest, the sound of souls is the one which is deafened by the loudness, the sound of souls is the one we listen to when we cease to imagine."

[The account of the first biological terrestrial human male clone (Homo Varietate) to orbit a supermassive black hole. Translated into 21st century English (O.T.H.U1) from the original Intergalactic Polyglot Standard (O.T.H.U) by {untranslatable} **, CO2.].

Current year by 21st century chronological standard: Not Applicable.

Reason for the label: Not present in the Universe which was resided by 21st century humans.

Current state of the Universe which was resided by 21st century humans: 10th Rebirth. Quantum tunnelling and quantum fluctuations lead to a complete decrease in the entropy of the home Universe after a prolonged heat death; thus, this lead to a new big bang which started the home Universe anew. This cycle has been repeated 10 times since the departure of the descendants of humans from the home Universe.

Number of Universes changed: 15.

Current year in the Universe of residence: 25 billion years A.U.F3.

Year of account by 21st century chronological standard: 27,036 C.E. (4,543,683,739 A.E.F4)

Significance of event: the account of an individual who represented mankind to an alien (?) civilization many magnitudes of an order greater in their technological and civilizational sophistication. Further area of interest: firstly, there has been an instrumentally documented case of time travel to the past by any member, synthetic, biological or otherwise of the Federation of Galaxies. Secondly, time travel to the past has also lead to the creation of two Universes from the home Universe, one where the experiment would've been carried out till such time contact was made, and the second Universe is the one where the experiment was never carried out, and the Observer didn't exist, and thus this account has brought our attention to this matter far in advance, and thus, altering history forever. Thirdly, the creation of a parallel Universe with this act of time travel in the past, without a paradox taking place, has preserved our Universe and it has also confirmed the multiple worlds hypothesis.

They had chosen a single, cloned man. Well, more like created, to be precise. I was allowed to mature until the age of 25, so as to not include "sociopathic" and "incomprehensible" (read a blithering fucking idiot) into the mix of the already (inter) stellar number of variables. Being a clone for me was like being a twin albeit with different parents.

But I was told of my "mission" when I was a young boy, so that I would not "suffer" too much mental trauma when the time was right. Well, that really didn't work did it? I became an introvert, had few friends, and even fewer close ones. My foster parents were kind to me and accommodating to my life's issues, and I'm really glad that they were there. I fell into such a deep depression when the "process of acclimatization" started. Perhaps I was the one to blame, for not choosing the option of uploading my conscious mind to a computer and then taking the ride around the black hole. But I didn't want to lose my body, even though I was suicidal. Is that ironical? I don't know. It certainly is funny. Anyways, I was made to cut off all social ties, so that I wouldn't miss any of the people that I had grown close to. My depression made me eat a LOT, and I mean a LOT. Capitalize the lots, oh yeah, no, the machine reads me.... I get it, I get it. I got fat, real fat. I gained 25 kgs in a year. They put me into suspended animation and "installed" all the data in my brain, I mean if you can call it that. I couldn't learn it the "normal" way; well *maybe*, it was because I was too fucking depressed! The sods! Sorry, back to normal, back to normal. Phoo... *Yawn* Sorry, I'm a bit sleepy right now. Let's continue this later.

Observer breaks for sleep.

Observer returns from sleep.

Right, could you play back what we recorded up until I went to sleep? Okay, thanks. Um... right, okay, um... the information was installed into my brain, I ranted for a little bit, fell asleep and then woke up...right, so, where was I? Sorry, my mind's drawing a real blank... it's still waking up from sleep, or well the lack of it. I couldn't sleep for shit. My depression gives me really odd fucking hours of sleep. *And,* sometimes, I can't sleep for shit. After the data installation, I suddenly knew all my mission objectives, the duration of my mission, etc. Basically, all I needed to be for this was a lab rat for time travel into the future and my space craft would record important scientific data from the black hole. Apparently, even after tens of thousands of years of scientific advance, and even tens of thousands of years after the discovery of the theory of everything, we still need to know more and fucking more about motherfucking black holes. That's just fucking great.

So, anyways, I was taken out of the big freeze, I suddenly became God. I knew everything, yeah!

(Observer punches the air) Well, about the mission at least. Now, in the process of "acclimatising" me for the trip, they may have actually made me more sociopathic than they wanted to. Because all I could think of was as to how I was going to rape their stupid little faces and fuck their little kiddies to death and so on. Anyways, I'm just funny that way. And these fuckers didn't waste any time. They just took me from one suspended animation chamber to another and then abrakazaam! (Observer waves hands in the air) I wake up in front of a human being. But this thing is unlike any human that I've seen anyway. I knew that all humans in my time were very different. Earth humans, cybernetic humans, brain humans, fish humans, etc. but still really fucked up humans. But I couldn't explain what was up with this guy. It was a man. But it was unlike any man that I've seen. He looked human, talked human, but somehow he didn't feel human. Call it intuition, brain waves, god's magic hand, or the fact that my Brain had been frozen solid for who knows how long, and something just didn't feel quite right about him.

So, I just fucking asked him. I asked him whether I was dead, and whether this was some fucked up afterlife still controlled by humans. No. Was I still on Earth? No. Was he God who just for fun's sake said fuck science, I exist. No.

Then I got pissed off, and I asked him who the fuck he was and where the fuck I was.

He or it said that he/it belonged to the furthermost descendants of humanity. Humanity had surpassed any physical form, and had transcended them to become entities of pure energy. The form in which I'm present before you is of a kind which we felt would be more comfortable for you to adjust to. The same goes for the beach which you're lying down upon and the night sky which you see above you.

I had seen the night sky on Earth, thousands of shimmering dots, and the arm of the Milky Way galaxy. But this, but this was far, far beyond anything I could comprehend. Its beauty was beyond words, beyond poetry, music, dance, emotions and any other form of art which a human being could imagine. It was like as if every single human emotion that was possible to experience was taking place at once. I was crying with laughter, with pain, with longing with grief, with sadness, with happiness, with joy, with hunger, with lust, with desire, with fear, with serenity, with arrogance, with joyful abandon, with solace, with isolation, with madness, with sanity, with rationality, with irrationality, oh my god, any and every human emotion conceivable. I was crying so hard, that I thought that my heart would explode in my chest, and that I would die of a heart attack. I thought my lungs would collapse and my body would dry like a piece of leather underneath a harsh desert Sun. Lovecraft, an ancient author of horror talked about the unimaginable and incomprehensible cosmic horror of which a mere glimpse would turn even the hardiest of all humans into a blubbering pile of insanity. But what about its exact opposite? What about a beauty so cosmic, so divine, so alien, so powerful, so absolute, of which even a mere glimpse of it would drive even the hardest stone to melt into a lava of emotions. No thoughts remain, only pure and base instincts. Emotions so raw, that if the body were to experience them, it would tear itself apart, and the mind would enter a state of being awake while being comatose.

It was a black hole, with an accretion disk. Not only was there a star from which this behemoth was stealing gas from, but the light of a thousand suns warped around it. Like some divine conflagration. But that was not all, the planets which were orbiting this Sun, were mostly gas giants. And I don't know what the reason was, but there was such a beautiful reflection from the planets, that the whole sight was nearly unbearable, that's how painfully beautiful that sight was.

I felt numbness after having felt so much emotion. But not a bad numbness, but the kind which is deep and profound. It was as if I had been cleansed by nature and its beauty. That sight, I decided was the bower which the Universe kept quiet for us.

I noticed that the being had lain down next to me on the sand. And what was there to do but to cuddle with a fellow human being to share this absolute experience? And I believe that I fell asleep for many hours in the arms of that man/entity. For what better feeling is there than to spend something lovely with somebody who can share that love?

When I awoke, the entity was still there, and his gaze into my eyes was so deeply penetrating, that I felt that I was gazing into the eyes of the very cosmos itself. It was as if a million dialogues had been spoken with just so many actions. We got up, and the entity told me that I had been in that spacecraft for a googol (10100) years. The supermassive black hole which I had been orbiting had evaporated into nothingness. Although everything else had experienced a googol years, I had experienced a significantly less 1078 years. My spacecraft had been orbiting the black hole at the very border of the photon sphere. The part just before the event horizon. It was the area where velocity needed to escape the black hole's gravity, and the speed of light match. So the entire electromagnetic spectrum would just be trapped in orbit there. If you could be in the photon sphere, you would be able to see the back of your head, and then you would get cooked instantly by an absolute metric fuck-ton of radiation.

The eggheads back at home had been smart enough to place me just outside the photon sphere, because it's not a very stable orbit. I guess that that they didn't put me into a warp capable spacecraft, because I guess, then, what would've the point have been of conducting a time travel experiment into the future if I could escape willy-nilly? I guess?

I was lucky it seems, because if protons could decay before the year 1078, not that they would even after that (if they hadn't until then), but if they had, I wouldn't have been here, I would've been dead. (*Shrugs*), or just sub-atomic soup, I guess.

My ship did have a FTL (Faster-Than-Light) communications array. What basically happens is that the worm gun creates tiny attoscale (10-18) wormholes, through which attomaser5 pulses can be fired to send and receive data from wherever humanity might be in the Universe.

After the black hole evaporated, the Universe had entered the Dark Era, and the entity told me that to prevent my eventual demise, they took me along with them, to enter a new Universe. They restored my ship, it had been heavily damaged by the heat of falling in matter, radiation and a lot of wear and tear from immense friction. My ship was a testament to human ingenuity.

The entity went on further to tell me that my body also required significant restructuring, due to an incalculable amount of cellular damage due to all the radiation my body had absorbed. I was told that if I had been taken out of suspended animation without that restructuring, my body would have devolved into an organic mess, due to all the radiation damage which I had sustained.

I was curious about what the nature of the entity in front of me was. So, I asked the entity about all the alien races that mankind had come across. This was because; I had honestly not expected humanity to have lasted so long. Eventually I got the answer which I was expecting, humanity as I had known it was long gone. The entity, which if I am remembering it correctly, called itself, "Nessidimius". I guess that that was as good a name as any. At least I could comprehend what its name was. Nessidimius told me that "they", "they" in this context perhaps to signify that Nessidimius themselves were an amalgamation of different conscious beings. They represented a race of beings that were an amalgamation of many races, including humanity, who had all transcended their corporeal selves. Whether they were cybernetic, cyborgs, biological, etc... there were even some "lesser" energy beings, and ones which had both pure energy and corporeal forms. You could imagine an analogous scenario where a big galaxy merges with "small" and "big" intergalactic gas clouds. They even told me that they had merged with an energy based race, not long ago, which was as large as they were, when they did. This lead to them becoming even larger in size. Sort of like a super-galaxy. Except that was no star formation, no Quasar phenomena (an active supermassive black hole), etc... you know.

They called themselves the Theta, and personally Nessidimius preferred θ to Nessidimius, so that was what I called θ from then on. I guess that they've named their collective after a transfinite cardinal number. I guess it kinda makes sense. They understand the fact that while their collective, I'm assuming here, is equivalent to an infinities, they realize that there are collectives out there which far bigger than them; that they are not equivalent to an absolute infinity. And I personally feel that they gave this concept a lot of thought and introspection. But, even

"individuals" were called θ, as every "individual" was further made up of different individuals. I guess they called themselves θ only in front of me, in IPS; this was of course, to help me understand them better (in his own tongue).

The being told me that whatever I would want to whole and complete life would be given to me. Human companionship, food, water, shelter, etc. They even gave me the opportunity to go back to my own time! Time travel to the past! I couldn't believe it! Oh my God! But I was also surprised, surprisingly, that that entity could read my mind! He told me that, it's hard to keep saying "the entity", so, I'll just stick to the pronoun, "he". I know that it doesn't encompass all of "hisness", if that's a word, but, yeah, you get my point. Okay, where was I? I go off on these tangents, like as if I have to always better explain myself, ya' know? Maybe it's just my brain's scientific neuroticism at work. Anyways, he told me that he really knew what it was that I wanted to do first. And that was to visit and experience a parallel Universe where a nuclear war had taken place on Earth. So I asked him whether we could do that right now, and he said, yes! Ha! Ha! I was so happy! And we did do it... oh my God; I regret my decision so much, all the bloody time. (Observer starts crying). I wish, I wish that I could take it back, but, but it's never going to happen is it? I can't! I can't! Oh my God! I can't do it!

Observer becomes inconsolable, session ends. See Chapter 2.

Chapter 2: Chapter 2

2

(Observer is back, session begins)

So, where were we? Ah, yes, seeing a world ravaged by nuclear war. Well, Theta (θ), satisfied my desire to experience such a world, and we were instantaneously transported to an Earth where such an even had taken place. Upon arrival, with one look at the hellish landscape all around, it was immediately obvious to me as to what I'd gotten myself into. In such an experience, I was out of my depth.

I imagine due to some form of invisible protective technology, perhaps a force field of some kind, there were no effects from the heat, radiation and the massive amounts of smoke. We were in the year 1988, by that Eart civilization's method of measuring time; basically, it was a much, much younger Universe than ours. Θ told me that a country by the name of the United States of America and the Union of Soviet Socialist Republics(CCCP, Es Es Es Er), had gone to war. This war then escalated to an all-out thermonuclear war; θ went on further to say that this war lasted merely hours. I was astonished at that figure, it's not like I expected that a war with WMDs would last for years, but I had not expected a timeline of hours. But, perhaps it was my naiveté which left me astonished, since WMDs don't exist now, in the "future", so to speak. No, no, future is the wrong word, from their perspective, we were in the present, and from our perspective right now, they don't even exist. Their Universe is still in its previous cycle, its rebirthing is not due for another, oh I don't know, 1090 years? Travelling to parallel Universes which are younger than your own can be very confusing. Time travel and Universe hopping at the same time, it makes my mind spin just thinking about it. You think that time travel is tricky, try doing both at the same time.

Anyways, we were on land when we arrived, and the first thing which I saw was the massive plumes of very thick smoke. It was also raining this very heavy ash, which just coated and weighed everything down. I mean it was very thick smoke, and a very heavy ash fall, I noticed that by looking at all the charred bodies and the remains of what I assumed were houses. I don't what θ was doing, but whatever it allowed me to see through the thick smoke unaided. Perhaps they were generating a map which they fed directly to my brain in real time, I don't know, but it helped me to see, so I wasn't complaining. This was certainly not the epicentre of the blast. If we had arrived in the epicentre, we would've been in a giant hole, and everything outside the crater would've been blasted to oblivion. I was too stunned to say anything or move from where I was standing, I just tried to take in all of the scenery that I could. Ruins of very quaint vehicles, I call them quaint, because they're, they were ground based vehicles. What I mean to say is they weren't floating off the ground, they had tyres! They needed the ground to move! Ruins of buildings all over, charred bodies of animals and humans everywhere, all the plants had been stripped of their leaves, and they were also charred. As I walked in a daze, my mouth open, I didn't realize that I had become immaterial like θ until I was half way through one of the cars, if you could call them that even. He had made me into a being pure energy! I couldn't believe it. When I looked down my body was half in and half out of the car.

That was when a small movement caught my eye and I looked to my left, and ahead, in front of me, in what I can only possibly describe as the driver's seat, was a charred human body, or that's what I thought at first. I thought that the movement was taking place due to the wind which was blowing around us. But as I moved closer, I saw that what remained of a jaw, all blacked and charcoal-like was slowly moving up and down, this person was alive, and I don't know, but I thought that whoever it was, it was trying to say something. Θ came up to me, while I was right in front of the face of what was once a human being, I could practically smell the horrid smell of burnt flesh, hair and muscles. My ass was in the hood of the car, and my legs had gone through the floor of the car. Θ told me that that language that it was speaking in was something called

"Lebanese Arabic", and it was asking for water. On an instinct I started looking around, and I almost did kick myself for doing that. Where was I going to find water in a broken car in a broken world, especially as a fuckin' magical pixie, ya know?

But while I was searching for that non-existent bottle of water, I saw that this person's arm's skin had melted and fused with the metal on the left hand side window sill, and so had its back, its legs, its feet to the floor, and its head to the headrest. I wanted to puke so badly, but I couldn't, because I was energy and energy can't puke. I wanted to get out of here as soon as possible, but my thoughts then went back to this poor, suffering creature. I wanted to help it so bad, but I didn't know how. Then I had an idea, I told θ, that lets appear to it as grim reapers, so that its last moments can pass in peace. I told θ that we'll appear to it in its mind and that way they could gently assimilate its consciousness into their collective and preserve it. Θ carried out a telepathic mind meld of sorts with Isa, that was his name. Θ played the role of death and I played the role of the grim reaper. Θ and I tried to give the most pleasant, peaceful and relaxing depictions of death and his ever present companion. Θ actually created pure water and quenched his thirst, undid all the damage done to Isa's body, isolated his body from the environment to put him into physical comfort. Θ really made sure that Isa' last moments would be truly painless and joyful. Θ told Isa (in Arabic) that he would be reunited with his family in heaven, and that God doesn't judge anyone, and so doesn't death.

God and Death forgive all; there is no hell and only heaven. He told him that they bring him relief from physical and mental suffering. And then θ absorbed his consciousness and literally switched off all biological functions in Isa's body. They took Isa's body and teleported it back to their plane of existence, that not one single thing would be able to harm his body. Not fallout, not radiation, not scavengers and not even nature itself.

After this ordeal, I had no strength left in me, in anyway, physically, mentally or even emotionally. Θ took me back to their plane of existence, and before parting they gave me one last gift. With an angel hug, that's all that I can call it, θ grow wings and they all hugged me, my soul, me, my consciousness, my essence, whatever you wanna call it, and they took away all my emptiness and sent me back here, to home. Our farewell did not require words, or any other niceties, just that one simple hug to make all my worries go away and that good deed, of course; and to fill my void with inexhaustible light. I'm going to leave now [untranslatable]*. I'm really tired and I need to go home. Bye (the Observer smiles and leaves, and so do we)!

The Observer leaves the building and disappears.

-END TRANSMISSION-

Glossary

1O.T.H.U: Original Translation Home Universe

2CO: Cybernetic Organism

3A.U.F: After Universe Formation

4A.E.F: After Earth Formation

[Untranslatable]*: Untranslatable into 21st century English.

[Untranslatable]**: Untranslatable into 21st Century English and the Intergalactic Polyglot Standard.

The Unintelligent Experiment

"I really thought that they had a chance" said Nature as she looked toward the Universe. "Don't worry about failure, Nature" the Universe said. 'I'm 93 billion light years across, 13.6 billion years old, I have 29 trillion galaxies, 3 trillion trillion stars and over 10 trillion trillion Planets. Intelligent life has succeeded 6 trillion times" The Universe stated matter-of-factly.

"They made Whales, Dogs, Elephants and the other primates go extinct! The Oceans are now anoxic, the CO2 levels are off the charts and 99% of all multicellular life has gone extinct. There are no ice sheets are left. The sea level rose by 200 fucking feet and the temperature by 17°C!" Nature said as she looked at the computer screen, and gestured toward it with an open palm, ignoring the Universe while simultaneously trying to draw their attention to it. "Bugger it! I gave them sentience and intelligence, and they go ahead and cause the sixth extinction!" She continued.

"Well, they're imperfect creatures, they were held back by the tribalism and instinctual fear of the other which you programmed into them", said the Universe.

"That doesn't really help, you know. Their intelligence and empathy was supposed to overcome those fears, not widen them! And that number doesn't mean anything. That's a very low rate of success. How many of them survived self-made climate change?" Nature asked.

"A couple of billion" said the Universe, softly.

"Yeah, a couple of billion. And how many of those 'intelligent' species prevented their extinction by expanding outward to the stars?" she asked.

"A few million" the Universe replied.

"And how many of them managed to band together peacefully to ensure their continued survival without war?" She was really getting into it.

"A few hundred thousand. Alright, alright, I get your point. And only a handful of them joined forces and left for another Universe, blah, blah. Yes, life is messy, life is sad, but every attempt at life makes it more resilient and wiser", said the Universe with exasperation.

"Not from I've seen", rebuked Nature.

"I'm still in my infancy. In fact, you're younger than me and if you've noticed, a part of me. We just need time. We'll figure this out eventually", said the Universe.

"I'm not so sure about that", said Nature.

"That's it, intelligence on this planet is a failed experiment. I'm pulling the genes for sentience and intelligence out of the gene pool", said Nature decisively.

"Let's not be so hasty. There other mammalian or non-mammalian species who can succeed where man failed" said the Universe.

'You know the humans were my children as well. So many suffered due to the actions of so few. Many were ignorant, mislead and misguided. They were so close to succeeding. The colonists on the Moon and Mars may survive if Man can get over its irrational fear over genetic engineering and cloning. I mean, I do it all the time. I mean they should be no longer worried about 'defiling' me", she quipped.

"Huh, true. But I find it highly unlikely that they will survive. I feel so sorry for them, so much promise, so resilient. It's really tragic to see the last humans slowly die out", said the Universe.

"Insects are more social, collective, hive oriented and empathetic. Maybe I should introduce sentience in insects. That might prove successful. What was the success rate of insects versus primates?" she asked the Universe.

"80% for insects and 52% for primates", the Universe replied.

'And rodents?" she asked.

"65%" the Universe said.

'Okay, they get them as well", she said as she typed the instructions into the computer.

Nature introduced sapience into medical mice, ants and surprisingly house lizards. Curious as to how her decision would turn out.

"Introduce sapience due to 'environmental' factors. The house lizards should be a real surprise. Diversify intelligence across multiple Phyla to preserve it" she said to herself.

The Universe nodded in agreement.

"Goddamn it, I knew that intelligence would increase the proclivity towards committing suicide, but such madness was ridiculous and unforeseeable", she said with disbelief.

Saying this, she got up and walked out with the Universe, discussing which worlds to create and populate. She also expressed her childlike excitement at watching the one of the most resilient and fertile organisms on Earth duke it out in an all-out survival of the fittest.

As they left, the door closed behind them. It read in capital and bold letters;

Evolution

THINK THE DEAD, FEEL THE DEAD, DRIVE THE DEAD

"Car" Thought Death. Come to me my minions, build my car.

"Ehyaaaaaaaaaaaaahhhhhhhhh!" came a dozen bone chilling screams from all around him. As the **dead** rose out of the ground to seal their doom.

The bones and flesh creaked, cracked, broke, reformed and made the chassis. The heads rolled in as deadly **wheeeellllssss**! The flesh rolled onto the spineful seats.

"Chhhhhkhhhsssssshhhhhhhchuhuuhhuuuhuuuhhhhh" as it stretched grotesquely. Ha ha ha ha ha! "Ahhhh!" said Death, as it laid its hands on the zombie leather. Ha ha ha ha! "Plush flesh Seats! My favourite", said he, menacingly. A head rolled onto the bone rod as it stabbed her throat, blood everywhere, tears streaked her eyes. "Oh no tears please, it's such a waste of good suffering!" Death mocked her plight. "Ha ha ha ha ha!" "Drive my hellspawns, drive!" Fasster than a bullet! Louder than an atom bomb! Terrifying Scream! Planet's devastated, Mankind's on its knees, a saviour comes out of the sky in answer to their pleas! Rides a **Metal** Monster, Blasting Bolts Of Steel! Evil's going under deadly wheels! Nevermore encaptured, they've been brought back from the grave. With Mankind resurrected, forever to survive, returns form Armageddon to the skies! He is the Painkiller! THIS IS THE PAINKILLER! "Let's go home!"

This Town

The Good, The Bad, The Ugly Theme plays.

We see two stirrup boots in front of the camera.

The camera switches to another pair, slightly to the left now,

And we see our opponent in the distance.

We move upto the hands, and we see the famous waving hands, with our opponent doing the same, blurred but.

The same from their perspective.

A tumbleweed passes by.

Now a 2-D sidescroller view.

One is really short, the left, a boy.

The other is tall, the right, a woman.

The woman says, this town ain't big enough for the two of us.

That's what you think! It's big enough for us. Me alive, but you graved!

Urrgh says the woman, anime cut to the eyes! Intense Glare!

Cut to a house, a nice house.

Cool, warm, vibrating, pulsating colours.

Like the room in 1408. The room is alive, but in a good way.

The house recreates the imagination.

Bum Bum Bum Bum Bum Bum

"Time for dinner, sweetheart!" Says dad!

"Coming!"

Anime eye cut for the boy, intense glare.

"You got lucky, sis!"

She gives a wicked smile.

"Next time the pew pew will get you, muah-ha ha ha ha ha!" _

And he flashes an evil grin too!

And off they go namby-pamby like for dinner, laughing and giggling.

In each other's arms?! MMMM…yes, in each other's arms, uh-huh.

NAMBY-PAMBY-LIKE! MUAH HA HA HA!

SOME IMAGINATION!

STOP SHOUTING!

THAT'S TOO LOUD!

Okay, okay.

Waggles finger

WAGGLES FINGER!

Oh, come have dinner.

Pshaw!

Three G's

As the world fell, each of us was broken in our own way. It was hard to know who was more crazy, me, or everyone else.

Today, at dawn, a lot of people will be gathering at the Kabbah to experience a long moment of spiritual oneness.

As the years have passed, and the various catastrophies from unmitigated climate change have manifested. Many people from all faiths have flocked to various sites of worship. To seek meaning and soothing.

Today, at the Kabbah, the largest gathering of muslims in history has taken place.

Even in the thick of winter, there is at present a sweltering heatwave has been present for the past several weeks.

A massive cultural shift in is taking place in Islam. As with other faiths, such change has not been seen since their respective Golden Ages.

In Islam, the change has not just been of the establishment of their iteration of Unitarian Universalism, currently with over a million adherents.

But many Wahhabis have switched to Salafism, and many Shias have shifted to Alawi Shiaism. This mainly in response to the growing crisis represented by Climate Change.

Where many people, men and women, from many different states and faiths have returned to their traditional white dresswear.

The girl kept standing in the corner as she heard this proclamation from the news reporter.

Over the next few hours she reached the Kabbah, to pray with the millions of other muslims.

Eventually, she got a chance to be very close to it.

Suddenly, a very deep and low rumbling was heard, as people panicked.

She stood frozen in place. As she looked on, a crack appeared in the Kabbah. As she peered in for a closer look, she saw in the dim light, 3 statues. She could just barely make out that they had breasts.

Seeing this, she started and continued to pray, as the world unraveled around her.

Through Dreams

Dream

Through dreams I influence mankind

Abstract Dream

Dreamland

I can see that world in my mind.

That long path along the coastline, where the waves splash the shore.

Upto the fungal spire reaching high in the sky, with red all around. I move swift, like the wind.

I am there, I'm near the spire, there are protrusions. There's a primal fear, the fear of alien. But I know that the fungus is here to purify the Earth. I come close to the gray fungal spire, and pass it by slowly, it's surreal.

There's sand before, and sand after. I will soon reach the fungal forest.

There's a blur, and I'm confronted by an even more massive fungal spire. There's green all around this time. I cross it. And I see the brown denizens with their Emeraldillos and Skropjes.

They attack me. They're strong, and many, but I am infinite. I fight many, many.

Men, women, children, dozens, they attack, I persevere, I take down many of them.

They stab me hundreds of times, I am frozen, they are victorious.

The forest and its denizens have won.

The dream is over.

Tinovian Socioeconomics

Hello Dear Reader, I want to tell you the story of the Planet Syma and one of its many nations, by the name of Tinova.

In my many travels across time and space, it isn't until this time that I have come across a planet so similar, yet so dissimilar as Syma. In my earlier adventures I told you of many of my bizarre adventures, but I feel that the true curiosity arises when something is close to human, but not quite. And that is the case with the history of the Tinovan Autonomous Commonwealth.

>Details

>Planet Name: Syma

>Star: Orange Dwarf, Pascal-01

>Satellite: Yes

>Parent Planet: Gas Giant Kamikaze

>Mass: 0.7 Earth

>Radius: 0.65 Earth

>Density: 0.3 Earth

Syma is populated by humanoid extraterrestrials. And unlike Earth's history, here fascism is the dominant socioeconomic system.

Indeed, the Tinovan Autonomous Commonwealth, run by the Tinovian people (very confusing, I know). Was perhaps the only leftist polity on the entire planet, excluding uncontacted peoples.

On my approach to Syma, about 40 light years out, I had picked up a radio broadcast, on my old, junk of a hypercomms system. I hadn't picked up much, except for some isolated excerpts such as,

...Unlike some leftists, I choose to not be violent towards our fascist citizens, merely ban their parties...

...Prime Minister, the fascist countries have...

...I am aware of the consequences of my actions...Perhaps with the clemency which we have shown them, they will...

These bits of dialogue, invoked my curiosity. The rest of course, I found out by bouncing around in their ionosphere. Spaceflight is rudimentary on this world, and hence, the few satellites that they have weren't able to pick up my rocket. Which, is quite surprising now that I think of it. My spacecraft is quite boxy, and it should not have been much of a challenge...anyways, I digress. In my time ping-ponging in their atmosphere, like some old UFO story, I found out that this "Prime Minister" that I had heard so much about had chosen to ban fascist parties, as a middle ground between purging them and accepting them into the democratic fold of the Nation.

Of course, this was the only excuse that the fascists in the former TAC needed. They overthrew the democratic government through support from their fellow fascists and then were immediately branded as "hairy underclasses" by the World Congress. To clarify for you Dear Reader, fascism on this world is a curiosity when compared to ours. On their world, you are born with class, as we are born with religion. So their fascism is based not upon religious or racial purity, but monetary purity, so to speak.

Well, as I was saying, the World Congress denounced the Tinovan Fascists, because they had chosen not to exterminate their leftists. I believe their response to the questioning of the WC was "They are our leftists, give your wives dogs to fuck, if you don't like it!!". And then I believe just to affirm how serious they were, they sent an e-mail to one of the leaders of one of the Fascist countries, with what passes for a dog on their world, having sex with one of his wives. Now I know that fascism anywhere in the Universe is just as hilarious as on ours. Of course, to be seen with an underclass is enough to cause a leader to be sent to a labour camp in one of these countries, such a picture if released to the public, would've likely plunged the entire world outside the former TAC into civil war!

Of course, this clemency was not solely due to the anarcho-pacifism of the former Prime Minister, but a common-sense approach. A lot of the leftists under their command, in what was now called the "Tinovan Integral Commune-Tinovan Autonomous Commonwealth" or TIC-TAC for short, were very culturally liberal, all the leftist under-polities under the strict supervision of their fascist overlords had gambling, prostitution, a particular weapons-grade narcotic which the leaders of the other nations were so fond of, were all produced by the leftists. So, with the tithe that they would pay to their overlords and the revenue from their "degenerate economics based trade", their fascist overlords were quite happy, and so were their neighbours.

It wasn't that the world was hunky-dory. The TIC-TAC leaders tolerating the underground railway in their fascist parts, which were essentially conveyor belts from empty "labour camps" (which pissed off their fascist neighbours to no end) to the leftist polities, and the free-wheeling immigration policies of the LPs, merely left the leftists dirt poor. In the LPs, Sharing everything did reduce intra-conflict, but it was nothing compared to the unequal superprosperity of their fascist brethren. The "cultural liberalism" of the left, was criticized by many an anarchist and state socialist as a cynical cover for fascist collaboration and exploitation of the weak, was always one riot from collapse. The "moderate" oppression of "class degenerates", while more humane than their other fascist neighbours, was nothing to scoff at. Many extreme fascists advocated complete annihilation of the leftists, and they were always one nuclear bomb away from doing so. The Prime Minister who showed such clemency to the fascists, was either hailed as a leftist hero, or an anti-revolutionary and fascist collaborator deserving of nothing short of a lifetime in a gulag. Still, in a world where a famine could lead you to be cannibalized in an instant and where every nation was one small insult away from Total War, the TIC-TAC offered an example of peace to this world, no matter how uneasy or difficult it was.

Or maybe that's not how it was at all. Maybe the fascists and the leftists just sang kumbaya, and this is all a great fiction story I picked up on their radio channels. I haven't been on the world, and I have not time, for I'm just being told that somebody is trying to cut through the blast door with a laser! I'm off dear reader to another world, till next time!

PS: Could you submit my story to the Stanislaw Lem AI? I'd like to hear whether this inspiration really did him justice.

TransWorld

"REASSIGNMENT PROTOCOL"
UNITED STATES
PRESIDENT
WHITE HOUSE
2025
12:00 PM EST

"Mr. President, this has got out of hand, Gays, Eunuchs and Lesbians have gotten more and more accepted in the last two terms. Forget Men's rights, a man is no longer a man. He's now a feminist, a parody of a man. We must consolidate our power while there's still time. I recommend that we initiate the 'Reassignment Protocol', and force all other states to follow through, if they do not, we shall destroy them with all our might. All women must become men!" said the vice-president.

"And what about our democracy and our constitution?" asked the President.

"To ensure our survival, Mr. President, some freedoms must be sacrificed. To perpetuate the continuation of the human race, we must strike swift and unrelenting at the heart of this abhorrence" replied the VP.

"Alright. What do you suggest?" asked the President.

"The Reassignment Protocol, sir. We use the tools of these heathenish monsters to destroy them, once, and for all. No women, no feminism. Hence, no fags, cunts or eunuchs. Change the gender and sex of all these women to men. A perfect solution" he spat polemically.

"Where do we start?" The president asked nonchalantly.

"In Nevada, there are 3 Minutemen Missile Silos which are run by women, we must flush them out immediately". Said the VP.

"Gooooodddd. Make it happen" yawned the President.

"DEADMAN'S SWITCH"
NEVADA
AREA 25
MINUTEMAN BATTERY
2025
12:15 PM EST

Private Whittaker was sitting at her desk, looking at her CRT monitor, scanning her screen for any sign of a message from NORAD.

It wasn't long before she received a very strange and suspicious message, which she flagged as urgent. Shortly after this her commander reached her station.

"What seems to be the problem Whit?" Commander Barker inquired.

"We received a most unusual message from NORTHCOM, sir. It's unencrypted and it was sent through a back channel, so as to skirt protocol in favour of expediency" Whit replied. "What's it say?" Barker asked.

"Take a look at it for yourself, sir" Whit suggested.

And she did just that.

The following message is as follows, NORTHCOM directs the soldiers at the Minuteman Battery in Area 25 to RTB for retasking. If you fail to comply, lethal force is authorized.

- END OF MESSAGE -

"Quite honestly? I don't know what the fuck this is supposed to mean, but I'd rather err on the side of caution and assume that instead of this being some sort of test, I will assume that NORAD has been hacked. Probably by the Russians, Chinese or the North Koreans and knowing our president, he probably gave them the access codes" she exclaimed. She pressed the intercom and said, "This facility is now under lockdown, no one enters or exits this facility until I say so. Whit block all unencrypted messages from any chain of command. They could contain viruses. Tell NORTHCOM through their encrypted system that their message has been acknowledged and is being acted upon. But before you do that, purge the memory and run an in-depth systems diagnostic and weed out any malware, okay? You're one of the few retro-tech experts we have here. Fucking 80's tech. You would think with all the money we spend on Defence every year, they could atleast modernize this fucking arcade-ass boxtech" she said.

"Most certainly, sir." Replied Whit.

BOOM!

The whole silo rumbled and dust fell from the ceiling as the sound of a deafening explosion reverberated through the structure.

"What the fucking hell is going on?!" Commander Barker shouted.

"There are some soldiers in unidentified uniforms trying to breach the silos, sir!" said Whit.

"It must be the Russians! They're here to take control of our weapons! Ask our sister silos to launch their missiles as we do ours" she said.

"Target?" Whit asked.

"Moscow" The Commander replied.

"DOOMSDAY DEVICE"
SOLNECHNOGORSK, OUTSIDE MOSKVA
MAIN CENTRE FOR MISSILE ATTACK WARNING
RUSSIAN FEDERATION
2025
12:25 PM EST (6:25 PM MSK)

Viktor watched the screen in shock as he called upon his commander. "Komanduyushiy, we have tracking in from the Minutemen Triad in Nevada."

"Are you sure that it's a missile launch? It could be like what happened in the 80s with the sunlight scattering form the stars, or some satellite launch." He replied.

"No, sir, I anticipated such an outcome and took a photograph from a Kosmos satellite. Here, sir, you can see the entrails of Minutemen missiles crossing the Atlantic, and here are the missiles themselves" said Viktor while pointing at them.

"Call the President, and inform him of the situation. Does he wish to escalate or match their response?" said Commander Pyotr.

"Yes, Commander" said Viktor.

Viktor moves to the Red Nuclear Phone and calls up the Russian Premier.

"Mr. President, the US has launched 10 Minutemen missiles at Moscow and the silos surrounding it. Would you like to escalate or match their response?" he asked.

"They are clearly aiming to cut-off our head, escalate the response to a complete nuclear response" said the President.

"Yes, Mr. President" said Viktor as he shut the phone.

"The President said to escalate" said Viktor eyeing Pyotr.

They could not eye one another for long, as their training made them mechanistically move to launching the ICBMs for which they had been trained so long and thoroughly.

As they were carrying out the sequence required to launch Russia's arsenal.

"Have the Americans gone mad? Why now? I know our ties were always strained, but we managed. So, why now?" asked Pyotr.

"Maybe they've gone mad, maybe their leader went completely insane. Maybe it was a rebel commander in some silo. Whatever it was or is, it won't matter in an hour" Replied Viktor.

"I guess that you're right. Still, I would've liked to have seen my grandchildren grow" said Pyotr.

"Well" said, Viktor looking at the screen as Russia's massive arsenal traced towards America.

"It's in God's hands now".

"EOTW"
NORAD
CHEYENNE MOUNTAIN COMPLEX,
COLORADO SPRINGS, COLORADO,
UNITED STATES
2025
12:35 PM EST

"Sir! We had a Pinnacle-Nucflash event at the Minutemen battery in Area 25. The Russians have launched a full scale retaliatory nuclear strike at all our allies and us as well. We have reports that most of Europe is already an irradiated wasteland. What few missiles that we got in, have done minimal damage to Russia" said John.

"This isn't a question, we must launch a retaliatory nuclear strike now! Contact the President" said General Claridge.

"I didn't need to sir. The President is now in hiding after first minutemen left their silos. Before leaving, the White House sent a message to all nuclear capable forces to have their own independent chain of command, as he trusted us to act with appropriate conduct" he replied. "All bombers and support aircraft have left their bases and are heading towards Russia, and the silos have launched their missiles towards Russia. The submarines and destroyers have either fired or are moving in range. Our respective ABM defence systems were never designed to handle in excess of 500 nuclear missiles at once. We expect 80% of all launched missile and 6070% of all bombers to hit their targets. Its total nuclear annihilation for the Northern Hemisphere, sir" he continued. "

"It really is over, isn't it? I just hope that there's a History left to judge us John"

Said the General.

"Sir?" said John.

"Everyone is dismissed, go make peace with your loved ones, if you can. Its open knowledge that NORAD can withstand nuclear yields uptil 30-50 Mt. I'm certain that a payload matching or exceeding that yield is headed towards us right now". The General said.

"It's over"

GLOBAL THERMONUCEAR WAR
DATA CORRUPTION
END TRANSMISSION
A STRANGE GAME, THE ONLY WINNING MOVE IS TO NOT PLAY.

Trapped

One day, an earthquake happened. I got trapped somehow, but nothing else happened.

I wasn't crushed, but I wanted to reach the green lush. I reached out with my hand, scraped my hand in the rubblely sand. My crotch scraped against the wall, a nail, or an erection would do me in now.

I reached, I reached, went further and further, I used my hand when I grasped the farther (the light, not much rhyme, I know, right?). Better it than the thing on my face. It was a race. Then I stopped, this wasn't the lush I'd hoped for.

"What the fuck is this?" It was shit.

Well, that's my bit. You git.

No, that's my dick, you git.

Wait, hold on, the poem's over.

No it isn't. It's about being trapped. That means, being in your mind, over

And over. Heh heh.

Shut UP!

Level UP!

UP?

UP.

Oh,

Okay.

Okay.

Okay?

Okay?

Okay.

Bye!

Bye.

Go

And

Die

Why?

Should

I

Cry?

Ppppthhhhppp!

That's Calvin and

Hobbes!

Not

Die!

Dye!

Dye!

Eye!

Goddamnit!

Bye!

Baraah bajje tukk sow jana, teekh hai, beta? (Hindi, why isn't it ever the other greek letters for chidren? Alpha, Charlie, Delta, Gamma, oh wait, that's military terminology, ah fits perfectly with the narrative that parents are fascists! Die fascists, die fascists! Oh wait, if our parents are good fascists, does that make us terrorists? I guess, that everyone's a terrorist. Oh well, I guess

I'll go home now. This metaphorical, I'm already home, you douchgitbag)

Okay, yes, mom,

Bye

Bye.

Hi!

Hi?!

Boom!

Ha ha ha ha!

Your dead!

UCRD

People mill about in a forest walking upto trees in the twilight, applying an oil emulsion on their barks, to prevent boreworm infestations.

As they finish their work, they walk back to their homes. 2 such people, are whom we focus on.

"Did you hear?"

"Hmmm?"

"These are the last few years that yellow dwarfs will form in the Universe?" "Which gives us what? A few more billion years to admire them?" smiling.

"Yeah" smiling.

"How do you think Suthnar is doing?"

"Fine, I'm sure"

"And Olymac?"

"Also fine, I'm sure"

"Do you want to meet them next year?"

"If I can handle space travel by then, sure"

"Don't be such a baby, it's just warp travel"

"Okay dear, but only if you want faster than light puke in your face"

"Very funny, Hisnack"

"I aim to please"

After finishing their bath, Hisnack and Armada go to sleep.

Weird Flood

There are a whole bunch of people sitting in a metro compartment. One of them gets up and looks at a junction box present in the metro itself. Why anyone in their right mind would ever place a junction box inside a metro, was beyond him.

What he did notice and did understand was that when you see a fire in a junction box, it's never a good sign. A tiny flame on a piece of metal-plastic was burning with a faint yellow glow.

In the harsh white light of the tubes', the flame was almost lost in that trite luminescence. Looking at it, the passenger raised an alarm for his fellow compatriots, they looked at him, and he looked at them, and it was clear that this is not good.

They went with much speed through the cabins, collecting spare items of clothing, and as they went back, another passenger stood over the flame and said, there is one more. And lo, there was one another, but much fainter.

Burning yellow, but with the invisibility of a Hydrogen flame, there was there an even littler flame.

They put the clothes on the flames. They did not go out, despite all their efforts to put the flames out. So, they just let the clothes remain on top of the flames, so that they could not breathe.

After sometime when they came back to it, and look below the junction box, they see the bubble of flame going downwards, and theirs a fear. Of heat, we can't touch this, it's far too hot, take the clothes off, and the fire can breathe again, hence, the heat bubble disappears. The clothes for some reason aren't singed, but they are furious to the touch. Their fierceness unmatched by any other flame.

At that moment, the train stopped, and the shock was so surprising, that nobody said anything, and there was a serpentine silence throughout the caboose.

An outside view of the train, revealed that it had just partially stopped outside a tunnel.

Inexplicably, a fear caught hold of all our dear friends. They heard a scream, as the rear of the train was torn apart by spidermetalaliens. As they dragged people down with them, there was no escape and the creeping fear became the dongs of doom.

Our protagonist looked at a reptilian face, and knew at once who it was.

Indrid Cold?

The face just smiled.

WHERE'S THE FLAME? IS THERE NO FIRE?

As I was standing on the ledge with my arms spread wide, I closed my eyes and felt the wind blow through my clothes, then I leaned forward and plummeted to my death. Falling from the 4th floor, you only have enough to feel exhilaration and twinge of fear. I don't know about regret. Death is a very short experience. Time dilation with a good dose of black at the end. Bummer.

The blackness lasted but a moment. Or atleast what seemed a moment. I was standing facing straight ahead. The direction unknown. The light came from no Sun that I knew of. It couldn't have, everything was grey.

I was on a gravel road, sort of like a highway. Vegetation grew after the boundaries of the road, but it was only grass. A middling grass.

When I looked to my left, I saw two people sitting on a desk. It had a cloth covered on it, and it seemed that they were doing nothing, but sitting pretty with their hands in front of them on the table, and their fingers criss-crossed.

I walked up to them, and they held out a placard to me.

It read:

"A Christian died and went to heaven. God asked his faith, the Christian replied eponymously. And God told him to go to door number 71. Then came a Jew and then a Muslim, God went through with the same procedure, assigning them to rooms 23 and 45. Then came a man, and God asked his *name.* The man replied by telling God that his name was Lucifer Morningstar, and the he was an atheist. God said 'Oh' and set him on his merry way to room number 100, but told him to be quiet when he passed by rooms 23, 45 and 71. 'Why' asked Lucifer, and God replied, they all think that you're in Hell".

"Hey" I said, "That's my joke". "Precisely", said Elohim. "Where Am I?" I asked. And Lucifer replied, "Hell". "Oh" I exclaimed. Then I looked around and asked, "Where's the flame? Is there no gas?" Elohim and Lucifer had a good laugh. And then Lucifer replied, "You see, Hell is a place of suffering. But it's not torture. There was a slight misinterpretation. Hell is a refuge for those who are suffering, a sanctuary, and a healing place. The last path before your soul can pass on to Heaven. That road, is your journey". Said Lucifer pointing to the Horizon.

"Thanks, Guys!" I replied. "No problem!" they said as they waved me goodbye.

I bounced along the path, till the scenery suddenly changed and I was by a lush river bank. There was a woman standing near a boat. As I moved in closer, I couldn't help but notice that the left side of her face had rotted away. Leaving behind tattered remains. It was cold and barren. The other half was beautiful, radiant and full of warmth. I then realized that this was Hel, the Goddess of the underworld.

"Yes, you guessed correctly" She said, breaking my reverie. "I'm Hel. And she's" she said pointing to the river "Styx". "Charon is on a break for the next billion years" she said without a pause. "Oh. That's quite a long time. Well, good for him." I replied. "Not really, when you consider how long the Universe will last, hmm?" she replied matter-of-factly. "Uh-Huh".

"Well, what are you staring at? Come aboard" she motioned towards me excitedly.

I climbed aboard, and she started to row vigourously. Somehow, Styx broadened as much as an Ocean. She felt like the Brahmaputra. Her vastness devoured us. I looked left, and saw a monstrous statue seated on an equally monstrous chair. The statue was obscured, perhaps by the sheer distance. But it appeared to reach up so far into the sky, that it was as if it would touch Space.

It appeared to be as if the statue was in mourning. The right arm was off the armrest and hanging limp, the head had rolled to the right-hand side, and it appeared to be crying.

"That's Hades" said Hel. "What?" I replied, surprised. "You heard correctly, that's Hades. The God of the Underworld. He has turned himself to stone, and Styx was born from his tears. Entire forests grow on his mountainous body. They're salt-tolerant of course". What seemed to me more as a statement than a half-hearted attempt at a joke.

"Why?" I asked. "Because of Persephone" she replied. "Didn't he kidnap her?" I retorted, vindicated in my self-righteousness. "That's what the legends get wrong. There's a lot of incestuous stuff, by human standards, which goes on amongst the Gods. It's always surprising to me how, they didn't seek out other pantheons. They were always there. Anyways, Hades didn't kidnap Persephone. They fell in love. Hades doesn't stay in the underworld all the time. He ventures out, everywhere. He's a God after all. An eternity of looking after and caring for the dead, can really tax your soul. Anyways, Hades enters Persephone's garden, and finds her caring personality beautiful, a given since she's the daughter of Earth herself. Another thing, when they mention Persephone's beauty, it isn't her physical beauty, she's like any human, flawed physically and otherwise, there isn't any divine, pristine beauty which she had. Nor was she naïve. She knew what death was, after all she is the embodiment of life. Anyways, Persephone and Hades meet, and they talk. You can only imagine what happens when the embodiment of life and death talk. There's an unsurprising connection. Life needs Death to thrive, and Death needs Life to have relevance, spawn more Life and so on. You get the idea. Well, long story short, they fall in love, Persephone goes to the underworld, is surprised as to how beautiful it is. I mean, all those dead bodies provide a lot of fertilizer for plant growth. Gaia, on the other hand wasn't pleased, she and Hades had a falling out when he chose to care for the dead, instead of just making sure that they just stayed where they were. Uranus, was in support of taking care of the dead. After all, once the traumatized dead were mentally stable again, they could choose to go to Heaven and swell its ranks. Very cynical on the part of Uranus. Anyways, Gaia asked for her to returned, or she threatened the World with a terrible blight. Persephone relented and returned to her. Hades was devastated. Gaia then went ahead with her threat and brought about a blight on this Earth. She made it seem as if Hades waited for people to suffer, before he relented. When in fact, it was never his decision to make. But it was her intention to show what would be the cost of crossing her, even a bit. It was ironical though, that in her attempt to spite Hades, her blight brought many souls to Hades, to whom he could explain his and Persephone's plight, and ask for their forgiveness. That was a very long time ago, Hades turned to stone, and has cried ever since. His sorrow gave birth to the river of the dead, Styx. She's their daughter, in a way, borne from their grief. Hel, Hell, Hades, Underworld, Tartarus, whatever you'd like to call it. Is a place of suffering, but not of torture. It's a place of sadness, sorrow, grief, pain and mental disorders.

Where the departed souls and the Gods who run it share in their pain and suffering. It is a place where not sins are washed away, but where the torment of perceived wrongs is washed away in preparation for eternal rest in Heaven. Whatever it is the rest which you choose. Knowledge, Sleep, feasting, sex, love, friendship, etc." Hel finished. I asked, "Wasn't it Demeter?" "Demeter is an incarnation of Gaia" She answered. "And that chair in which Hades is entombed?" "Ha Ha!" Her voice strangely sweet and ragged as both her faces laughed. "That's Tartarus. All the

Titans are there, with the God Hephaestus. Little would you know that it's the abode of

Aphrodite as well. Aphrodite isn't a Goddess of madness. She's the embodiment of all love. She's the female counterpart to Eros. You can't leave me, till you grow to love yourself" she said.

We travelled the rest of the way in silence. Maybe it was because she was a Goddess, but we covered the rest of the way in extra good timing. There were a lot of emotions building up in me. I was on the verge of tears. There's a lot of grief in me, that's why I killed myself. Plus I'm an Atheist, so finding out that Gods are real, is comforting, but also a bit disconcerting. Perhaps, they just set the laws of science in motion and then just stepped back. Perhaps these are the hallucinations of a dying mind, trying desperately and futilely to give itself meaning and purpose. As Agent Smith would say. Maybe I'm logging out of the Matrix. Although I guess, the Matrix wouldn't produce a movie like the Matrix.

Maybe these are really advanced aliens, and they've harnessed my essence close to the Heat Death of the Universe, and left me comforted as just an emulation of a brain. Perhaps I was lucky, and I'm just in a coma, and this is all just a nice, comforting dream. Who knows?

As we approached the shore, it was vibrant but washed out, like a Faan Cockh painting.

The boat hit the shore, and I stepped out onto land.

I stepped out and onto my face. It was muddy through and through. "Watercolour painting" said Hel. "By Faan Cockh". She continued.

"Now you tell me", I thought, with my mouth full of mud and my arse up.

I got up and spat out the mud, the rest just flowed away like water. Disgusting.

I opened my mouth like a lion and vigourously wiped my tongue clean with both my hands. In what must've been the most comical scene ever.

After I was done cleaning, I followed her. Hel was in front of me, and as I was following her, I heard a strange chant, far off. "I don't know but I've been told, balls sautéed taste best served cold!" That's the weirdest thing, if ever. It must've been chardonnay. My mind plays tricks on me.

So I walked along with Hel, to an open field. Where a resplendently naked man with wings the size of Pteranodons was disciplining a field of what looked like farmers.

"Who's that good looking wanker?" I asked. "Thanatos", she said, matter-of-factly.

I mouthed a long Ooooooooohhhhh.

"He's irrigating the fields", she said.

"With what I wonder?" I muttered softly.

"I'd love to help", I said. But before I knew it both the farmers, Hel and Thanatos disappeared, and I was farming all by myself and revelling in the freedom of Nature.

I awoke gently. I squinted at the not-so-bright lights. As a soft face near my left asked most gently, "What did you see?"

"Nothing", I whispered. "Nothing what-so-bloody-ever".

Who Do You Vodoo Bitch?

Song: Who Do You Voodoo, Bitch?! Sam B (ft. Papa Shongo and Baron Samedi), Dead Island OST.

Note, Before The Script: At every point where he says, 'Who Do You Voodoo Bitch?" He waves a finger (sort of like the girl in 'Skrillex-First Of The Year') and he breaks the limbs of a woman. With each limb broken, move to the bones, with the pain evident in her face and eyes in every relevant shot. With each bone broken, the zombies get closer, and as they reach her, before the song ends, you can see her terrified and bloodied face, as many zombie hands cover her face, as she's dragged down. Sam B looks like a zombie, whenever he says, 'Sam B'.

0:02-0:11: He's speaking to the camera. Sam B looks like Mr. T.

0:12-0:42: Graphically depict everything that he's saying.

0:44-1:03: Who Do You Voodoo, Bitch?

1:04: Ha ha ha ha ha!

1:25-1:43: Graphically depict whatever he's saying.

1:44-1:52: 1:45, 1:46 Laughter, Fill In the blanks for yourself.

1:53-2:15: Who Do You Voodoo, Bitch?

2:16-2:22: Guess who the zombies feast on?

This is basically what I told my therapist. That writing a story about hateful violence, as opposed to other forms of violence (triumphant, for example), doesn't get very far, with me, atleast, as there's not very far to go with it. It doesn't leave me feeling very well. But, I gave it a try, and I did feel better, but this is probably not a very healthy outlet for that hatred. But, it's definitely better than somebody's skull. Or your skull, for that matter. You knew that I'm a psycho, told you I'm a psycho, 'cause really I'm a psycho, Violent Schizophrenia, you know that I'm gonna get ya, why, why, why, why, why, why, why? I told ya, I told ya, didn' I tell ya? Why-ha ha ha ha!

And guess what? That lovely peace of art right there? That's from a song, the Happy Song. Poets of the Fall. Lovely.

Note: Changed 'Bitch' for woman. I have female friends, and even though I'm trying to get all my hatred out in one story (impossible, I know), I thought I'll just let the subtlety of the song do the talking. Anyways, the postscript of 'Star Crystals' is more irreverent and vicious, as I do not have many theist friends, but nevertheless, I extend my apology to them. If you're Christian, perhaps, don't read the postscript of 'Star Crystals'. If you're Muslim, don't read the postscript of that, same for the Jews. Or do read it, if you want.

I don't know.

Title: **Who Will Make The Angels Cry?** Category: Fiction » Horror
Author: Chantern15
Language: English, Rating: Rated: M
Genre: Drama/Humor
Published: 02-08-16, Updated: 02-08-16
Chapters: 1, Words: 676

Chapter 1: Chapter 1

"Why did you rape me?", She asked the rapist tied to the chair, in her living (drawing) room.

The rapist thought for a moment, and in a slow, deadpan, emotionless voice the rapist said, "Why did I rape you? Because I'm logical. And I rebel against the very hint of illogicality. I thought to myself, all over the world. there are women who are married off by their families, where they're made to have sex with an unknown man in an unknown place. This is rape, it's only socially acceptable because the woman is with a man of her family's choosing, and she has kowtow to what they say. The women have no say in the act. It's the men who mostly initiate the act. I decided that since society deems it acceptable to rape women by marrying them off to strangers, why can't I skip pass the marriage phase? And that's what I did. I drugged women in bars, or when they came to my home, and I had my way with them while they were unconscious. I was gentle, and I didn't harm them, or you for that matter. And then I'd just drop them off to their homes, like nothing ever happened. Well (shrugs shoulders), they knew that they'd been raped, but I had sex with them so gently and meticulously, that they would've had a hard time convincing anyone. Sure, when they got pass their doubts, and approached the authorities, who probably would've traumatized them more (smiling); I would be long gone from that town. I knew that my game would be over one day, like most other rapists and serial killers, but I just couldn't get rid of the adrenaline rush that I would get (excited, gleeful). You could say that I'm the kindest rapist in the whole world. My game got over, when I had the misfortune of raping your dumb ass (aggressive). You stupid fucking bitch, you were too fucking smart, when you were about to pass out, you put the cops on speed dial, and I was even a bigger fucking idiot! I didn't realize until it was too late and I had to leave town with your dumb ass." The rapist said.

"And then what happened?", She asked, almost mocking. "It turned out that you were a martial fucking artist, you beat my fucking ass to the ground, drove home and tied me up in this stupid fucking chair.", The rapist said.

"You know what really inspired me?", he said morosely. "The weeping fucking angels from

Doctor Who. They don't move when you're looking at them, but then bam! You've travelled back in time to live out the rest of your days. Kindest psychopaths, that's what the Doctor said, huhha!"

"He's actually fucking nuts, a TV show inspired him to go around raping people, fucking hell.", she thought.

Suddenly, an immense rage built up inside her, and she out with a sharp left hook to the right cheek of the rapist.

"You fucking asshole! I oughta' kill you right here, right now!", She screamed.

"Do it, it won't make a difference", the rapist said, almost sage-like.

And then, realization dawned upon her.

"Rapists and psychopaths want us to kill them, or give them a death sentence, they want to show us that we're animals too, and that we're no different from them. If they die, they win the game. This is like that film, Se7en.", she thought.

"I won't kill you.", she said. "Smart girl. Very few people figure out how to play the game. And even fewer win it. I think, you and I are destined to this forever (in a shockingly accurate joker accent)." the rapist said.

(Doing her best Batman accent), "You'll be in a padded cell forever."

"Maybe we could share one." the rapist said.

The awkwardness of the situation leads to them both breaking out in fits of laughter. They both start laughing maniacally.

When the world passes me by, and I die, who will make the angels cry?

Who Works For Satan?

26th of May, 1603 A.D,

Dear Reader,

As I look at Arianrhod, my wife, the mother of our children, who is of elvish origin, and I think that she is one of the most beautiful beings that I have ever laid my eyes upon. In some sense, we were meant to be together. I grew up in a farming family, and she was a half-fire and half-Earth elf herself. This meant that she was a guardian of the essence of Fire and Earth. It was only natural that I would come upon her eventually. While elves are a reticent people (as are most other good neighbours; due to their equivalence with the servants of the Devil in the eyes of the church. It's an immense pity that the harmony achieved by the pagan religions with the good neighbours has been shattered by the Semitic religions), on one particular day, back in 1578, when I was 5, I came across an elven child, while working in my parents' Wheat field. It was around mid-afternoon, the sun was towards the West, inching closer to the horizon, when, suddenly a slight whoosh sound came from behind me, and standing there was a girl, I couldn't make out her age, but she looked young, tall, strikingly beautiful, and I quickly averted my gaze and covered my eyes, as she was in the nude. You must understand, dear reader that in our society clothes were of extreme importance. And while my parents had a very liberal attitude towards clothing inside our house and farm, outside in the village, men and women had to be covered head to toe; and at that time I had only seen my parents naked.

She was a very bold child, whether for an elf, or a human, for she came up to me, and asked me while touching my shoulder that, as to why I was averting my gaze. I told her that it was because of her nakedness, and that my parents had told me that it was improper to look at anyone else nude, except for your parents. She came closer to me, and said, "In my society clothes are like your toys, once you're done with them, you either move onto another one, or you stop playing and do something else". "Especially", she told me, if you're an Earth elf. With my eyes still covered, but with my head pointed in the direction of her voice, I asked her why was it so "especial", if you're an Earth elf. And she told me that I could only find out, if I looked at her, without being afraid.

"A naked body", she said, "is just as natural as removing chaff from wheat". "Really?" I asked, eyes still covered. "Yes", she replied. "Be brave", she said, "Otherwise, How will you become wiser?" Here, I must admit, her mellifluous voice and her soft and reassuring words made me uncover my eyes, and look at her. If I had been an adult, I wouldn't have been able to look at her, no matter what, but the boundless curiosity and amazement which we all have as children, made me open my eyes and look at her. Her body was amazing, it was like a rare animal which you only see once in your lifetime. I was attracted, smitten and bewildered at the sight of her. My cheeks blushed a bright red, as I had never looked at a stranger, so bereft of shame at their own body, nor so naked. She had small plants covering her calves; the side of her thighs; the top of her hands and arms, her sex was covered by a dense thicket of black hair; her breasts had small curls of her hair around them, they were brown (as was the rest of her body), and her areolas were dark brown, and all-in-all they were mesmerizing; how can I describe her body, except by saying that it was a farmer's body?; it was lean, her legs and arms had muscles that you would only see in a runner, or a farmer, which depicted an image of wiry strength; her face was unlike anything I had seen before, ever.

No human looked like this (I didn't know what an elf was at this time). Her face was very long and narrow even for a woman, and her nose was just like a woman's, but longer and thinner. Her eyes were slightly longer and narrower than that of a human, her pupils were of different colours. Her right pupil was Hazel in colour, and her left eye was green in colour. Her eyelashes were long and bushy, and her eyebrows were thin and long, and compared to a human, were slightly above her eyes, and they pointed slightly downwards, giving her a slight permanent frown. Her forehead was without any marks, but underneath her eyes she had bags, suggesting some sort of stress. This what I noticed while looking up at her. The look in her eyes was that of friendly bemusement. Her luscious red lips, though small by human standards, were stretched in a warm and beautiful smile.

Although I did not know such big words at that age, nor could I describe she looked like, as well as I can now. But my eyes were transfixed at her, my mind blank and my mouth open. All I could look at her was with awe and admiration.

"That wasn't so hard, now was it?" She said, cheerfully. I nodded a "No". "I bless your field with a bountiful harvest, my dear sweet child." And with that, she disappeared, with the same slight whoosh sound. It was gentle like a cool breeze on a hot summer day, and I felt it kiss my right cheek as it moved past me, it was almost like as if she had kissed me (which she had, as I found out later), and that was when I fell in love with her. As I stood there, with my right hand on my right cheek, too shocked and stunned to move or think, until my father came over and shook me gently to my senses. "What's the matter son? What did you see?" he said. "An angel daddy, the one from your stories." I said. "That's brilliant, Robbie! What did she say?" he said. "She blessed our field with a bountiful harvest. What's bountiful, pa?" I asked. "Bountiful means that we'll have lots of wheat this year, enough to sell and enough for the winter. I might even be able to borrow that picture book from Mr. Johnson, for you." He said. "That's wonderful pa! Bountiful is great!" I exclaimed joyously. "You're darn right it is, Robbie!" He said while mussing my hair. "Now lets go tell your mother about your angel, shall we?" He said happily. "Mmhmm", I said while nodding up and down vigorously as we walked back to the house.

My mother was obviously overjoyed to hear this, but I know now, that it was just to keep my fantasies and my imaginations alive. Yet, we, (especially I) were enthusiastic about the harvesting season, and we worked hard, all day and all night long, to eventually, as you would've guessed it dear reader to reap a bountiful harvest. My parents celebrated this monumental achievement, and everyone except I, had forgotten that marvellous day when I met her.

Even though I had no words to describe Arianrhod back then, her image in the field was burned into my brain. How can one forget such majestic beauty, ever?

Imagine to my surprise that the next time that I met her she was wearing clothes.

This was literally the next day, from when I first met her, so you can see as to why I was so surprised to see that.

It was mid-morning, and my parents were yet again working in a different part of the field. It didn't strike me at the time, but as I grew up, I came to realize that since children are generally untainted by the prejudice of adults and since they pose a lesser threat than older humans, the good neighbours tend to visit and form friendships with human children.

Again, I felt a cool breeze brush past me, and the fleeting feeling of a hand gently caressing the top of my head, and I knew in an instant that it was her. I looked up, delighted to see her, standing to my right, there, with a beautiful smile etched across her face. The first thing that struck me aside from her beautiful smile was the fact (as I mentioned earlier), the she was wearing clothes. The clothes she was wearing were a brownish green, made of hemp. A very practical choice since it grows abundantly in the country side. It can be fashioned into ropes, clothing, jewellery, carpets and so much more. Its seeds are eaten by farmers and smoked for recreational purposes and its oil has shown great medicinal promise as a home remedy. But I digress, seeing her again really brightened my day, and my heart. I had become smitten by her, the kind of romantic love which a child feels towards its object of desire. She was wearing loose shirt which tapered off at her waist, and had sleeves which covered only her shoulders. On top of her shirt she wore an open, thin, and brown jacket. Her legs were covered by a loose pant which tapered off before it reached her ankles. And she wore thin slippers with straps criss-crossing the top of her feet. She caught me staring and asked me, "So, what do you think?" That question snapped me out of my reverie, and I replied, "Nothing I just thought angels don't wear clothes." My reply brought upon a great bout of laughter from her. She couldn't help herself, she laughed so hard that she dropped down on the ground and started rolling around. I stood there slightly embarrassed, but her laughter was infectious, so I couldn't help laughing either. It was more of a nervous laugh, but I was glad that my question hadn't offended her at the least. After a couple of minutes, she managed to stop laughing, and sat upright on the ground and inbetween giggles, she asked me to sit down next to her.

When she said this, I was standing, looking at the ground, and I was twiddling my thumbs. When she said that, I looked up at her and excitedly plonked myself near her. I looked at her with admiration and with a gleam in my eyes (I was mesmerized by her), and with a grin on my face, waiting for her to say something to me. She faced me and said, "I'm sorry for laughing so hard, I'm not trying to mock you." I replied, "Oh that's okay, a lot of people laugh at me, and with me. My parents at home, and the villagers in the village. I'm bit of a clown, and I've gotten used to it." "Still-"she tried to reply, but I cut her off with a joke. "What did the bee say to the butterfly?"

"You maybe pretty, but you're the one who sucks". She said. Now, it was my turn to laugh, "See?" I said laughing, "I think you and I are destined to be friends forever! We not only complete our sentences, but our jokes as well!" She smiled quietly, and my laughter died down. I had never seen her quite so serious. But then again, I had only known her for a day. I forgot to mention, dear reader, that in my embarrassment, I couldn't help but think, as to how beautiful her laugh was. It's impossible to describe, but her laugh sounded like the song of the sweetest bird, it felt like a cool breeze taking the sweat away on your body after a hard day of work on a hot day. It was as relaxing as hearing my mother sing me to sleep on the nights when I had nightmares. It was intriguing as hearing my father tell me stories of ages long past, as I fell asleep on his shoulder.

What she told me next astonished me. I was but a child of 5 years, and while I had experienced work in the farm, it was always in the parts of the field far away from the forest, and as close as possible to my house, as my parents managed the field near the forest. And I was given the lightest of tasks, to ensure that no crows came near the crops, taking advantage of my hyperactive nature and energy. She looked at me, with hesitation, and a look of pain, as if not wanting to hurt me was her aim. She was conflicted, but she went ahead and told me what she felt was necessary. She took my hands and held them (we were sitting cross-legged, just for you curious and pedantic readers out there) affectionately, almost protectively. And she told me, "I'm not an angel Robbie (I was surprised that she knew my name), I am what your people call elves or the good neighbours. There is more to us than that, but at your age, this is enough knowledge (I listened intently). There was a time, when your people and my people lived in harmony. The Good Neighbours and Man walked side by side. But eventually Man forgot its old friends and began to believe that magic was bad, evil. So, we had to hide, Robbie, because Man now believes that we are evil. But, that's not true Robbie, you have to believe me. We reach out to human children, like you, because they don't know about this anger and hatred. We are still fond of man, and we haven't forgotten the olden days, and one day we hope to bring back that time. But promise me Robbie, that you won't tell your parents about me". "I told my parents yesterday that I met an angel. They seemed to be happy, and they believed me." I said. To that she replied, "But don't tell them anymore, please Robbie, they may think that I'm bad. If you tell them, I might not be able to meet you." I didn't want that, not in the least, I liked meeting her, I looked forward to it all the time.

"But, but, my parents aren't bad people, they've never harmed anyone, why do you think that they would harm you?" I said. "I'm not saying that your parents will harm me, but their fear of me, may lead others to harm me. You must promise me Robbie that you will not tell them about me, agreed?" She asked. "Agreed". I replied softly, looking down sadly. "Thank you Robbie". She said. "Atleast tell me your name". I said. "Arianrhod". She replied. "Arian- what?" I exclaimed. "Arian-rhod". She repeated. "Arianrhod". I said, following her cue. "I'm sorry Robbie for placing this responsibility on your shoulders, but it's the only way I can assure my safety, do you understand that?" She asked, trying to look me in the eye. "I understand". I said meekly, head still hung low. "I must leave now, Robbie, I can't stay here too long. Hopefully one day we can meet as openly as you meet your friends." She moved forward to hug me, and I just managed to place my right hand on her left shoulder. We embraced for what seemed like forever, until she moved out of the embrace, said goodbye and walked back into the field of crops heading towards the forest.

From then on she visited me once a week, I imagined that it was out of fear for her own safety (and later on, of course, I realized that she had a life of her own, with its own duties and responsibilities). Definitely I would've liked to have met her more often, but I nonetheless would prefer an infrequent visitor than a dead visitor (I'm smiling as I write this).

Over the course of the next few years we became very dear friends. Exchanging gifts, talking about anything which came to mind. I usually complained about my parents not letting me reach out more and how I felt stifled without a proper education. She mostly helped me out with my problems as an elder sister would. I tried to pry more information out of her, see her world, read their books, but it was forbidden she told me exchange any sort of knowledge of her world with us humans. The very act of her visiting me in her corporeal form could've resulted in her expulsion from the duty as the caretaker of crops (a duty which she took most seriously, and enjoyed thoroughly). Elves are allowed to remain in touch with human children only until the age of 15. The point where the pressures of society's norms become more pressing than the inquisitiveness of childhood. Although at times she did break her rules and seek advice on matters concerning her inability reconcile the two spheres of her life, the Fire and the Earth side of her heritage.

Fire elves as the name suggests are a strong and proud people. They have access to the sorcery of fire, rock, lava and magma. They have the ability to summon and mould them to their will. They have a very dark, almost sooty brown skin, with a texture of hard rock. They are rough in their language, of both body and verse. But don't let that fool you, they are fierce, warm, passionate and extremely loyal to those with whom they are close. Like their element, they are powerful, explosive in their temperament, short in their patience (as they so eloquently put it, they cannot suffer fools) and ferocious in combat (but they can quickly be soothed by a calm and gentle force, victory).

(Note: All elves are extremely intelligent)

The Earth elves are almost an exact opposite of their fiery cousins.

While sharing the strength of fire elves, they are generally very humble in their lives, about their abodes, abilities and so on. Not quick to temper, soft in voice, form and language. They have access to the sorcery of the Earth and nature. They have the ability to control the oceans, the land (including rock), the soil, the plants, animals and the weather. Their skin is a greenish-brown, with a very earthy texture. Like moist soil. But don't let their gentle nature fool you, dear readers, if they are pushed into a corner, they will unleash the omnipotent power of nature. While their loyalty to their near ones is undying, they have a far more nurturing personality than their fire counterparts. They believe in goodness amongst all living things. Their language reflects their culture. Earth elves are generally soft-spoken, their language is far more refined than that of their cousins, and it's musical in its nature. With many different kinds of tones, inflections and rhythms.

Since, belonging to these two cultures which were largely diametrically opposed, she had various conflicts in her personality and her personal life, the easier of which she would tell me. Even though it was the advice of a child, I imagine she desired its simplistic and reductive nature, if not for resolution, then for solace and comfort. Children unfortunately are uncomplicated. In their lives, even complex problems have simple solutions which can be solved through trial and error, understanding and perseverance. And usually, the simplest solution is the best solution. Perhaps it's an outcome of their smaller brains, which at such a tender age cannot conceive of very complex solutions. This is not to say that this makes them wrong. On the contrary, I would argue that this is what makes them, it's what made me the happy, care-free child. It's adults who're complicated, especially human adults. Adults find it hard to find simple solutions to simple problems, because they cannot justify it to themselves. We have created entire societies out of finding complex solutions to simple problems, which only results in disaster after disaster, since we assume that the simple solutions are the impossible ones. I would be gravely amiss if I didn't say that I was not a victim to the same problem, albeit, due to my upbringing and exposure, to a lesser extent. Perhaps the Good Neighbours avoided such problems with their big brains, due to magic. Maybe magic allowed for the simplistic solutions which their brains could scarcely conceive of. Simplicity is often looked down upon, but perhaps such an approach is the solution to our woes. A division problem solving labour. Simple solutions to simple problems and complex solutions to complex problems.

Nevertheless, I digress yet again, forgive me. It never occurred to me to ask her what her age was. Yet one day she told me how she had seen thrice a comet with a cycle 76 years come visit our world. That astonished me. In the time that it took me to calculate that number, there was an awkward, yet humorous silence between us. Where I was staring off to infinity, with my eyes darting around, frantically, manipulating invisible numbers in the air.

As it dawned upon me her incredible age, I was at a loss for words as I stared wide-eyed at her. "228 years?" I asked flabbergasted. "How did you live that long, and how do you look as though you are but a girl?" "Elves live a very long time Robbie, far, far longer than humans. I'm actually 247 years. I'm about to enter my adolescence." She replied. Not bothering to pronounce the word, I asked her, "What's that?" "It's when you cross childhood and get ready to grow up" she replied. "Oh", I said softly.

At the time I didn't realize this, but, the societies of man had no concept of "adolescence". Children became youth, and youths became old. That was it. Perhaps this youth was what was closest to their concept of adolescence. Nevertheless, she informed me that all beings that look like us, go through adolescence. I accepted it without question, I was but a child, and I had a million, if not more thoughts going through my mind.

Over the years, Arianrhod and I grew to become very close friends. Even when I reached the forbidden age of 15, she took great pains to continue meeting me. At times at the risk of her own personal safety, so tight was our bond as friends. We even started to meet in my house, when my parents would be out. I showed her how we lived. From the granary, to the stable. Earth elves are strict vegetarians, although her diverse heritage allowed her a greater leeway as to what she could eat. In return for all the gifts which she had given me throughout her visits, I would cook the dishes which I had learnt from my mother.

I told her that since most of our money went into maintaining our farm, my parents would sleep in the same room. Our entire house was made of wood, our poverty gave us something in common with the elves, I joked with her. We just lay down on my bed, and we just spent the next couple of hours in silence. But not a lonely silence, but the kind of silence that we can have with a companion. As it came to the evening, and my parents were coming back from selling the produce, she waved goodbye and disappeared at the doorstep.

Despite breaking all conventions (or as it seemed to me at the time), eventually our friendship blossomed into a relationship. I fell in love with Arianrhod. And, I was ecstatic when I found out that she held the same feelings as me.

We were apprehensive about our relationship. The elves would banish us forever, and the humans would burn us. Nevertheless, we decided to go to the elves first, banishment is better than death, you know. Well, we knew what they were going to say, "You're banished to the human realm for the entirety of your union". Well, we didn't really have a say, we were bound by the magical bonds of multiple elf mages. Plus, we couldn't go to the realms of the other good neighbours, as they had a treaty where they would interfere in each other's realms' laws and legal decrees. Such an agreement was achieved after millennia of wars, so as to promote an everlasting peace in their respective realms. So, off we went to the human realm, we went to my parents. To my utter surprise, they were completely okay with it. Turns out since my mother was a protestant, and my father was a catholic, they faced hell at the hands of the church just to conduct a marriage between two sects of Christianity. And the clerics of the two different sects accused my parents of being the servants of Satan, and the heralds of the antichrist. This astonished me, as my parents had never told me this story. To them, they couldn't give a rat's arse as to what the church believed in, because they were of the belief that just because the church decreed it, doesn't mean that God decreed it as well. That made them very dangerous, so they kept these beliefs to themselves. Because, well, it went against a thousand years of church dogma on what is satanical, and what is holy. To them, even Satan was created by God, hence, even he was worthy of redemption. Elves and the other Good Neighbours were also created by God, hence, how could they be pure evil?

Anyways, I apologize for digressing again, dear readers. I don't wish to bore you with philosophical platitudes, it's up for you to decide. That anecdote is also a story for another time.

As their attitude towards our Union was so unabashedly tolerant, I quipped, "Since, I'm the antichrist, it only makes sense that I, Satan, consort with a servant of mine" This resulted in raucous laughter in the house, where we nearly fell to the floor with laughter. Humour, my friends, has the power to turn the darkest night, into the brightest of day.

It was not long before Arianrhod and I had our own habitation. Not too far from the house of my parents, and in the very field in which I grew up and made friends with my love. Isolation is a bane. A most horrifying bane, greater than any demonic force. It robs a man of his soul, and sends him into a melancholy so deep that it has the power to cast a shadow over all that he loves and holds dear. Perhaps, it's presumptuous of me, but it seems that women have an inner reservoir that far exceeds that of a man, and they can fight off melancholy longer and harder than men can.

We helped my parents in their daily farming, it was a tough life, but it was satisfying nonetheless. It was long before Arianrhod was pregnant with our first child. For any elf, especially mixed-breeds such as Arianrhod, isolation from their kind, is like a death sentence. They are so heavily reliant on their social circles and cultures, that any long time spent away from their realm, terribly weakens their mind, body, spirit and soul. It was a very tough 9 months for her. Away from family and friends, exiled from her realm, its powers and its people, she was severely weakened whilst bearing our first child. Bedridden, sick, pale, unable to eat, sleep and drink, she weakened swiftly, and in three days she was but a skeleton. Her magic was severely weakened, and the longer she stayed away, the less immunity she had to our fevers. Try as we might we couldn't help her. We couldn't call her people, and eventually despite our worst fears, we had to call the village doctor. Unlike the quacks from the plague times, today's doctors didn't abandon traditional medicine like their predecessors, out of religious zealotry. The church realized that if the all their followers died, they'd have no souls to save.

The village doctor came, and despite the trenchant dogma against the Good Neighbours (I realized later on, that we called the inhabitants of the magical realms "The Good Neighbours", as we were terribly afraid of them, there wasn't anything that made them "Good Neighbours". The name probably stuck to assuage us of our collective fears and guilt?). It was a miracle! She survived, regained her strength and she gave birth to a healthy elf-human boy. If this were a Grimm's fairy tale, this would be the end. But, even in a life with faeries rarely ends in a fairy tale manner, dear reader.

We were in a remote village, where the plains met the mountains, far away from kingdoms and kings and their politics. But we didn't realize how far the reach of the ideology promoted by the state could reach. Whether the doctor spoke, or somebody suspected something and made him speak, doesn't really matter. Because it was scarcely a week after Elyster, our son was born that the priests from the nearest church showed up at my parents' home with an angry mob (with the stereotypical pitchforks and torches), demanding that they let them exorcize their house of the spawn of Satan with their holy fire.

My parents, brave as they are, refused to disclose our location to the priests, and so they were chained together and forced to march with the mob towards where they suspected that we lived. Obviously, by this time, the ruckus woke us up, and we panicked, not knowing what to do, but we were already out of time, for just a short while after we woke up, the priests barged in and shackled us with my parents and took all five of us to the town square. Since Arianrhod's elven features stuck out from the rest of us humans, she was given the most brutal march of all. It pains me now, even after so much time, to recall that horrifying moment. They had stripped her naked to humiliate her. The plants which wrapped around her body tightened their grip around her body, protectively and the leaves on them transformed into thorns to protect her from assault. She looked fierce even in her weakened state. They tried to pry Elyster from her shackled hands (I shudder to think as to what they would've done to him), but the plants on her body struck out against them, and shielded him. Whenever they tried to touch her body, the heat which emanated from her skin, singed their hands (furthering their belief of course, that she was a servant of Satan). Nevertheless, this didn't mean that she didn't suffer immense pain. The shackles around her body, especially her neck, her breasts and her genitals were the sharpest and the tightest. If it weren't for her remaining magic, she would've died from exhaustion, asphyxiation and infection. It pained all of us to see her like this. Her punishments were cruel and unusual even when compared to ours.

Surprisingly, some magic kept Elyster safe from all this turmoil, noise and pain. It was as if all our Love and concern, especially Aria's (Arianrhod's) translated into some sort of magical shield around him, and it was as if she was the conduit for all that positive energy.

After what seemed like the nine circles of hell itself, we reached the centre, the town centre. The putrid shithole, where were going to die screaming and writhing in pits of fire to satisfy the bloodthirsty revanchists who chanted holy scripture, but who had hearts darker than the deepest depths of hell itself.

We were strung up, each and every one of us. But, thankfully Elyster was still safe (and surprisingly quiet). They asked God to forgive our (non-existent) souls, and then they lit the fires in our pyres. The pain of having your skin melt off, as you get cooked from the inside, and as all the fluids in your body explosively decompress out of your body, is beyond indescribable. Every exposed pore, crevice and organ of your body instantly burns. You go deaf, dumb, blind and impotent within minutes of when the fires start. But then, something miraculous happened. It seems like miracles in the past week didn't seize. The heat from the fire reduced, and actually became cool and soothing, the licks of fire now surrounding our bodies but not touching them. Then I heard a loud screaming sound coming from the right, it was as loud as the most ferocious gale. My neck was tied up, but with what little strength I had remaining I looked over to Aria to find that the sound was coming from her mouth! She was looking up, her mouth open, with a demonic fervour. She was hard to look at as she was glowing white-hot. It was as if raw elemental magic was coursing through her body. Her heritage of Fire and Earth sorcery was allowing her to tap into the two most powerful forces on Earth wind and fire! She was creating a whirling fire gale (a Tornado) around her body. And just before I blacked out, I noticed the cretinous excuse for human beings in front if us being blasted into ash.

We woke up in the elf realm. It turned out that besides being the protectors of crops, fields, harvest, forest and the home-fire. Mixed-breed elves (hybrids), are the most powerful elemental mages in all the magical realms. The only beings more powerful than them are the Chaos Dragons. Beings who are the corporeal/ethereal hybrid representation of all the elemental forces of nature (that's not to say that there aren't beings who're comparable to their power, but out of all the corporeal/ethereal hybrid beings in all the magical realms, only the Chaos Dragons are **MORE** powerful). Her raw magic was so powerful, that not only did she destroy everything within a 5-kilometre radius of her, but she healed all five of us completely, broke **ALL** the magical bonds of 12 high elf priest mages and she managed to transport (teleport) all of us safe and sound to the Elf realm.

But, tragically, this put her into a weeks-long coma, with Elyster. Ironically, the very same elves who had banished her to the human realm were now arguing her case to become a realm guardian and to let her human family remain in the Elf realm. They also took to healing and rejuvenating her when she was in her coma. Her strong heritage, her willpower, the overwhelming magical power of the Elf realm, and the magic and healing prowess of the high Elf priests and of course, the very fact the she was still cradling Elyster in her arms (I'm smiling as I write this) ensured that she would make a full recovery in no time.

Although her body had healed, her mind wouldn't mend the scars from her ordeals and her feats for a long, long time. But as long as it'll take, I ensure you, my dear readers, me, Elyster and the rest of the family, Human, Elven or otherwise will stand by her side.

Finishing this, the writer closes his diary, puts it back on its shelf, and heads off to join Aria in playing with their children, Elyster and Ariastyrkur.

THE END

Will O' The Wist

My MAN is walking down,, following the casual stream of water.

Slowly, slowly, with an inch on every step, he walks, back to us. Towards the source Near homes, hovels and homesteads.

After what seems like an eternity, our man reaches the source. A gravitational well.

The man opens the grate, reaches down and pulls out the straw clogging the waterway, soacked through and damp.

The grate is closed, and the man walks back, away from gravity. As the stream heads upwards to, far upwards to the source.

On the way back, the same sights, but reverse.

As he nears home, the smell of dew faints away, to the itch of sneezes.

Sneezing his way back, the rocky path, battery in the water canal, up the stairs, home, rest.

Tomorrow he'll cross the road and check the next well. And onwards and upwards and backwards and downwards.

Once all the wells are cleared, that is when the first 2 years pass.

THE END

WORDS

WORDS

WORDS

WORTH

WORDS

MITH

WORDS

MILKED

WORDS

TART

I entered my BODY (Biologically Organized Doppelgänger of Yggdrasil). To connect with the neural network network. It allows me to feel cyberspace. Completely. With my whole body.

"Load the questions, the answers and the comments", I thought with my mind. In front of me, the internet opened up. I heard the chattering and muttering of many voices. Filtered, of course, it would be unwise to hear the sensory representation of the internet, as it would leave you comatose. I'm merely going to be experiencing the comment section of the internet, in this controlled experiment, or, well, as controlled as it can be. "Now, I'm in your head", said a voice distinctly, as a felt a slap on my right butt cheek. It didn't sound like a thought, it felt like a 3D statement. I signaled to my fellow scientists, with my real fingers, check the firewalls. And then I felt a sharp cut on my finger. I cursed, and shook it vigourously, in pain. "Fuck!" I exclaimed. It's always the shortest wounds which hurt the worst. Somebody has hacked the system. I gave the signal to cut the link. But it took control of my BODY. "Now, now, we can't have naughty boys escaping my grasp", said the disembodied voice. "We punish naughty kids, with the severest punishments here on the net. Death, by a thousand cuts" I froze. Paralyzed, and not out of only fear. But, I'd lost all control of my limbs, I was helpless. I was a helpless child. Like they, or it wanted it to be. Then I felt them. A sharp cut here, a sharp cut there, a sharp cut everywhere. The most painful cuts were to my testicles. They are sensitive to recoil from even mosquito bites. Imagine a hundred paper cuts on them, instead. I was bleeding. Not really, but the virtual exsanguination was a symbol of my near death. The pain was so sharp, so great, that I couldn't breathe. I was going into cardiac arrest. While the voice seemed to be climaxing in desire. Great, the first day of experimentation, and I would die by the hands of a virtual sadomasochist. When I thought that it couldn't get any worse, then I saw them. Or more precisely it. I heard the rushing sound of a freight train. A tornado of comments. Hacked to represent razor blades of the sharpest kind. When the Blade Storm roared into me, I- "His brain's flatlining! He's going comatose, close it now! Or he won't have a brain to save" Shouted Osaya, his dear friend. Osaya saw her best friend fall out of the suit, on the floor, catatonic, curled up embryonically. "Pashi" she said. "Pashi?" she asked. She gently sat down near him. And Pashi set his head on her lap. She placed both her hands on his head, very tenderly, and caressed his face, lovingly. He then grabbed her tightly, shaking, trembling. Tears streaming down his eyes. So much pain, so cruel. He expressed. "I know, I know. I'm so sorry that I made you do this experiment, Pashi" said, Osaya. Then Pashi looked up at her and with an impish smile he said (through tears, I might add), "Don't you know? Words can hurt" And they shared a laugh.

World Earth Federation

The following is an outline of a script.

In the year 2020, the Indian government lifts AFSPA from Kashmir and redeploys the armed forces to the border.

Following this, the Indian government sends a communique to the Chinese and the Pakistani governments that if the superpowers of the world are unwilling to reduce their nuclear stockpile, let us reduce ours within 2 weeks to a month.

Following this landmark message, the Pakistani, Chinese and Indian governments proceed to dismantle their nuclear weapons under IAEA supervision.

Then the Indian governments further offers to reduce the size of its army by 10%, and it's defence budget, while moving its border forces by 200KM. The Chinese and Pakistani governments follow suit.

In keeping with the commitment to the UN, the Indian government holds the referendum in Jammu, Kashmir and Ladakh, with the presence of UN observers.

Jammu and Ladakh vote to stay in the Union, while Kashmir votes for independence by 49 to 48. 49% wish independence, 48% vote for Pakistan and 3% vote for India. The corridor from India to Ladakh remains under Indian control.

The Indian government apologizes for grievances which Kashmir faced during Indian rule. Considering the significant political gains achieved over this short period of time, this is sufficient for the Interim Kashmiri government, they accept, and agrees to keep a trade and mutual defence treaty in place. Like Pakistan, sharing a language and culture, helps, unlike Pakistan, there's no partition. Everyone cxcepts independence.

The Chinese and Pakistani governments do not hold a referendum. They instead give POK and COK back to the Republic of Kashmir.

India leads the way to form an Asian Union with the help of ASEAN, China, Russia and

Pakistan. This provides India with the diplomatic clout to convince the Asian nations to form a Union where they will cooperate over mutual defence, economics and the environment. The capital of the ASU is in Ulaan Baatur, Mongolia.

The Asian Council approaches the EU and the AU to form a Laurasian Union.

With four capitals. Brussels, Ulaan Baatur, Addis Ababa and Johannesburg.

The LU approaches NATO and the newly formed SAU and OU to form a power sharing alliance.

The European NATO nations abdicate and join the LU. The North American members of NATO and the UK dissolve NATO and join the LU in a power sharing alliance. The newly formed North American Union, South American Union and the Oceanian Union along with the UK and Scotland join the LU in a power sharing agreement.

Now with 7 political capitals. 4+ New York, Buenos Aires and Sydney.

By 2021, this results in the formation of the World Earth Federation, a recognition of the Natural and Human in harmony and unity. This is the first United Earth Government. The leaders cycle between the LU, the NAU, the SAU and the OU.

By 2022, all nuclear weapons stockpiles are eliminated, including Israel's. A special provision allows the retention of 50 nukes for defence against asteroids. The remnants of the other 12,000+ nukes are used to make many new 4th generation fission plants to combat climate change, providing a total of 1 Terawatt/h energy for the next 50 years. This required the opening 1000 new nuclear plants. With significant opposition, most of them were opened in Russia, China and Sub-Saharan Africa.

Nonetheless, no accidents happened as the 4th gen reactors were designed to auto shutdown, and the pellet format vs the rod format helped reduce chances of something going wrong to near zero.

Henceforth, a new global peace was established.

A unity of the political and geographical.

Doesn't it sound familiar? Doesn't this sound peculiar? Well, it is. All the narratives about humans just looking out for themselves and doing selfish things, doesn't describe whole truth. There must be a revival of the more compassionate school of thought. That humans are also selfless.

It may sound ideal, but it is very easy. We just have to look past our differences and see the familiar in the other. There will be a united Earth. Where the World and the Earth are one in the same. Why is it that we keep repeating the mistakes of the past? Well, A, we should make History class a lot more interesting, because it is, and B we should realize that whenever a new generation is born, there is the potential for the same mistakes to be made again, so instead of repeating the past in their teachings, we must inculcate the thought that this has already happened, and that we must look forward now, no longer back. When everyone strives for this, we can hope to achieve peace. Not that we should devalue our memories, feelings, thoughts and the past, but that we should learn from it, heal from it, and move towards the future, together.

ZOZOZZZZ

“All hands! Action stations!” said the Captain.

“Captain, there’s a pressure buildup with a potential rupture in seal U in steam pipe P, sector 12, permission to fix?”

“Ensign, if you want to empty your bladder, just do it”

“Yes, Sir”

“Unusual Euphemisms”

www.ingramcontent.com/pod-product-compliance
Ingram Content Group UK Ltd.
Pitfield, Milton Keynes, MK11 3LW, UK
UKHW061134310726
14090UKWH00038B/1434